REVENGE OF THE STAR SURVIVORS

Michael Merschel

Holiday House / New York

For Melinda, Krista, Gabriella and Jacob

Printed and bound in February 2017 at Maple Press, York, PA, USA.
www.holidayhouse.com
First Edition
1 3 5 7 9 10 8 6 4 2
Library of Congress Cataloging-in-Publication Data
Names: Merschel, Michael, author.
Title: Revenge of the Star Survivors / by Michael Merschel.
Description: First edition. | New York : Holiday House, [2017] | Summary:
"When his family relocates to a new town, sci-fi enthusiast Clark Sherman
uses his encyclopedic knowledge of the hit TV show, Star Survivors, to
both endure and battle the evils he encounters in his terrifying new
middle school"—Provided by publisher.
Identifiers: LCCN 2016028383 | ISBN 9780823436675 (hardcover)
Subjects: | CYAC: Middle schools—Fiction. | Schools—Fiction. |
Self-confidence—Fiction. | Science fiction fans—Fiction.
Classification: LCC PZ7.1.M478 Re 2017 | DDC [Fic]—dc23 LC record available at
https://lccn.loc.gov/2016028383

"I have a fear of moving....I think it's one of the two worst experiences that you can have as a human being—moving or dying. And I think moving is a little worse, because you're there to experience it."

—Norton Juster

MAYDAY...MAYDAY...

This is a Priority One distress call.
Can anyone hear me?
Anyone?

My situation is desperate. I have crash-landed on an inhospitable world. Communication with my commanders has broken down. My shields have been compromised. I am critically short on vital supplies. I am isolated. Adrift. Cold.

Lonely.

Worst of all, I am surrounded by aliens. Hundreds of them. All hostile. They *look* humanoid, but so far I have been unable to make sense of their primitive social order, which is filled with arcane rites and rituals that no advanced life form could hope to comprehend.

It wasn't supposed to be like this. I was told I was the best and brightest of my generation and could handle whatever the universe flung at me.

I have learned, painfully, that was not true.

And so I find myself curled up in a corner of my shelter with only the barest necessities for sustaining life: an archaic computer, on which I recently started recording my observations; a supply of space-themed books, salvaged from the wreckage of my previous life; and a few chocolate snack cakes, which I smuggled from the kitchen.

My entire situation reeks of despair. That, and cardboard. From all the moving boxes. They are everywhere, most of them still packed. From the day they arrived in my life, my universe has been a mess.

My future appears as bright as the far side of a small moon of a dying planet near an imploding star.

By which I mean, not very bright. I probably do not even *have* a future.

I cling to one small hope: That if I write down what happened, perhaps I can analyze the data. Find a way forward. Or, in the likely event of my demise, leave a record for whoever comes across my remains. So others can learn from my mistakes.

There were so many. Beginning from the moment I landed.

EXPEDITION LOG

ENTRY 1.01.01

We were hurtling across the planet's surface, seconds away from the drop zone, when my commander spoke.

"You really want to do this by yourself? You're absolutely sure?" The tiny crease between her eyebrows told me she was as worried as I was.

"I'll be fine," I replied. By which I meant, "No, I don't want to do this at all. I have never been so terrified in my entire life. Please take me home immediately."

Unfortunately, I sent that second part via psionic mind blast, forgetting that I was not technically capable of telepathy. So if she received the message, she ignored it.

"OK, then," she said, as our *Odyssey*-class transport entered the parking lot. "You just need to find the counselor, and she said they would handle the rest. You're sure you don't want me to...?"

"I'm fine," I lied. I tried to scan the terrain, but my breath had fogged the window. I quietly traced an *SOS* in the condensation, then wiped it clean.

"OK," she sighed. She brought the landing craft to a halt. "Well, good luck then, sweetheart. I'll see you when you get home."

She reached across the seat to kiss me, but I quickly slid out of range, pulled the handle and opened the door. Icy, dry January air stung my lungs.

I set my foot on the frozen firmament. *That's one small step from a van*, I thought. I was too nervous to add more.

The commander drove off, leaving me standing on the curb in a thin fog of exhaust.

I lifted my eyes toward the fortress-like structure ahead of me. It was a long, rectangular complex, constructed mostly of rust-hued brick, and it sprawled atop a low, wide hill. Its walls were punctuated at regular intervals by thin windows, kept narrow, I suspected, to prevent escapes.

I swallowed, trying to keep the taste of fear from rising in my throat, and stepped toward the building.

At least I'm properly provisioned, I thought, as I clutched my supply kit. It bore the bright green logo of a major league athletics organization known as the Cosmos. Not being much of a sports fan, I was not entirely sure where or what the

Cosmos played, but I assumed that allegiance to such a team would help me blend in. The backpack was covered in cartoonish rockets and stars; I had felt very lucky the day we found it wedged in the back of the bottom shelf in the clearance section of the department store.

My uniform was certain to hold universal appeal with the natives as well: Jeans with the logo branded onto a small leather patch. A fuzzy brown sweater pulled over my favorite *Star Wars* T-shirt.

During my preflight research, I'd learned that things could get chilly here. So I had prepared by acquiring thick, insulated shoes that protected me from moisture, cold and gamma rays. Moon Boots, they were called. They hissed reassuringly as I walked.

And I had wrapped myself in a forest ranger–green thermoprotective parka, freshly purchased for this expedition. I had specifically requisitioned this model, because the description in the PBS catalog where I had first seen it made reference to the great Antarctic explorer Ernest Shackleton, who knew a thing or two about surviving in hostile environments. It had a big, furry hood, which I thought might shield me from sudden snow squalls. And with the bright yellow reflective stripes around the sleeves, there was no risk of being lost in an avalanche.

Also, it had the nice touch of being certified for high-altitude use by the RAF, as made clear by the circular insignia on the back, between my shoulder blades.

So attired, I was confident I would quickly blend in.

Yet somehow, I still noticed wary stares as I trudged forward, up the long walkway, past the flagpole, to the entrance.

"Excelsior," I whispered.

I arrived on a concrete dock, where I faced a set of steel doors. Passing through them should have been simple. But three natives loitered there, watching me. I fixed my eyes on the ground. If I could just slip past them without engaging in any kind of communication, I would be perfectly—

"Nice jacket," one said as I reached for the middle door. The tone of his voice registered as somewhere between "less than sincere" and "extremely sarcastic." His companions began to either laugh or choke on something, I couldn't tell which.

I did not return the greeting. Not drawing attention to myself was key to achieving my first-day objectives.

I kept my head down and eagerly tugged on the door.

I failed to open it; it was locked. But my efforts did set three reactions in motion: First, the bolt rattling against the doorframe made a tremendous *CLANG* that drew the attention of every being in the courtyard (so much for not drawing attention to myself); second, my shoulder painfully absorbed most of the energy from my tugging, which caused me to blurt out something akin to "GAHH!"; and third, my clanging and GAHHing set the three loitering natives to a new round of guffawing.

"The door's *locked*," one said.

I raised my head, slowly, and tried to scan him with a sideways glance. He was tall—at least compared to me. He had stringy blond hair, long, whiplike arms and a thin, cold smile. His narrow eyes made me think of a big, carnivorous reptile. Only more dangerous.

"Thanks for telling me," I said, staring at the door. "I could kind of...yeah. Locked. Heh."

"*Everyone* knows this door stays locked until first bell," the reptile boy said.

"Uh, I guess I'm new around here," I said.

"Yeah, I guess I could tell. What's your name?"

"Clark," I said.

He snorted. "What kind of name is that?"

I turned to face him. "Uh, the one my parents gave me?"

The looks on their faces indicated I was dealing with simple creatures. So I tried to explain. "My dad liked the explorer."

Silence.

"You know, Lewis and...?"

Stares.

"He also liked it because of, you know, the Superman thing."

The reptilian native appeared to think this over, then asked, "So I guess your dad's a real douchewad, too?"

Derisive snorts.

I didn't like the way this conversation was headed, so I turned back toward the building. "Umm, I guess I'd better, maybe, try another door and, ah, find the office," I told it.

The reptile licked his thin lips, as if he had just been served a delicious meal and was about to devour it. "I think they'll be able to find you just fine, as long as you're wearing that coat. Jeez, is that a dead skunk hanging off the back of your neck, or what?"

I tried to process this data. The coat? That's what this was about? But...how could the coat be a problem? When it came to blending in, I had expected a few difficulties—the sort that always occur when a being of superior intellect makes first contact.

But the *coat*?

I scanned the courtyard. Hmm. I *did* seem to be the only person in an Arctic-ready, fur-lined, RAF-certified parka.

YELLOW ALERT, went my brain. Because if my intelligence reports had failed me on the coat, why, they could be wrong about any number of things, such as my—

"And did your mom get it for you at the same Goodwill store where she got those boots?" the reptile asked.

RED ALERT. DANGER. DANGER. I looked down at the Moon Boots, which suddenly didn't seem all that protective. Another quick scan of the courtyard revealed that everyone else had opted for athletic shoes with a curvy stripe along the side.

And their jeans? All of them bore red tabs. *Not a single branded patch of leather to be seen.*

My mouth went dry. Just minutes into the mission, and I was already outed as an alien interloper!

Stay strong, I told myself. And think fast. But do what? A display of confidence—yes, that could only help.

"My mom. Yeah. Ha," I chortled. "Well, you know, she probably shopped at the same Goodwill that *your* mom goes to."

I smiled weakly. It was not a world-class retort, but I had been hoping it would buy me some time until I could figure out how to *make* the doors *open.*

Instead, it somehow made the two sidekicks stand up straight, electrified. They watched the reptile, as if awaiting a signal.

His face, which had appeared pale in the wintry air, flushed red. He stepped toward me.

"Did you just...*insult* me?" he asked, in a voice that seemed a lot deeper than someone his age should have been capable of.

I thought, No, technically I just insulted your mother, but I stopped myself from saying that out loud. Instead, I just sort of stumbled away, until I could clutch the handle of the door farthest from him.

"It sounded like he was picking you!" said the smaller of the sidekicks excitedly.

The larger sidekick nodded. "Nobody's been that dumb since—"

"Um, 'picking?'" I interrupted, confused. I had neither seen any scabs nor come near his nose.

"You come into *my* space, and start talking about *my* mom, in front of *my* friends? I think it's kind of clear you're picking me for a fight," the reptile said.

Oh. *That* kind of picking.

"You got any smart responses to that, *Clark*?" he asked with a sneer.

I suppose if I had packed a universal translator droid, I might have opted to stick around and try to explain that I meant no harm and came in peace. But all I had were my own wits. Which led me to say, "I'll be careful?"

I was hoping he would get the cantina scene reference and decide I wasn't worth the effort—or start worrying about a lightsaber attack from Obi-Wan, which is what had bailed Luke Skywalker out of a similar situation.

But it was apparently the wrong line to have chosen. Because instead of backing away, he glanced at his friends, then stepped closer and said, "You should have *been* careful, *Clark*. People who insult me—they *pay*."

I didn't need a translator droid to explain *that*. I just needed to get away, fast. I grabbed the door and yanked with all my strength.

At which moment, the air was pierced by a strange metallic buzz. Which I would later come to understand was the sound of the door being unlocked remotely.

I did not understand that at the time, though. Which is why the now-unbolted door responded to my exertions by flying open with great force—at least until it met resistance.

Which it did, from the side of my face.

I saw stars.

Not the inspiring kind.

1.01.02

Apparently, instructions for entering Planet Festus, a.k.a. Loretta T. Festus Middle School, were posted on a sign right beside the front doors. Next to the buzzer that would have alerted the office to let me in. The buzzer someone had pressed right as I yanked on the door.

I had seen none of this because the reptile and his posse had been blocking my view.

I learned about the buzzer after the aide who saw me lying in the doorway had escorted me to the Festus sick bay, which was operated by one Nurse McDowdy.

The nurse was a large, soft woman whose shape reminded me of a giant pear, although this particular pear had a swirl of reddish hair where the stem would be. Also, her eyebrows were missing, and had been replaced with thick, brownish lines apparently drawn by an old Magic Marker.

Nurse McDowdy communicated with a series of clicks and clacks:

"(*Click*) I don't know what it is with you boys. (*Clack*) Always roughhousing and ignoring the rules. (*Click*) Don't have the sense God gave a chicken. (*Clack*) And on your first day, no less. (*Click-clack.*) This is no way to make a good first impression."

Perhaps I would have thanked Nurse McDowdy for her wisdom had she not been pressing a little too hard on the cloth ice pack she was applying to the swelling flesh beneath my right eye.

The good news is that Nurse McDowdy's quarters were situated in the "office" area I had been seeking. So that much of my mission was done. Maybe she would just provide comfort and a place to rest and let me make a fresh start tomorrow.

But here is a quirk about the chief healer of Planet Festus: She was remarkably disinterested in doing any actual healing. After a few minutes, she reclaimed her ice pack, dispensed some more wisdom—"Maybe that shiner will teach you to pay attention to the rules next time (*click-click-click*)"—and declared me fit for duty.

With that, she pointed me across a narrow hallway to the office of the person who would determine where I would be stationed within the facility: Counselor Blethins.

As I flopped into a seat and tried to process everything that had just happened, I found myself thinking, How did I get into this mess?

This mission, as you might have guessed, had not been my idea. The commanders and I had been based on my home planet for many years. It was a small, predictable place in a part of the galaxy that was remote but secure. Think of Tatooine, but with oil wells and orange trees instead of Jabba the Hutt and Jawas. Also, we did not actually maintain any moisture vaporators.

One commander was a reporter at the town's newspaper, and the other had a little photography studio where she shot portraits for people who, I presume, did not have friends to take snapshots for them.

Anyhow, a little more than a solar year ago, the commanders acquired their second spawn—me being the first—which somehow ignited a series of events that led to our relocation. They explained the reasoning to me; I can't say I was able to process it at the briefing. All I had really heard was: new job for Dad at a great big newspaper. In a big new city, a thousand miles to the east and a mile higher than our home base.

Then the changes had come at faster-than-light speed. At Halloween, I was tripping over John Kerry and George Bush yard signs while trick-or-treating in my homemade robot costume. By Christmas break, life was a blur of cardboard and bubble wrap and sweaty men with packing tape and my commanders yelling into phones demanding to know why the moving van with everything we owned had first been diverted to Winnemucca and then gotten snowbound in Boise. And now, here I was, a stranger in a strange school, trying to check in two weeks after the start of the semester.

I closed my eyes, trying to recall all the friendly details of my old planet. I could tell you how many steps it took to get from the light switch in my bedroom to the safety of my covers in the dark (four), how many Jules Verne–era balloons were on the peeling wallpaper border above my door (13½), how many spots in the ceiling were missing those little popcorn bumps because of ill-advised efforts to launch rocketlike projectiles indoors (three), how many movie posters with the words *star* or *galaxy* in the title hung on the wall next to my bed (seven).

Like I said: home.

But for all my affection for the place, I had not been totally opposed to the idea of adventure being thrust upon me. Life on the home planet was not entirely...stimulating. Maybe I felt a bit like an alien among my classmates. They had known me a long time, and most of them usually left me alone with my books, which was nice. But that meant nobody ever really wanted to talk with me about my books, either. A few people even went out of their way to mock me about them.

I had a couple of friends, sure. When I was little, I'd get invited to birthday parties, although that had sort of tapered off in recent years, as almost everyone I knew got attached to some kind of sports team, and that was not exactly my crowd. Of late, maybe I had not exactly *had* a crowd.

Maybe what I mean is, it's possible everybody there had been counting down the days to my departure as eagerly as I had.

I knew that fitting in at a new place might take time—at least a couple of hours. But amid my fears I had also thought, How bad could it really be?

1.01.03

I pressed my fingertips against the cold, swollen flesh on the side of my face. I winced. I could have used some more time with that ice pack.

I distracted myself by surveying Counselor Blethins's office. It was a small space, just across from the nurse's quarters, with pea-green walls and a poster showing a kitten dangling from a tree limb. HANG IN THERE! the poster read. Somehow, this was supposed to encourage me.

It is a bad sign when a civilization's chief form of encouragement comes from the torture of fluffy animals.

"Welcome to Festus, Sherman! Sorry that we weren't ready for you," said Counselor Blethins as she dashed in, dropped some papers on her desk and plopped into her chair. She was younger and more spry than Nurse McDowdy, but then I suppose most life forms that were not, say, Galapagos turtles or giant redwoods would be. She had mousy brown hair and a pointy nose and a nervous way of looking around that reminded me of the pet gerbils I once kept.

"My name is Clark," I said, pointing to a folder that held my "academic records," which was upside-down in front of her, atop a pile of similar folders, and wire baskets with still more folders. "Clark Sherman. Sherman is my last name."

"Oh yes, sorry." She laughed. It was a high-pitched, nervous sound. "Clark. That's kind of an old-fashioned...well, I mean, I haven't met many Clarks here."

"Yeah, my dad, um, liked the explorer."

She looked puzzled, so I added, "You know, Lewis and...?"

"Oh yes. Of course. Well, that should be easy for me to remember. Which would be nice. There are just so many students, and so much paperwork to shuffle, that sometimes I think I should just give everyone a number so I can keep track of who's who."

She looked me in the eye for the first time and let out a little gasp of horror at the bruise on my cheek, then glanced at the nurse's office, then back at me, and then apparently realized what she'd just said. "Oh! I didn't mean to suggest that you should be a number....I mean, your name *is* rather..." Her voice trailed off, and she pointed her gerbil nose into my folder.

She read with intensity. Probably awed, I thought. My course of studies back home had been the most rigorous and sophisticated offered. And, I might add, my marks had always been of the highest order. Perhaps she was questioning whether I even needed to *be* here. Perhaps I would soon be discharged and left to my own devices. Perhaps—

"This is so odd. Our computer has you down as a zero!"

Perhaps things were about to get even worse.

"A zero?" I asked.

Counselor Gerbil-face blushed again. "Well, not you personally, Sherman." She started to correct herself, stammered and looked back down. "No, I mean your credits. Our district's computer talked to your old district's computer, and it's as if you haven't completed any work at all!"

I stared at her while she typed something onto a keyboard so old that many of the letters had worn off. She stared at her screen.

"Hmmm. Well, hmmm," she said. "If you'll excuse me, I just need to clarify something with the principal."

As any galactic traveler knows, *hmmm* is a universal

warning that something unpleasant is about to be announced. While she stepped out of the room, I held my breath and hoped I was wrong.

It didn't take long to be let down.

"Well, Clark." She smiled with an excess of sweetness as she returned. "I'm afraid this is going to take some time to sort out. In the meantime, I need to enroll you today. But only certain courses are available at the zero level. So...well, it—it may not be what you're used to."

The worried look on her face told me I was not going to like what was about to happen. "Are you, uh, sure we need to do this today, then?" I offered. "Because I could, you know, come back when the computer has—"

"Oh no!" she said. "No, really, we should do this today. I have to. Principal Denton thinks you..." She paused for a very long second, during which I swear she looked like she wanted to wrap her tail around her face and bury herself deep in a pile of cedar shavings in the corner of her cage. "Principal Denton has made it very clear that enrollment paperwork needs to be completed as quickly as possible. And really, around here, what Principal Denton says, well, it pretty much has to happen."

She looked sideways, cleared her throat, took a deep breath and pressed a button. Her printer groaned and screeched and a piece of paper came out. She cleared her throat again and handed the printout to me.

"Now, later today I'll be contacting your old district to see if we can't clear up some of the confusion. But in the meantime, I've enrolled you in the best courses available."

I read the printout.

I looked up at her.

"Um, I don't see any of the electives I asked for."

She sniffled. "Yes, well, all the things you were interested in—Latin class, computer lab—were either full or unavailable to, um, zeros."

I looked down at the schedule again and then back up.

"You have me in something called Independent Study."

"That was the one elective that *was* open. You'll just, ah, be spending that time in the ARC. There's plenty to read there."

Which didn't sound so bad. "What does the little number next to some of the classes mean?"

The counselor shifted in her chair as if she were sitting on something hard and lumpy. "Um, that's just the course level you're enrolled in. Level one courses."

"And that means, like, advanced?"

"In this case, it means more like remedial."

I shot her a laser death stare. I screamed, "You have GOT to be kidding me! Here I am, a highly intelligent life form from another world, and you have me in REMEDIAL classes?"

But something in the dry atmosphere made the words catch in my throat, and what came out was, "Ummm...remedial classes?"

She squirmed again. "That's right."

"But you know I was, like, in advanced classes and all, you know?"

She laughed that nervous laugh. "Yes, well, like I said, I'm sure we'll be able to work it out soon!"

I stared at the paper in my hands. I stared a long, long time, not quite believing what I saw. And then I raised my eyes, slowly.

"You put me in PE *twice*."

Silence.

"I didn't sign up for PE *at all*."

There was no laugh this time. Just the resigned voice of a person bound to do her duty, no matter how much of my life she had to sacrifice to do it.

"Yes, well, we do require a certain number of physical education credits to graduate. And as I said, no other electives were available to you. So I enrolled you in Physical Education in the morning and Athletics in the afternoon. It's for people interested in trying out for sports teams. Everyone likes playing sports, right?"

She looked at me, realized I would be considered a ninety-eight-pound weakling only if I managed to gain a few pounds, and cleared her throat.

I stared at her. These aren't the classes I'm looking for, I thought, pinching my thumb and forefinger together. I can go about my business.

No effect. The Force apparently had the day off.

"It won't be so bad," she assured me. "I'll be working on updating things right away. I have the form right here...." She looked left, and right, and under three other folders, and on top of her computer, and under her keyboard, and then found it still in my folder, which somehow had already slipped beneath the pile of papers on her desk. "And as soon as I get the paperwork cleared up, we'll find a way to adjust, if necessary. In the meantime, why don't we just get you on over to the gym and let you start making your first Festus friends?"

Friends I could have used.

I did not expect to find any in the gym.

1.01.04

We left the office and entered the heart of the compound. As we walked, Counselor Blethins kept her head down, and I kept looking for emergency exits.

I did get a good overview of the place. It was basically a pair of extremely long, parallel hallways that were linked by a couple of shorter bisecting hallways. If you were looking down on it from orbit, it might seem like a giant *H* with two lines across the middle. The office was on the lower-right part of the *H*, like a boot, and the gym was at the top-left part, like a large rectangular execution chamber.

Just a thought.

The halls were lined with metallic lockers sunk into cinderblock walls that were decorated with posters that read WOLF PRIDE in the school colors of silver, black and blue. I thought the sign was the work of a particularly inept biology teacher—it's lions that move in a pride, right?—before I realized it was a reference to the school mascot. Breaking up the rows of lockers were doors with thin, rectangular windows laced with wire. Through them I could glimpse either classrooms or holding cells. It was hard to tell which.

Too soon, we were facing a pair of swinging doors. I thought of a medical drama I once watched where someone was always being bashed through such doors on a stretcher, often right before they died.

Counselor Blethins pushed the doors open, and we walked in. I smelled sweat and floor wax, and saw an assemblage of young males who had been engaged in an activity involving a rubberized ball. They stopped. And stared. At me. It occurred to me that this must be what a womp rat feels like right before it gets bull's-eyed by a squadron of T-16s.

Counselor Blethins walked me up to the sector's regional warlord. He was a tallish humanoid, with a blue cap on his head, a rectangle of facial hair on his upper lip and a whistle resting on the slight paunch at his midsection.

"Coach Chambers?" asked Counselor Blethins, sounding unsure.

He answered with eyebrows raised, as if he were annoyed. Then his eyes scanned me and his nose crinkled a bit, as if something distasteful had just crawled into the back of his throat.

"Keep moving, everyone," he barked at the immobilized players, who seemed to be anticipating some kind of showdown.

He put on a smile that reminded me of the man who sold my father our last car. "What can I do ya for, counselor?"

"Coach Chambers, this is Sherman Clark." She looked at the folder, then over at me. "Sorry, this is Clark *Sherman*. He's new. And he's going to be in your class."

"Clark, eh? That's a name you don't hear very often any-more. Kind of old-timey, isn't it?"

As I started to explain that my dad was a fan of the explorer, the coach got a faraway look in his eyes. It was as if he were staring through me. No, it was as if he were staring at something *behind* me. I turned to look.

He'd been staring at a ball that was flying toward the back of my head. It smacked into the side of my turning face. Right where the ice pack had been.

"GAHHHHHHHHH!" I said.

Coach Chambers blew his whistle. "Who threw that?" he called.

There was a moment of silence. Everyone in the room turned toward a tall, thin-lipped person whose face, even through my one working eye, looked regrettably familiar.

"Sorry, Coach," Reptile Boy said. "I should of caught that. I was just distracted by the appearance of Miss Blethins and her daughter."

The class laughed. The counselor blushed. The corners of the coach's mouth twitched. He didn't think that was funny, did he?

"Hunter," he said to Reptile Boy. "Watch it." He turned his head and coughed. It sounded a little bit like laughter.

The counselor looked unsure as to what should happen next. She started to walk toward me, as if to offer aid, but balked. She looked up at the coach. "Perhaps, Coach Chambers, you could take a moment to assign someone who would be able to help guide—"

"Blethins," said the coach, in a tone that was partly derisive, partly dismissive, and just a touch malevolent, "you can go. He's on my turf now. We'll take care of him."

He made a little flicking motion with his fingers. Some of the class laughed.

The counselor looked at him, and over at me, then bowed her head as she thrust a map of the school at me and walked out.

The coach sized me up for about two seconds, grunted, "Get a uniform by tomorrow or be ready to run laps," and told me to sit in the bleachers.

I looked at my chronometer. I was 33 minutes into the

mission. If my gear had included a self-destruct button, I might have broken my finger pressing it.

1.01.05

For the rest of the day, I was directed to and from a series of exhibit spaces. The signs on the doors read, ENTER AND GAWK AT THE BLACK-EYED ALIEN FREAK. That's how I felt, at least, as I was introduced to each class. And at the end of it all, I had to go back to the gym. It was like the least appealing time warp ever.

Coach Chambers again parked me in the bleachers. As he divided the class into scrimmage squads, I noticed another kid in the stands. He had made his way to a high row, far behind where I sat, and had avoided being chosen for any teams. I was ready to climb up and ask how he had managed that, but when I looked his way again, he had disappeared.

Before I could figure out how, I heard squealing.

Some other sort of uniformed group had occupied a space at the other end of the gym. The uniforms were blue, and the persons wearing them were engaged in ritualized chanting.

A stray ball bounced toward their zone, and one of the uniforms caught it. The uniform, it turns out, was wrapped around a girl. She took a few steps toward the basketball chaos before she returned the ball with a gracefully executed underhand volleyball serve.

Wow, I thought. Life forms like that could make this planet a lot more hospitable.

She had skin that made me think of a commercial for tanning oil, the kind that smells like coconut pie. She had hair that made me think of the cover of a fashion magazine. And she looked back at me with a curious smile that made me think—Wait. A *smile*? Is she *smiling* at me? Why, yes, I think she is indeed—

THWACK.

A wildly errant basketball hit the side of my head.

"Hunter!" Chambers yelled.

"Sorry, Coach. It just slipped out of my hands."

When I could focus again, she was gone.

And it was clear that my explore-and-establish-contact mission had transformed into something entirely different.

My new objective: survival.

1.01.06

When the final bell rang, there was nothing I wanted more than to flee the premises. Well, almost nothing: I urgently needed to find a way out of my double-PE predicament. So I ran back to the office, where I hoped to ask Counselor Blethins about fixing my schedule. Fast.

I got lost twice on the way, but I arrived just as she was packing up her things.

"Oh, hello, Sherman. Is everything OK?" she asked weakly.

"Uh, no, actually," I started to say. But then her face fell, as she stared at someone, or something, that had walked into her office right behind me.

Her lower lip trembled slightly. A voice as deep as space and cold as Pluto spoke.

"Ms. Blethins?"

"Yes, Principal Denton?"

"Is this the new student Coach Chambers called us about?"

"Yes, Principal Denton."

"In my office, please."

My stomach lurched as if a thousand middle school voices had cried out in terror and were suddenly silenced.

She nodded at me in a way that said, You'd better follow, or we'll both regret it.

I turned and found myself walking behind a large humanoid. His stiff movements reminded me of a stormtrooper, one who had let himself go just a bit. His suit was brown, and his hair was shoe-polish black, styled in stiff, tiny, orderly curls—so orderly that they might have been stapled into place. I thought—cyborg? He did move somewhat mechanically as he led me to his office.

We entered. He turned and gestured at me to close the door. I took a seat in a hard black chair that faced his desk. He stood, looking at a folder. He surely could hear my racing pulse and shallow breathing, if not the trembling of my very DNA.

"I heard about your little run-ins today, Sherman."

Oh, thank goodness. He was actually here to help!

"Well, yeah, there were a few, I guess," I said, relieved. "In the gym—"

"Yes, Coach Chambers told me all about what he saw in

you. And I can see for myself," he said, lifting a folder off his desk, "what a record you have."

To me, that could only mean he had my actual permanent record, the one that showed my exemplary scores on several state tests, or my second-place finish in the Pack 85 Pinewood Derby, or the science fair project where I made a battery out of a—

Then he dropped the folder, and as it slapped against his desk, he almost, but not quite, sneered: "How does one manage to get to eighth grade with virtually no credits?"

And *CRASH,* there went my final hopes of easy resolution.

"Sir," I said, as my stomach did a somersault, "I think somebody made a mistake."

"Yes, he did," he said, as his steel eyes—definitely cyborg— bored straight into the fear center of my brain. "Starting with your picking a fight the moment you arrived at my school."

Picking a fight? *I'm* not the one who had picked anything. There had been a big misunderstanding, and then a door had hit *me.* Hard. Wasn't it obvious that I was in no position to be picking any fights?

I should have said that out loud. But all I could do in actual response was rub my bruised face and stare blankly.

"Sherman," he said haughtily, "I was hired to maintain order and discipline around here. To keep the peace. And I will use whatever means necessary to keep order and discipline intact. Do we understand one another?"

I understood that I needed to get out of there as quickly as possible. So I nodded.

"Good," he said. "Then we won't need to see each other much."

"Keeping away from you would make me incredibly happy, sir," I said.

This seemed to anger him.

I wanted to tell him that I meant no disrespect, but I had run out of strength.

So I just ran.

1.01.07

I tried to summarize everything for the command unit on duty when I made it back to base. She was in the kitchen, unpacking dishes, as I walked in. The younger spawn was in a restraining seat, pounding a cracker into a brown, paste-like substance.

"Hi!" the commander said cheerfully. "You made it home, right on time! That's great! How was—" She halted, and gasped. "Your face!"

"It's nothing," I said. "Can I have some medicine? The grape kind?"

"But what *happened*?" she cried, rummaging through boxes that held spices, silverware, glassware, oven mitts, a never-used fondue pot and her collection of hand-tinted post-card images of several jackalope, a Paul Bunyan statue and America's Largest Ball of Twine—but apparently, no pain medicine.

"It was an accident," I said. "I hit a door. And then a ball."

I probably should have told her about the scheduling fiasco, and the additional "stray" balls that hit me as I was leaving the gym, and how I got lost going to three of my classes when the counselor forgot to arrange an escort. But I was still in shock, and embarrassed about being chewed out by the principal. And I thought, I'm too old to be crying. In front of her. Over this.

"Oh, Clark!" she said. "Sit down! I'll find the medicine. And I have a box of cupcakes here somewhere. Just sit! And let me—"

At the same moment the spawn began to scream, and the commander's phone buzzed with someone from the mortgage company, and as she was hanging up from that, the doorbell rang and some workers arrived to install the new dishwasher.

I made my way to the sofa, pushed aside some bubble wrap, and sat.

From the kitchen, the commander kept trying to question me. But it was becoming clear to me—she was busy. She didn't have time to worry about things like cupcakes, or how klutzy I was, or my mission in general.

I needed to find a way to take care of myself.

I had a *duty* to take care of myself.

And I therefore *would find a way* to take care of myself.

I turned on the TV.

The channels were wrong, and there were not enough of them; the cable company said it would be weeks before they could get an installer out. I recognized some of the network logos as I flipped through the over-the-air offerings. What had been Channel 4 at home was now 6. What had been 12 was now 2. There was nothing on 8. And at first I thought the same of 31, which was barely coming in at all.

But then, when I twisted the antenna slightly to the left, I saw it.

STAR SURVIVORS.

And for a moment, all was right in the universe again.

Allow me to explain.

Star Survivors is the story of the USS *Fortitude,* a twenty-third-century space vessel that, cast across the cold universe by the shock wave from a freak ultranova, spends each episode in a desperate search for a way to rejoin humanity.

Along the way, the crew—led by the resolute Captain Aristotle Maxim and his loyal, inventive first officer, Commander Conan Steele—battles various life forms and navigational hazards that make survival a day-to-day struggle. Only by luck, wit and courage can they hope to live.

The episode I stumbled across was the one where the shuttlecraft is sent to a planet that is supposed to be a tropical paradise. But it turns out the sensors are being jammed and the landing site is really a barren desert with these land-squid things that surface unexpectedly and drain the life force out of the guest star.

As I watched his corpse get slurped into the sand, I could totally relate.

This is why you should ignore anyone who tries to tell you that *Star Survivors* is an entertainment program. It is so, so much more.

It is a guide to orderly behavior in a confusing world. It creates role models in places where they do not otherwise exist.

Don't tell me that it's just a bunch of actors in funny costumes. I'm not stupid. Or crazy. I know the difference between Apollo 11 and Ceti Alpha XII. One happened on a soundstage. One did not.

Star Survivors is a refuge. It is a beacon of hope that my future will be something entirely different from my present.

Which, like a life force–eating land-squid, completely sucks.

"Damn the gravity mines.
And the asteroid field. And
the tractor beams. There is
one way home for us and that
direction is: Full speed ahead."

—Captain Maxim
Star Survivors Episode 3,
"Where Space Angels Fear to Tread"

EXPEDITION LOG

ENTRY 2.01.01

Each morning I wake up and tell myself, *this is the day things start to get better.*

Each day I do my best to charge into battle the way Captain Maxim would want me to.

Each day my results are less than...stellar.

Today, day ten of the mission, unfolded in typical fashion:

0800 hours: Exited transport. (I can't always count on a ride, but today was pretty cold, and the commander took pity.)

0801 hours: Sought cover.

0803 hours: Was discovered by Ty Hunter, Jerry Sneeva and Bubba Pignarski. You met them in the earlier report. I meet them every day at the entrance, where they often provide a fashion critique. Or other observations on ways I might improve myself. I would quote them, but these guys use words that are fouler than the inside of a tauntaun.

Sneeva is small, curly haired and rabbitlike, in a twitchy way. When he plays defense on basketball, he is constantly poking, prodding, reaching and slapping until the ball comes loose. On offense, he spends a lot of time looking around at what everyone else is doing, and dishes the ball to them.

Bubba is built round and strong, like a boulder. He is possibly almost as intelligent.

Ty is the long-armed Death Star they orbit. He's always smiling with those razor-thin lips, but his eyes stay narrow, like a sniper getting ready to pull the trigger. I saw a face like that in a comic book once. The villain's name was Sinister something. He was a cold-blooded killer with nerves of steel (literally, on account of some kind of nuclear accident) who kept blasting and maiming and wounding and—

Where was I? Oh, yeah. Dodging them before school. It's a significant part of my morning.

0810–1505 hours: Attended school. My days are a blend of me seeking out Counselor Blethins; me being avoided by Counselor Blethins; me being induced to sleep by my remedial classes; and me being exposed to torture by various spherical instruments in PE and Athletics. Classes that I happen to share with my three least-favorite life forms, who also seem to be maxing out on their PE credits. Lucky me.

1505 hours: Sought route to home base that would not go past Hunter, Sneeva and Pignarski. Failed. Endured further verbal abuse.

1530 hours: Arrived at base. Sought high-sugar nourishment. Assured command unit that all is going according to plan.

She is shockingly easy to fool. After particularly bad days, I tell her I have a lot of homework, and I close the door to my quarters so I can "focus." This buys the solitude I need to recharge.

You might be wondering why I haven't gotten around to debriefing my commanders about what I am experiencing. "Are they even fit to lead?" you might ask.

In their defense, they *do* ask about my classes. I tell them things are fine. This is true, from a GPA standpoint. They see 100s on my quizzes, same as ever. They believe all is well. And it is what I want them to believe—that I can handle things myself.

Here's how I see it: They have so much to worry about. His new job. Her new studio. All these boxes. Oh, and the little spawn, who is extremely loud and frequently smelly.

With all that going on, eighth-grade interpersonal relations should not be their priority, right?

Which is why, when they ask me about making friends, I tell them I'm seeing lots of interesting new people. And why, when they pressed for details about my black eye, I blamed only my own clumsiness.

Half-truths like these seem to make them relax. And I hope it keeps them out of my affairs while I sort things out on my own.

After all, I am supposed to be an explorer of superior intellect and ability. Doctor what's-his-name was able to save the universe who knows how many times with not much more than a telephone booth and a sonic screwdriver. Shouldn't I be able to figure out middle school?

1600 hours: Shut off overwhelmed emotional centers by engaging *Star Survivors* on the vidscreen.

I wish I could spend my whole life here.

Granted, the worst problems the USS *Fortitude* must face are radioactive comets, antimatter-reactor meltdowns and fanged, leather-skinned aliens with plasma beams—nothing as bad as what I am up against. But at the moment, the crew is all the companionship I have.

2.02.01

Planet Festus seems fraught with peril in every quadrant. Except one: The Academic Resource Center.

For starters, it is a large room filled with books. My kind of place.

Second, those books are on high shelves. It is easy to hide there. And when people can't find you, they can't hurt you.

Third, there is Ms. Beacon.

Ms. Beacon is the commander of this zone. She answers to the title of ARC Coordinator, but the plate on her desk identifies her as LIBRARIAN. Which would make sense, because on other planets, this zone would be called a library. I suspect she was promoted some time ago and is just waiting for the new deskplate to be assigned. From the looks of things, she has been waiting a while.

She is fairly old. My guess is at least forty. Her hair is streaked with gray, and she keeps it cut short. She has glasses of the type that allow her to scowl at people up close *and* far away. When she adjusts them a certain degree, her irises seem to take up the whole lens.

Back on Day One, when I was escorted into the ARC for my first Independent Study class, the intercom summoned Counselor Blethins to an urgent consultation with Principal Denton right in the middle of her introduction. The counselor had scurried off midsentence, leaving me and Ms. Beacon staring at one another. She looked me up and down, adjusted those glasses, looked me up and down again, and adjusted her vest.

"So," she said. "They messed up your schedule and

Counselor Blethins has parked you here for an hour because she can't figure out where else to put you."

I was stunned. It was the first time at Festus that anybody had spoken to me with what seemed to be honesty.

"Yeah," I said. "I think that's about it."

She furrowed her brow and puckered her lips in distaste. "Well," she finally said. "What do you think we should do?" She enunciated each consonant precisely.

I looked into those glasses and caught a reflection of myself staring up at her. "Well," I said, "if you've got a place where I can sit and read, you can go about your work. I'm kind of at home in libraries."

Although it would not have registered on any photon sensor, at that moment I do think I detected a twinkle in her eye.

"I am certain I can arrange something," she said, and showed me where to sit.

Since then, Independent Study has been the one hour I look forward to. Ms. Beacon pretty much leaves me alone, except when she asks about the book I have brought. Usually, it's a collection of science fiction stories, or something involving an apocalypse. If it's a tie-in to a movie or a TV show, she suggests that I might want to look for something a little more illuminating next time. But other times she listens to me summarize a plot and nods approvingly.

And those tiny bits of encouragement—I cling to them. I cling to them the way the people in those post-atomic wastelands cling to the sight of a lone, colorful insect buzzing over the ashes, or to a hint of something green and growing on the distant horizon.

In other words, it is not much. But we look for hope where we can get it.

2.03.01

Sunday nights are the worst here. After a thrilling weekend of helping the commanders move furniture or hang pictures, I lie awake, dreading the week ahead. Sometimes I just flip my phone open and closed, like Commander Steele's communicator, and wonder what it would be like if anybody called, or texted, or just acknowledged I was alive.

On this particular Sunday, I was reflecting on things I had overheard the commanders discussing when they thought I was out of earshot.

The initial topic was their concern about me, and I immediately went on full alert status. Some kind of awkward intervention from them was the absolute LAST thing I wanted.

I could make out questions about how I was adjusting and concerns about how distant I had become since the move. There was discussion as to whether this was normal teenage behavior, or whether I just needed space to sort things out.

Then they started remembering things from the ancient past: The time I had broken down in tears in first grade when I saw that the reading list was nothing but picture books. The way they had pulled me off the second-grade soccer team because I kept ducking and crying when the ball was kicked my way. And the way I reacted the day we visited Disneyland and found that Space Mountain was closed for repairs, when my sobs actually made an approaching Tinkerbell turn around and run the other way.

Listening to them was dreadful. And made worse by my fear that they were going to come in and hug me at any moment.

Luckily, talk quickly devolved from concern about how I was coping with the change to how the whole family was going through it. They discussed Unit One's latest big story and the lights Unit Two was going to hang in the bedroom that would become her studio. They used words like *opportunity* and *finally arriving,* and how they hoped they had made the right choice, and how they were sure things would be better for me and the baby now, and how they had waited so many years for their break, and how young they had been when they started. And then they lowered their voices and started giggling and that is when I stopped eavesdropping and started thinking about how much they were depending on me to be strong.

I've been doing my best. But earlier, while scrolling the TV listings, I came across an old movie about a scientist who spends too much time in an isolation chamber. Deprived of human contact and with only his own thoughts as company, he emerges as a crazed half-human beast.

I am worried that this might turn out to be me.

2.04.01

Some observations on local fauna, as I mark one month since my crash-landing:

When dinosaurs ruled the Earth, small, ratlike creatures scurried beneath their feet. These creatures were too small to attract attention. They provided insufficient nutrients to the large carnivores, and this is how they survived in a world clearly not meant for them.

Similarly, on a TV show I once watched that was set on the planet Koozebane, tiny furry beings survived assaults from larger, alien invaders by hugging gaps and craters in the surface of the planet.

On Planet Festus, there is Les Martin.

Les, I have learned, is that kid I saw briefly on Day One in Athletics. The one who keeps disappearing. I have caught only fleeting glimpses of him outside the gym. He walks with his head down and his shoulder brushing one wall. He does not make eye contact. I've never gotten near enough to say hello, much less start a conversation.

But today, while I was slipping into the ARC, there he was, checking out some books from Ms. Beacon.

"Ah, my other charter member of the science fiction book-of-the-week club," she said. "Clark, this is Les. Have you met?"

He looked me in the eye for the first time. His head was round and smooth and pale, with thin strands of blond hair clinging limply to the top. His eyes were wide and blue, and constantly darting.

"We have Athletics together," I said. "I've seen you in the bleachers."

"And I've seen you get hit by a lot of stray balls," he replied.

Awkward silence followed. Ms. Beacon had to break it.

"Well, then, I'm sure you two will enjoy talking about all the books you've been consuming lately. It's as if you've been going down the same reading list."

I examined what he was checking out–*Tales of Time and Space*, one of the Asimov Foundation books, and a battered copy of *101 Home Electronics Projects*.

"Cool stuff," I said, genuinely impressed.

He stared at his feet, looked at the door again, and looked at me.

"I gotta go," he said, scooping up the books and stuffing them in his backpack.

Using both straps, he slung it over his shoulders. He acted as if he were about to say something, then put his head down and headed for the exit.

He looked up the hall, then down, then over his shoulder at me.

"It's dangerous out there," he said, softly.

"I noticed."

"Try to stay low."

Before I could reply, he had slipped around a corner and disappeared.

2.05.01

After that, I looked for him everywhere. But he must be part phantom. It's like one of those *Star Survivors* episodes where the *Fortitude*'s sensors can detect some kind of energy fluctuation off the starboard bow, but nobody can lock on to an actual target.

So I continue to walk the halls with my head down, hoping that I, too, might disappear.

It has worked, in the sense that nobody besides Ty, Jerry and Bubba feels a need to push me, bump me, knock books out of my hand, punch my arm or give me body-part-related nicknames.

It has not worked in the sense that every time I pass Ty, Jerry and Bubba, they push me, bump me, knock books out of my hand, punch my arm and refer to me with body-part-related nicknames.

Looking at things logically, I suppose this means my approach is a bust.

But I am still determined to salvage some part of my original mission. Like the zero-g sharks of Rigel IX, I must move forward or die. I must be bold. I must take action. I must push the envelope and advance into uncharted quadrants.

2.06.01

I talked to a girl.

Not just any girl. That one I saw back on my first day. The one who cheers. She of the skin and the hair. And the smile.

Yeah. Her.

I learned that her name is Stephanie Spring. Spring, as in what hope does eternally. Spring, as in the time when flowers bloom and a young spaceman's thoughts turn lightly to love. Spring, as in what the coyote optimistically straps onto his shoe as he embarks on his latest effort to nab that roadrunner.

Stephanie Spring.

It happened as I was walking back from one of my check-ins with Counselor Blethins. She and I play this little game: Every few days, I show up right before first hour, pretending that I believe she can fix my schedule. She looks around the office nervously, then hems and haws and apologizes, saying that she is waiting for clarification on the new schedule-changing policy from Principal Denton, and that she hopes I am doing well and would I like to talk with her again soon? But she also writes me a hall pass to be late for PE. Which I take full advantage of.

I was maximizing use of just such a pass by ever so slowly making my way to the gym when it happened: I saw Stephanie ferrying paperwork to the office. Range: about fifty feet, course heading 355 Mark One. I calculated speed and trajectory and estimated fifteen seconds to intercept.

Hailing frequencies were open—but what message should I send? "I come in peace?" "Greetings and felicitations?" "That's a lovely skirt you're wearing?" "How about them…?"

"Hey," I said. Those fifteen seconds went by fast.

She smiled. "Hey."

We walked on.

What a great day!

2.07.01

Conversation! A whole conversation!

A day after that beautiful hallway meeting, I was at the checkout desk in the ARC, when who should walk in but Stephanie! Stephanie Spring! Spring, like the fresh smell of a garden after a gentle rain. Spring, like...

You get the idea.

I probably should mention that whenever I had observed her around the school, she was usually surrounded by friends. Lots of them. And I had been thinking—based on the way we had connected from afar, in the gym and in the hall, she could really help ease my way into the native culture.

Today, she was alone, apparently on an errand for another teacher. She approached the desk, and I just stood there, next to her.

She looked for Ms. Beacon. Then she looked at me.

I decided to seize the moment.

"Hey," I said.

She smiled. *Smiled*.

"Hey," she said.

I thought: Captain Maxim would totally approve of how well I am doing.

She looked back toward Ms. Beacon's office, expectantly.

"I'm Clark," I said.

She looked at me, bemused for a moment, but then the smile came back. "I'm Stephanie," she said.

This was the greatest moment I'd had since arriving on Festus.

"'Clark' is an...uncommon name, isn't it?" she said. "We don't hear it a lot around here, at least."

Isn't it adorable, how she mentioned my name like that? "My dad liked the explorer," I said, smiling.

A brief silence followed.

"You know, Lewis and...?"

Blank stare.

"We have Athletics together," I said, changing the subject. "Well, I have Athletics. You have cheer practice at the same time."

She leaned her head to one side, quizzically.

"Oh, yeah," she said. "I remember your first day. I think your eye has almost healed."

I winced at the memory, but kept smiling. "I haven't, uh, seen you, except in the gym. Much." I said, wincing again at my own awkward words.

"No, I guess not," she replied, perhaps warily. "You aren't in any other classes with me, are you?"

"Uh, no. I'm sort of, um, having an issue with some things, since I transferred in, and the office, well..."

"Oh. You must be a hero!" she blurted, saving me from trying to explain.

A hero! This was a surprise. I had thought of my struggles as difficult, and I aspired to be noble. But heroic? Wow. Here was a young woman who knew how to judge someone by his inner qualities, and not by the size of the bruise on his face.

"Well, you know—hero? Not much of one," I said, trying hard to sound modest as I stood a little straighter than I had been. "Although I suppose—yeah, some people would call me that."

She smiled. "I thought so. And we're probably not in any classes together because you've been gifted, right?"

I almost embraced her on the spot. She *knew* me. She really *knew* me. I might have swooned, if Ms. Beacon had not emerged from her office and accepted a packet from Stephanie, who turned to leave.

"Nice talking to you," I said.

She turned again, with a questioning look, as if she were surprised that I could speak. But then, that smile!

"You're an interesting person, Clark. I'll see you around," she said.

If you had told me that George Lucas had called to hear my thoughts on how he could improve his next movie, I could not have been happier. Interesting!

A hero!

Me!

2.08.01

Being a hero changes everything. I've started walking the halls with my head up. I've started noticing how the dirty windows in my remedial math class, where we have been working on converting fractions to decimals for *two weeks*, allow a lovely, golden light to filter in. And when Jerry Sneeva made fun of my parka, again, in the hallway this morning, I laughed and told him he was obviously jealous. I didn't even look back as I walked on.

Like a hero. An *interesting, gifted* hero!

It was such a nice day, I decided to walk right through the middle of the cafeteria. Just to see what things were like. And wouldn't you know it, I saw...Stephanie Spring! How lucky I was.

She was sitting at a table with three other girls. By some coincidence, they all had identical haircuts (Stephanie's looked best) and similar sweaters with black collars peeking out from them (Stephanie's seemed the most stylish to me). A suspicious mind would have been calling up data on clone armies and how to overcome them, but my guard was down. Dangerously so.

"Hi, Stephanie," I started to say.

"That's another *totally great* outfit! Way to rock the floral prints!" called the girl on Stephanie's left.

I halted, panicked, looked down and saw nothing but my usual attire before I realized they were talking to a dark-haired girl walking in front of me, carrying what appeared to be a nicely balanced meal on a tray.

"Yeah, nice one, Ricki," added the girl to Stephanie's right. "Hasn't anybody ever told you how we dress in *this* country?"

The dark-haired girl turned and started to say something in response, but amid peals of laughter from most of Stephanie's table, her shoulders sort of crumpled and she walked on. Leaving me standing alone, awkwardly wondering how to catch the attention of Stephanie, who was looking away.

"What do *you* want, geek boy?"

And I froze as the clone army now focused on—me.

Stephanie turned my way slowly. "Oh hi, Clark."

A clone's jaw went slack as she turned and looked Stephanie's way. "You know this reject?"

Stephanie let out a surprised gasp and glared at her. "Don't be mean!" she said.

"He's got to be *some* kind of reject," said the clone, whose sweater was blue and whose gold necklace identified her as "Kaitlyn." "I've never seen him in any of *my* classes."

"Give him a break," Stephanie said. "He's new and...he's a hero."

Yeah, Clone Girl. Did you hear that? Stephanie thinks I'm a hero! I waited for the girl to apologize, then make room for me at the table.

"Uh, Stephanie," said one of the other clones, whose sweater was yellow and whose necklace indicated her name was "Kaitlin," "isn't he Ms. Beacon's aide or something?"

"I don't *know*," she said, sounding annoyed and looking at me a little nervously. "I *guess* so."

"Stephanie," chided Kaitlin, "they don't *let* hero kids work as aides. Once you're 'gifted,' they practically lock you up." She rolled her eyes, as if this explained everything. "Doing nothing but gifted hero stuff."

"Nothing at all," said another clone, this one in a red sweater, whose necklace said "Katelyn." "Until you pass."

Something was not right here. These were no everyday clones. These were mascara-wearing, ribbon-bedecked, bubblegum-body-spray-scented weapons of ego destruction, genetically engineered to find their target's weakest point, then annihilate.

"Yeah," said Kaitlyn. "I had to do posters for hero last week for my volunteer hours. They made me do a cheer for some of them. It was the *worst*. But he wasn't there. I'd remember that *craptastic* parka he wears." She, Kaitlin and Katelyn laugh-snorted in unison.

YELLOW ALERT. YELLOW ALERT. RAISE DEFENSIVE SCREENS.

"Umm," I said, "I'm not quite sure what—"

"Clark and I have spoken only once," Stephanie said defensively. "It's not like we're *friends*. I was just being *polite*."

RED ALERT. MAN ESCAPE PODS.

"Hey, Stephanie, I thought that when we talked, you, um...," I started to say. But the words shriveled up and ran dry. So I just stood there with a hopeful, desperate, pleading smile.

"OHMIGOD!" said Katelyn. "HE THINKS YOU LIKE HIM! HE THINKS YOU LIKE HIM!"

There were peals of laughter. None of it mine.

"Nice meeting you all," I mumbled. I put my head down and sped toward the nearest exit.

Making my way out, I noticed a poster I had not paid attention to before:

STRUGGLING WITH STANDARDIZED TESTS?
Helping Everyone Reach Objectives
can get your scores back on target!
Just
Get In For Tutoring!
No matter how far behind you are,
You're a **HERO** to us!

I was glad that the HERO students had a chance to get caught up on things. Maybe a little jealous, too, that social skills were not subject to mandatory testing. Clearly, I needed the tutoring.

Later, as I left Athletics, Sneeva, Hunter and Pignarski were waiting. They wanted to talk about the lack of respect I had shown earlier.

As they began to play a tennis-like shoving game among themselves, using me as the ball, I had no witty responses.

"You say, 'We don't know what's down there! It might kill us!' I say, 'I know what's up here. It *will* kill us.' Prepare to dive."

—Captain Maxim
Star Survivors Episode 33,
"Occam's Laser"

EXPEDITION LOG

ENTRY 3.01.01

Have not had much to report for the past two weeks. The routine does numb the mind, and I have no interest in recording each bruise and insult.

I should probably begin some kind of classification system for them, though, distinguishing them by size, shade of green/purple and level of harm inflicted. I hear that Alaskans do this sort of thing with snow.

I should note that I have succeeded at keeping signs of physical damage hidden from my commanders, at least. Long sleeves are great at masking, say, the spot where someone might have punched me in the arm between classes.

The psychological damage? Well, it's nothing that a few hours of reading in my bedroom can't alleviate. The books transport me to much more manageable planets, and when my commanders knock on the door, peek in and see me behaving the same as I always have, it sends the message that all is right in my universe.

Even as it gets weirder by the day.

3.02.01

Today I entered the ARC to the sound of conversation. An intense one. I probably should have just taken my seat and pretended to see nothing, but I was curious.

So I walked up to the checkout desk and leaned in a bit to get a better view of Ms. Beacon's office. She was in a verbal duel with someone I could not see.

I felt the chill before I saw his brown suit.

"It's a simple matter of obeying a superior officer," he was saying.

"George, you might have impressed a few school board members with your military talk and business jargon, but despite your efforts, this has remained a public school, not a boot camp. And I will be treated as the professional educator I am."

"You're daring to question my credentials, again?"

"George, you can't bait me into rehashing that argument. The school board sold people on the idea that middle schools needed military-style leaders to instill values and raise test scores. That makes you my boss. But it does not make you *right*. Especially when I think your judgment is highly suspect. At best."

"One should be careful about what one infers in public, Edna. Especially about one's principal."

"The word you want is *implies*, George. I have *inferred* quite a lot, watching you order people around. But I know better than to *imply* anything. And while we are discussing grammar, one should not speak in the third person to make threats. It tells me that my principal is very flustered."

Principal Denton pivoted and marched out of her office. His face was red, all the way past his forehead to his hairline. He slowed long enough to give me an angry look as he went past.

Ms. Beacon emerged a few seconds later and watched him go. She was wiping the palms of her hands on her blouse.

"Today's theatrical presentation is over, Mr. Sherman. Take your seat."

I did. But I spent the rest of the hour looking over my shoulder every few seconds. It was clear: On this world, nobody, and nowhere, was safe.

3.03.01

And then Les rolled in. Literally.

We had a cold-weather lunch—that means instead of forcing the inmates out of doors for a few minutes of recreation at the end of lunch hour, they give us the option of going to the gym or the ARC. In the gym there is spirited play and abundant social interaction.

Which is why I go to the ARC.

I usually head to the .600s section, for a couple of reasons. First, that's always been one of my favorite Dewey numbers—it's where the technology books begin. I keep hoping I will find plans for a jet pack that will lift me from this place. Second, it's in a far corner, where none of my pursuers would see me even in the highly, highly unlikely scenario that any of them visited the ARC voluntarily.

On this day, I was so busy scanning the rocket science books that I almost stepped on him.

"Greetings," he said.

He was lying flat on the bottom shelf, filed somewhere between metallurgy and carpentry.

"Hi," I said, as if seeing him here were a normal thing.

"This is a good shelf, should you ever need a quiet place," he said. "Woodworking and metalworking books. The only person in the building who would use them teaches shop. And based on my experience, he's not that into literacy."

I nodded as if I understood.

"I need to tell you why I've been avoiding you," he said. His voice was only slightly muffled by the books on the shelf above him. "You have to understand that to be visible in this school is to be a target. If they can see you, they *will* hurt you. They have lots of ways of hurting you. I don't mean just the stuff with the balls or the doors."

I thought of Stephanie's friends as he continued.

"You and I are both targets. Together, we would jointly become one giant target. The assault would be constant and merciless. It is the opposite of finding safety in numbers; there is *danger* in numbers. We would merely provide them a target-rich environment. Are you with me?"

I nodded again.

"But I can call you, if you promise not to talk to anyone about it. Do you follow?"

I did. "You need my number?"

"Not if it's the one on the luggage tag of that Cosmos backpack you're carrying. You might want to clip that. You never know who might be tracking you."

"Um, I will."

"Good. Now, stay here and don't leave this aisle for at least five minutes. I will be in touch soon."

He rolled inward and slipped out of the shelves on the other side, probably in the mid-.500s, somewhere between space objects and natural disasters.

3.04.01

It took him two days to call. He did so right after *Star Survivors*.

When the command unit interrupted my inane social studies homework—*coloring*! They had us *coloring maps of the continents*!—to tell me my phone had been ringing, I assumed it was a mistake. I hadn't expected him to follow through.

"This is Clark," I said when she handed it over.

"I'm sorry it took so long," he said. "My...older brother and his friends have been around."

"I see," I said, snapping the tip of my green-for-rainforest pencil in surprise when I recognized the voice.

The conversation almost ended there. I couldn't think of much to say to a person who couldn't even mention my name in front of his family. This friendship seemed to have as much of a future as the unfamiliar actor in the red shirt whom Commander Steele had just asked to explore the unusual chewing sound coming from the nearby cave.

"I know that everything I have told you sounds really weird," he sighed.

"Yeah," I said. "I mean—no. You don't sound weird. This *place* is weird. You know? I haven't been able to figure it out. At all. So no. You don't."

"It's hard to find people who understand," he said. "In my family, they'd call me an anomaly. If they knew what that word meant. They're not so into...knowledge. They're more about sports. Which I am not."

"Yeah, I saw you at dodgeball," I said, thinking of one of the few days he had not vanished after roll call during Athletics. "I mean, um, well, you saw me at dodgeball too."

"Exactly," he said. "It's why I'm calling you. I knew you could relate."

"But...you couldn't say it in person?"

He paused before replying. "I've gotten used to working alone. Unencumbered. Logically, I can see advantages in some sort of...mutual cooperation pact. But it's like I said. There are...consequences. Unseen dangers. You're not a fan of *Star Survivors* by any chance, are you?"

I swallowed. "A little."

"You know that episode where they get trapped aboard the abandoned base on Ice Planet Nine?"

"The one with the walking, hemoglobin-sucking 'zombie' plants?"

"Precisely. You know how the plants start picking off crewmembers by honing in on their infrared signature every time they gather in a group? And Maxim and Steele have to survive on their own until they can find a safe place to come up with a strategy?"

"Yeah, sure," I said. "But I'm not sure how that applies to—"

"It's this simple," he said. "If anyone sees us together, they will eat us. I have watched this happen. The only survival strategy is to keep out of sight." I heard a door slam in the background, and his voice turned soft and urgent. "I have to go. Noon, Saturday, at Sand Creek Park. Meet at the bridge. Be sure you are not followed." The call ended.

I wasn't quite sure I understood what was going on in Les's head. He seemed slightly unstable, extremely paranoid and possibly dangerous.

But hey—I had weekend plans.

3.05.01

Les is right about the risks of being seen associating with the wrong people.

While walking from science to social studies today, I had to pass through a hallway that is a nesting ground for some of Planet Festus's most vicious native inhabitants. Specifically, it contains the adjacent lockers of Stephanie and her cloned friends—Kaitlin, Kaitlyn and Katelyn. They were engaged in some kind of preening behavior that involved applying a glossy liquid to their lips and staring at themselves in small mirrors.

Another girl, full of trepidation, approached the flock. She apparently needed access to her own locker, but the Kaitlins kept blocking her, while also ignoring her, which took some creative choreography.

"Come on. I said I was *sorry*," the girl implored as the

Kaitlins kept staring in their mirrors. "I was only talking to her because she was my partner in Spanish! We're not *friends*!"

One of the Kaitlins walked away and whispered something to Stephanie, who had moved off to the side. There was giggling as the whole crew gathered in formation and headed down the hall.

"Why won't you listen to me?" the girl pleaded. The group kept walking.

"I HATE YOU ALL!" the girl shrieked as the flock laughed together loudly.

They went one way; she slammed her locker door and went the other.

Which proved something I had already come to suspect: The natives here are cannibals.

And if they're willing to eat their own—just for talking to the wrong person—can you imagine what they have in store for me?

I redoubled on my commitment to Les's strategy: Keep to the shadows. Work alone. Do not become food for zombie plants. Or worse.

3.06.01

Received a timely communication in math class.

Remedial math is a challenging hour, by the way: challenging to stay awake in. But I have incentive to remain alert:

Ty Hunter and Bubba Pignarski have class across the hall at the same time. If I don't flee as soon as the bell rings, they often catch me and liberate something from my person—a notebook, or textbook, or anything else they can grab and fling.

Today I managed to slip past them on the way into class, where Mr. Schmidt was writing a problem on the whiteboard. This is his teaching method: He demonstrates a problem on the whiteboard, he works out the problem *again* on the whiteboard, and then he hands out worksheets so *we* can copy the problem. At the end of class, we turn in our work. If we are still conscious.

Being a math teacher, he is not that big on words. This is fine with me when it comes to listening to him talk about remedial math. It is not so good when he confiscates books he catches me reading when I am supposed to be doing worksheets. So the challenge is to hide my paperbacks in my lap and hold a pencil upright while I read. Since my brain is not usually otherwise engaged, I am up to performing such subterfuge.

I slipped my collection of Ray Bradbury stories into the desk and reached for the math textbook in my Cosmos backpack. As I was setting it down, I scanned the desktop graffiti. I was able to learn the names of several popular musical groups and the personal habits of one or two teachers. This was just like every other desk in the building.

But at the lower edge, I spotted something unusual: a doodle of a spaceship. And not just any spaceship: It was the sleek shape of the *Fortitude*. Beneath it was written *EPISODE 47*.

It was a coded message, from one fan to another. I was sure of it. And it constituted the single greatest word problem ever posed to me in Mr. Schmidt's class.

I racked my brain, running through the shows in order. Episode 47, was that the one with the bat people? The one where gamma rays give Commander Steele superspeed and age him at the rate of one year each hour?

No. It was the one where Steele and Captain Maxim are captured by Dr. Creatosid and are able to escape only when Steele unscrambles the communicator passlock code and slips it to Maxim...under the table!

I quietly reached under the desk. I felt paper—something had been stuck there among the petrified gum globs. I peeled it off, slipped it into my lap and read: *Need an escape to Andromeda? Try the closet.*

Another code!

As anyone knows, Andromeda is a nearby galaxy, but even so it's far beyond the range of the *Fortitude*. There's only one way to get there, as demonstrated in Episode 23, when, in order to escape pursuing Vexons, Captain Maxim orders the ship to plunge into...

A wormhole! Someone was telling me that the closet held an emergency wormhole!

Great, I thought. Someone who believes in wormholes wants me to walk into the math teacher's supply closet. The odds of this being useable information were approximately—

"Sherman?"

Huh? I thought. "Huh?" I said.

It was Mr. Schmidt. He must have noticed me deep in thought, which would not have been part of his lesson plan.

"You will concentrate on your worksheet, please."

Oh, yeah. The worksheet. Wouldn't you know it, he'd passed out an extra-long one. *And* he was making us show our work. Show our work! I could show him a thing or two about—

I looked at the clock. I had spent about a third of the class pondering the code. So I needed to get busy.

I raced through the problems, but I felt like an elite runner who was stuck in a sandpit. Not that I would know anything about being an elite runner. What I meant was, the math was simple, but to break it down into component steps was time-consuming. I plodded along, filling out lines, watching the clock, pacing myself so that I would finish at just the right—

There. I completed the worksheet with a minute to spare. Really not hard at all, for someone of my advanced—

"If anyone needs an extra moment to complete the problem on the back, I can write you a note for your next class," Mr. Schmidt intoned.

The back? The BACK? I flipped the paper over, and there it was—a big, gnarly word problem with at least seven steps to be written out, leaving me with an even bigger problem: how to finish it and get down the hall ahead of Hunter and Pignarski.

I scrawled, I rushed, I muttered Martian curses as the bell rang. I suppose I could have turned in an incomplete paper, but pride was at stake here. Also, there was the slightest chance that Hunter and Pignarski might get bored and move on without me. I chanced a glance at the doorway as I slapped my paper down on Mr. Schmidt's desk.

Not only were Hunter and Pignarski nearby, but Jerry Sneeva had joined them. The whole gang, together again. Like a reunion episode of the worst TV show in the history of ever.

I slowly made my way back to my desk. No sense in rushing now. Better to apply all my energy to an escape plan.

Mr. Schmidt already had his back turned as he prepared

his whiteboard for the next class. I briefly considered asking him for assistance. Then I reasoned—the adults on Planet Festus, with the possible exception of Ms. Beacon, had not demonstrated NASA-engineer-like levels of ability with solving my problems, and Mr. Schmidt hardly seemed like someone who would buck that trend.

No, I couldn't seek his help. I also couldn't walk out. And I couldn't stay in his class forever. That left...the wormhole.

Schmidt had his back to me. The triplets were distracted for the moment—their waving gestures indicated they were laughing at someone's gas-passing. It was as close to a smokescreen as I was going to get. With the noise of my actions drowned out by the chaos in the hallway, I carefully turned the knob on the supply closet and slipped inside, hoping for the best.

I found...darkness. It was an ordinary closet. One that smelled of pencil shavings. Well, this was just great. I hadn't expected to discover the actual Andromeda Galaxy, but I had hoped for *something*. I began feeling my way around, hoping to find at least a light switch, but there was little to see beyond the thin lines of light coming from the cracks under the doors.

Wait—doors? Did I say doors? By the nameless spirit of Ahor, yes I did. There was the door I had come through, behind me, and one in *front* of me that led to the next classroom over!

I felt for the knob. I opened the door a crack. The classroom I peered into was vacant, the teacher already off to lunch. I slipped out of the closet, slid along the wall and peeked into the main hallway. I had completely outflanked my foes, who had their backs to me.

I offered a silent thanks to my *Fortitude* crewmate and cruised safely toward the cafeteria.

3.07.01

It did not take rocket science to figure out that the person who had helped me was Les. I didn't want to think about how closely he must have been watching me to know where to leave that coded message, but his wormhole had totally saved me.

Some might call my escape maneuver "weak." Or "cowardly." Or perhaps "running away like a frightened bunny." But I'm not ashamed. Well, not *that* ashamed. Space history is full of heroes who spent at least some time ducking and hiding and sneaking away from problems. Isn't that the basic summary of Han Solo's entire career? And things worked out OK for him. I mean, aside from being thrown into a deep freeze and turned into wall art in the living room of his worst enemy and all.

Maybe Han Solo is not such a good example.

But survival: It's a star explorer's first order of business, Captain Maxim would say. And I have developed special tactics to help me get through each day alive. Such as being aware of my surroundings at all times. Knowing the terrain and the movements of my enemies. Charting high-risk zones and taking precautions for dealing with them.

Take the gym, for example. I am at particular risk after Athletics, at the end of the school day. Because when my enemies don't get to harass me in the locker room, where Coach Chambers is often not watching, they sometimes like to stalk me on the way home.

I usually just need to hide out for a few minutes. My predators have blessedly short attention spans, and simple patience is often all it takes to outwit them.

Except when it is not.

Like today.

It was my own fault. The gang had been entertaining themselves by putting one another in headlocks—the sort of ritual for establishing dominance one often sees among small-minded, feral primates—and I should have just made best possible speed out of the building.

Which I was doing, until I rounded a corner and was distracted by a most unexpected sight: Stephanie Spring slinking out of the ARC.

I started to hail her, but she turned away and put in some fancy-looking earbuds that meant she would not hear me or anyone else. I didn't know whether to be disappointed or relieved, but I was definitely curious: What could she have been doing in the ARC?

I decided to check things out.

It wasn't the first time I had dropped into the ARC after school. More than once, I had waited out my pursuers there. Ms. Beacon never asks questions. Sometimes she even lets me help with shelving and stuff.

As I entered the ARC this time, it's possible I could still detect Stephanie's delicate flowery perfume in the air—it's not a scent I could easily forget—but I saw nothing else that indicated her presence. The returns cart held only a couple of atlases, an *Encyclopedia of Classic Rock,* a couple of fantasy novels that I had read years ago and that same book of electronics projects I had seen Les carrying the day I met him. Maybe he had been here too?

I was about to turn and leave when Ms. Beacon emerged from her office with several public radio tote bags draped over her arms.

"Can I help you carry those?" I asked.

"Actually, I would appreciate that, Mr. Sherman," she said. "I am in a bit of a hurry."

I took a bag in each hand and watched as she locked the library behind her. Our footsteps echoed as we walked the near-empty corridors.

"I trust that I am not keeping you from any important extracurricular activities?" she asked.

I shook my head. True, *Star Survivors* would be on soon. But it was nice to spend a little extra time with another sentient being, even if she was a teacher.

In the parking lot we found her vehicle, a blue Subaru with one faded bumper sticker that said TREE HUGGING DIRT WORSHIPPER and another, fresher sticker that said, THOSE WHO CAN, TEACH. THOSE WHO CANNOT, PASS LAWS ABOUT TEACHING. We loaded the bags into the hatchback.

Ms. Beacon looked distracted as we did so. If I hadn't known better, I would have said she looked worried. As if an adult whose life revolved around books could have much to worry about. When would I ever learn to accurately read emotions?

"Thank you, again," she said. "It has been a long day."

"It was simple." I shrugged.

"Simple acts can reveal true character, in people who are of good character," she said.

I blushed a little at that. But I tried to keep up my end of the conversation.

"So, I guess you're probably headed off to home to like, read a book or something?" Which is what I assumed a librarian would do in her off hours.

She looked at me as if she were trying to make up her

mind about something. "A book sounds nice," she finally said. "But I'm afraid I have to visit a friend in the hospital."

"Oh," I said. "I'm sorry." I thought back to the time I had spent in the hospital to have my appendix out. My mom was in full hover mode all day, which got annoying, especially when I was just trying to watch TV. When she wasn't there, Dad was, and to my great disappointment I didn't get to sleep underneath one of those giant beeping computer screens showing all my vital signs like on the *Fortitude.* "You probably have to, like, crowd in with your friend's family and stuff."

She gave me another curious look. "Actually, I have to wait for them to leave. They don't particularly care for me."

This shocked me. What kind of person would have a problem with Ms. Beacon? "They must not be very…intelligent," I blurted out.

Her lips pursed as she held back a smile. "You are an observant and honest person, Mr. Sherman," she said. "I respect that."

I said nothing but was pleased to have earned her respect.

"And I suppose we all must deal with people who are not intelligent enough to accept us for who we are. But I take inspiration from a science-fiction book I once read about life on a desert planet, where water was more valuable than gold and expended only on the most precious things. When I have to deal with such people and am tempted to start engaging with them, I tell myself, 'They are not worth the spit.'"

I laughed at that.

"And now I must go. Have a good afternoon, Mr. Sherman."

"Bye," I said. "And, uh, good luck."

She got in and closed the door. Her Subaru buzzed out of the parking lot, through the perpetual puddle of snowmelt at the curb, down the street and out of sight.

As I turned to walk toward home, I spent a moment attempting to classify the emotional readings I was picking up. As I just noted, emotions are not my strong suit. It is a trait I share with Commander Steele, although I would trade this commonality for his pocket laser and mastery of the deadly Omegan combat technique known as the Fingers of Defibrillation, a skill that enables him to incapacitate enemies with an open-palmed thrust to the chest (accompanied by his signature yell, "K'HAHHHHHHH!" and the tagline, "Never cross paths with a determined Omegan").

I looked around the parking lot. I rarely left the school by this vector. My usual exit led to a sports field, which was adjacent to a rugged, undeveloped slice of land known as Sand Creek Park. Home base was on the other side of the park. I usually walked around the park by staying on a well-traveled road that cut to the south. The walk took fifteen minutes most days. The commander came for me in the transport only during particularly bad weather, as class dismissal overlapped with naptime for the spawn.

I sometimes cut straight across the park as a shortcut home—but only when I had a clear head start on my enemies. Today, they had fallen off my radar. I had no idea where they might be.

I had to make a choice. Cutting across the park would get me home fastest. But I dreaded being caught out in the wild, with nobody to hear my cries for help. Going home by the usual road to the south would require going around the entire school building—and my enemies could be lurking behind any corner.

Detouring around the park to the *north* was not the most direct route. In fact, I had never walked it before. But I had seen it roll by through the windows of the transport. This route *would* keep me safely on surface streets. Also, part of my mission was, still, to explore this strange new world. Taking a slightly roundabout way home would help me feel as if I were accomplishing something.

So with a determined deep breath, I plotted a northern course, laid the coordinates in, and engaged my feet.

It turned out to be a nice little stroll. The sky was gray, but a tiny bit of white sunlight was filtering through, and much of the latest snowfall was melting. The breeze coming off the distant mountains was just cool enough to redden my cheeks. I was in a happy mood after talking with Ms. Beacon, and I felt almost invigorated.

I started thinking that this was not such an alien place, all the time. The houses looked like houses anywhere else. Although often, they looked like each other, clinging to every curve and roll of the hillside, except for the long, open ravine that was Sand Creek Park. As I walked, I envisioned a machine from a Dr. Seuss cartoon rolling down the hillside behind me, blurting out one identical dwelling after another, which would be rapidly inhabited by one identical family after another, with identical cars parked in identical driveways. I imagined that this was comforting if you fit in.

I thought of a book I once read about such a place, filled with boys who came out and bounced balls in sync and girls who jumped rope at the exact same time. Their lives were controlled by an evil giant brain, true, but that seems a small price to pay for not having to worry about being a lonely weirdo alien freak who has to dodge tormentors who could materialize at any moment—say, in the form of three figures emerging from the park and heading straight for me.

It wasn't. Was it?

Aw, frak. It was.

Whether they planned it or not, it was a perfect spot for an ambush, right where the road cut through the park, which meant there were no houses for a hundred feet in either direction. I got that feeling in the middle of my chest where my heart melts into my stomach and starts pushing the contents up toward my throat.

But I could not retreat. I had no safe place to run. The only shelter was my home, which was through the three of them. I cast my eyes toward the ground and strode forward. My hands, inside the pockets of my parka, were clenched into fists so tight that my fingernails cut into my palms.

My enemies waited, three abreast, on the sidewalk.

I tried to walk around them. Ty blocked me.

"Where you been, friend?" The term he used was not actually *friend*, but rather something untranslatable that I assumed referred to a ball of tissue used to clean a personal area of one's body.

I tried to go to his left. Sneeva and Pignarski closed ranks and blocked me.

"What's the hurry?" Ty asked. "Rushing home for some *play time* with yourself?" He made a gesture that had some significance to his partners, who began to laugh.

I'm not sure what led me to do what I did next. I didn't think of the possible repercussions. I was just scared and frustrated and a hot flash of anger came over my face and the tears were forming in my eyes and everything was getting blurry. And I wanted it all to go away.

So I took all that hurt and fear and shame and looked up at Sneeva and Pignarski and opened my mouth and the noise came from the deepest, most primitive part of my being:

"K'HAHHHHHHHHHHHHHHHHHHHHHHH!"

I lunged, palm-first. They were so taken aback that they jumped out of my way. I walked on, forcefully. Not running, just striding with a little more purpose.

I dared a quick glance back. They were not following. I had actually stunned them!

Then the shouting started. Out came all their favorite insults. But with each step I put between us, I gained confidence. Something I had done had actually worked! I had taken action—bold action, at that—and made my own success! This was a first. I felt *strong*. I felt *proud*. I felt—

I felt the projectile as it hit the back of my head and turned my field of vision into a red flash of angry neurons. I felt the ice shards shower down my neck. And with my fingers, I felt the spot where the welt would form as I realized that someone had just scored a direct hit on my skull with a rock-hard snow-and-ice ball from thirty yards away.

No wonder the coach liked Ty. It was quite a throw.

I looked back to see what their next move would be. I saw Ty packing his hands together and winding up.

I broke and ran. Not bold. Not proud. Just as hard as I could.

It wasn't enough. The next iceball made impact between my shoulders, right on the RAF patch. I stumbled forward, trying to get out of range.

They kept firing and shouting until I rounded a corner, at which point they switched to just laughing. I sprinted another half-block, then paused to catch my breath. I ran my fingers along my skull again, felt the lump rising, saw the thin sheen of blood on my fingertips, wiped my runny nose with the back of my hand.

Once home, I went in through the garage and bolted to my room. I shook out the remaining ice from my shirt, combed the clotting blood from my hair and put on the one baseball cap that I owned—the one my aunt had sent from the Air and Space Museum—to hide the mess.

I didn't want to cause a scene with the commander on duty.

I filled my favorite Luke Skywalker stadium cup with cereal and milk and parked myself in front of the TV and tried not to think for a long time. The welling tears made it hard for me to focus on the screen, but I had seen this episode before. And I knew I would again.

3.07.02

Of course the entire home base gathered for mealtime that evening. Which was the last thing I wanted.

Usually, we eat in waves; one command unit feeds the spawn, then me, then later the other command unit comes home and picks through whatever is left.

I prefer things that way. Because when we are all together, the commanders insist on talking about my efforts to establish peaceful communications with the natives at Festus.

As noted, I work hard to mask my failures. But even as I assure the commanders, they still want reports about my daily experiences and my feelings about them. They want to chart my entire psychological universe. They are really getting on my nerves.

I have attempted to spare everyone a lot of worry by simply saying as little as possible. But to them, this indicates something is wrong. And when they sense that, they want to tell me how to fix it. Particularly the male command unit, whose advice tends to be spooled out in long, impenetrable discourses.

I think of these monologues as conversational black holes. Their advice is so dense that even the optics in the room are affected. At least, that's the only reason I can figure for why they start talking about me as if I weren't there.

"He just needs to reach out and talk to people more," the male commander said. "I mean, it's not that hard. At work, I just met this guy, a few desks over, who works on the cops beat—big guy, a veteran, grew up somewhere in the Pacific, actually did training at a base I helped cover back when I was an intern. Anyhow, you wouldn't believe how crazy he—"

The female commander mercifully cut him off. "I'm sure Clark will be fine and tell us all about everything whenever he feels ready."

I wanted to ask them whether they had any advice for how I could make use of this invisibility cloak they had flung over me, and if maybe there were a magical boarding school they could send me to where I could learn more such techniques, because the place they had me enrolled in now stank worse than the spawn's diaper pail. But I did not think it was the kind of remark that would lead to a positive outcome.

And I absolutely didn't consider telling them what my life was really like. Because if there is anything more humiliating than being a picked-on, put-down, insignificant carcass of weakling alien roadkill, it is being a picked-on, put-down, insignificant carcass of weakling alien roadkill who goes crying to mommy and daddy when things get rough.

I still had my pride.

Not much. But some.

So I just finished my meatloaf, cleared my dishes and went back to my room, where the books did not ask stupid questions.

"The universe is missing dark matter? I'll tell you where you'll find most of it: in the hearts of petty men."

—Captain Maxim
Star Survivors Episode 39,
"Space for the Devil"

EXPEDITION LOG

ENTRY 4.01.01

Principal Denton abducted me today.

It happened right before second hour. After a typically invigorating PE class, I walked all the way back to the office and was debating whether to approach Counselor Blethins when he stepped out.

"Sherman," he said. "In my office." He turned.

I obeyed. I would have preferred to have run outside, been picked up by the *Fortitude* and whisked into hiding in a nearby nebula *immediately*, but that seemed unlikely. So I meekly followed in his wake, watching the adult staffers make an extra show of how hard they were shuffling pieces of paper as he brisked past. The only being who did not move was a student aide in the corner, who was quietly reading a book. I recognized her from the cafeteria—she was one of the few Asian-American kids at the school, and I remembered how the Kaitlins had savaged her about her floral-print dress that day in the cafeteria right before they sank their fangs into me.

I shuddered at the memory, stepped into the principal's office and sat down on the black chair across from his desk.

"Have a seat," he said, before he turned to face me.

His eyes were the same steel marbles I remembered from

Day One. But something was wrong with his face. His lips. They were oddly twisted. As if he had just swallowed an ice cube and did not want anyone to know it. Then I realized—he was trying to *smile* at me.

"How are things going, Sherman?"

Something did not compute. Not at all.

"Uhhh...fine, I guess."

His face made that look again, which made me a little ill. "Good, good," he said, looking over his shoulder and off into the distance. "You've been here—what, a couple of months now?"

"Just about six weeks, sir," I said.

"Yes, I thought so," he said. "And how is...your Independent Study class?" He spoke as if this were a casual topic of conversation that he had chosen to bring up for no particular reason. During one of our usual, regular, friendly chats.

"That's fine too," I said. After a too-long pause, I added, "Sir."

His face snapped back to me. I think he thought I was being sarcastic. But he quickly realized that I was just scared out of my mind. This seemed to relax him.

"Good. Any...problems with that *woman* in the library?"

I paused, thought about what he might want to hear, what might release me to the halls the fastest. But what could I say? "No, sir. I think she's doing excellent work."

He gave a little grunt of disappointment, and my stomach gurgled in response.

He did not look at me as he began to pace behind his desk. "Sherman, you got off to a rough start here. But you're aware that I'm here to help you, I assume?"

No, I thought, I was not aware of that at all. "Yes, Mr. Denton. I am aware. Thank you, sir."

He drew himself up again. "Excellent attitude, Sherman. All together, on one team. Reminds me of my days in the Corps."

"The Corps?" It came out sounding more confused than I would have preferred, but frankly, I could not envision him playing either drums or bugle.

He chuckled in a forced way and gestured to a shelf next to his desk. It held a large portrait of a young Marine, standing in front of an American flag. Next to it was a small framed case that held a dog tag, some colorful rectangular pieces of cloth and a red, white and blue ribbon with a bronze medal, showing an eagle, hanging from it.

"United States Marine Corps, son. The most excellent fighting force on the planet. And how did we do it?" He waited for a reply, but I had nothing. So he went on. "We did it with unity. And teamwork. Every Marine, from the top to the bottom, carries his load."

His eyes rested on me again. "Semper fi. All for one."

I nodded, uncomprehending.

"Several years ago, when the school board urged the superintendent to hire me away from the private sector and put me in their new fast-track principal program, they looked at my military record and said, 'Denton, we need your help in restoring values at this school. Values like honor. And discipline. And teamsmanship.'"

I stared.

"You would agree that those are important values, would you not, Sherman?"

"I guess...yes. Yes, sir."

"Indeed. But unfortunately, as we pursue these values, there are people who would...challenge us, aren't there?"

"You mean enemies, sir?"

"Yes!" he said, a little too excitedly for my comfort. "Enemies. They abound. Even a decorated combat veteran such as myself can sometimes feel surrounded. But you know how we fight them?"

I did not. "How's that, sir?"

"Together!"

"Together."

"Yes, that's what I mean. I need your help to keep an eye on…enemies in our midst. It's not as easy as when I was in the Corps, when all I needed to set things right was my wits and my gun." He chuckled as he held an invisible rifle up to his eye, squinted and pulled the trigger. "So I need your help in watching our…enemies."

Given the number of enemies I had, this would not be a problem at all. I always had my eye on them—often right before they threw something at it.

"And if you're doing that for me," Denton said, lowering his voice and leaning on his desk, "I can keep an eye on things for you. Is that clear?"

Wait a minute, did he just make some kind of offer to me? Because I think that's what he did, and I had no idea what he meant.

"Yes, Principal Denton. Very clear."

He smiled again. This time it did not look forced. It was the smile of a man who had just achieved something that made him feel smug.

"Good," he said. "Anytime you have anything to report, my door will be open. As far as I'm concerned, from now on, we're a fighting unit—two buddies, sharing a foxhole. Together!"

This sounded a little gross. But I told him, "I appreciate it, sir."

"Dismissed, soldier," he said in a way that made me think he was going to chuck my chin and call me his Little Buckaroo.

I walked out. The staff looked my way, saw that I was not the principal and went back to chatting among themselves. The girl in the corner kept reading her book. Counselor Blethins averted her eyes. I didn't bother asking her anything.

4.01.02

One advantage of sitting alone at lunch every day is that you get time to think. Today I was thinking about how the other lunch tables had greeted my efforts to make contact. In short, I had not succeeded. At all.

I wasn't welcome at the table closest to the entrance because I cannot catch a ball, nor am I particularly speedy.

I cannot go near the tables occupied by clusters of females. When I approach, I definitely feel a deadly negative-ion force field being generated.

The inhabitants who are skilled with the blowing of wind into tubes, producing a primitive type of music, seem pleasant enough. But the one time I attempted to join the conversation, I suspect that I passed through a radiation zone en route to the table, because I was clearly invisible to them.

Each table is its own planet. Each planet has its own defenses. The tables of people who seem ready to hire on if a rodeo should suddenly set up outside. The tables of people who seem ready in case a rock festival does the same. There are planets within these planets, and absolutely none of them are described in any astronomy books I can find. I'm perpetually pushed to the periphery—unable to maintain an orbit anywhere.

At one point, cruising toward the dead space among the empty tables, I looked for the girl in the flower dress, the one I had seen in the office, but she hasn't been around the cafeteria lately. Come to think of it, she disappeared soon after Judgment Day.

That's the day, maybe two weeks ago, when a group of males situated themselves so as to monitor people exiting the serving line. The males armed themselves with index cards, upon which they had written numbers. As females walked past with their trays, the males would assign them a numerical value from one to ten. There was much laughter among the males, who enjoyed showing their appreciation for Stephanie Spring and the Kaitlin-Kaitlyn-Katelyn axis, and seemed to have even more fun assigning low values to isolated individual females. Some of the greatest laughter was reserved for the girl in the flower dress, who was not given a number, but rather a series of scribbles that looked like an attempt at Chinese characters. They discussed her appearance in a series of remarks that included the sound of a dog barking.

It was not fun to watch.

And I haven't seen her since.

"Captain, the shadows, I think they're— YARRRGHH!"

—Security Officer Hernandez
Star Survivors Episode 50.
"Plato's Cave of Horrors"

EXPEDITION LOG

ENTRY 5.01.01

It had been such a terrible week that I almost forgot how Les had told me to find him on Saturday. The command units exchanged glances when I said I was going out to meet someone at the park. I slipped away before they could interrogate me too thoroughly.

I should explain more about Sand Creek Park. *Park* in the local dialect does not mean the same as what it meant back home. There, a park was a place with swings, mowed grass, a few trees, and people. Sand Creek Park is something they call *open space,* which I think means that after the developers realized they couldn't build houses on its steep, scrub-covered slopes, they put a sign out front and called it a park.

It is wedged between two hills. To the east, Festus towers like something Sauron built. To the west, clusters of identical homes line curvy streets with identical names: Beechwood Street, Aspen Leaf Lane, Ponderosa Pines Drive. Also, Beechwood Drive, Aspen Leaf Circle and Ponderosa Pines Court. I wondered where all those pines, beeches and aspen had gone.

The middle of the park is cut by a tiny trickle of water that has, over time, gouged a jagged ravine in the rocky soil.

I would not describe the landscape as magnificent desolation, but the place did look about as lively as a lunar landing site. I should have felt right at home.

Standing on the rim, I saw no sign of Les. I started making my way down anyway.

The park is ringed with a running trail and bisected by a worn dirt path that dips sharply toward a small bridge linking the barren eastern half of the park with the equally barren western half. The builders had not wasted effort on making the bridge attractive. It was concrete, with a railing of steel pipe. A marginally functional bridge in a hideous spot that nobody could possibly have any use for. I empathized.

My windbreaker had seemed protection enough on this bright February day, but as I descended, I found myself zipping up and thrusting my hands into my pockets.

Once at the bridge, I paused to stare down at anemic Sand Creek, eight or so feet below. The water was not deep enough to cover more than a couple of minnows and a flattened Coors Light can. And the bridge was making an unusual knocking sound. Must have been the wind.

Wait—there was no wind.

I looked over the edge.

The knocking stopped.

I walked to where the bridge met the eastern embankment. The soil was eroded where the concrete pressed into the brown earth. Unless you observed closely, you couldn't see the chunks of rock that someone had pressed into the gouge, forming a crude ladder. The rocks looked sturdy enough to support me. I hesitated a moment, then muttered, "Here goes nothing," as I swung over the railing and stepped down.

The bridge, it turns out, did serve a purpose: it camouflaged the entrance to a huge concrete drainpipe. And Les was standing in its mouth, holding a large staff, which he had been using to tap the underside of the bridge to get my attention.

"Follow me," he said.

He dropped the staff and disappeared into the dark.

Walking into dark pipes with people I hardly knew was not something I usually made a hobby of. Come to think of it, it sounded more like something a *Fortitude* red-shirt would do. But again—what did I have to lose? In I went.

The pipe was just about an inch shorter than me, so I had to crouch. Dust covered the floor. Within a few steps, the blackness was almost complete.

I looked over my shoulder to make sure I could see my way out. Just as I started to feel really nervous, Les turned on a flashlight.

"It takes a minute to get there," he said as the light stabbed the blackness.

I thought of every dark cave in every movie scene that ends with a scream from someone just off camera, followed by shrieking violins and a quick cut to the body on the floor.

Then suddenly, things opened up.

My analysis suggested that the space had been built as some kind of juncture for a stormwater drainage system. It was a rectangular vault a bit smaller than the moving van that had hauled my commanders' stuff. A narrow access tube shot straight up above us, and a couple of smaller pipes, too small for me to walk through upright, sloped into darkness ahead.

Les reached into his pocket. The flashlight flickered. For a moment, all I could see was tomorrow's headline: "Missing

Boy's Mutilated Body Found; 'What Was He Thinking?' Mom Asks."

But then Les struck a match and dropped it into a coffee can. Which was filled with wax from old crayons. And a wick. He did this three more times, with three other cans.

"Well," he asked, "what do you think?"

He turned off the flashlight. The glow of the candles and the sweet smell of crayons made the room feel as cozy as...well, as cozy as a concrete shoebox several hundred feet inside a hill. Someone had dragged in a couple of fold-up camp chairs. And milk crates—almost a dozen of them—stacked neatly on the far side, filled with old comic books and paperback novels.

On the walls were clippings from computer and music magazines and some pictures of bands I did not recognize. The floor was littered with boxes of electronics gear—tubes from ancient computer monitors, speakers from discarded radios, clocks pulled from either garage sales or trash bins, smashed droids, a burned-out hyperdrive coil. Maybe. I didn't recognize everything. But there was a lot of it.

I saw one battered cassette player and some well-used tapes, most from bands of one syllable: Rush. Yes. Queen. A few, with shiny gold-foil labels, had nothing but dates written on them. Those were in a crate next to a couple of lantern batteries (the kind with the springs on top), some jumper cables and a spool of telephone wire. I thought about what happens when water and electricity mix.

"What happens if it rains?" I asked. It was an odd first question to ask about such a marvelous place, I know, but I suppose all those dead red-shirt crewmembers were still on my mind.

"I wouldn't worry," Les said, cupping his hand over one of the candles to nurture the flickering light. "These pipes connect only to the storm drain on the curb in front of the school. Which is thoroughly plugged."

"With what?"

"Beer bottles."

I looked at him, baffled.

"From my stepdad. He fills these big, plastic trash bags with them and thinks I'm loading them in my backpack for recycling." He paused. "Or maybe he just doesn't pay attention."

He reached down and picked up a length of thin blue wire, which he began winding around his finger. "I also threw in some baseball equipment that I removed from his truck."

"Enough to dam up the drain?"

"Yeah."

"That must have taken awhile."

He stopped spooling the wire while he thought. "The bottles I packed in over a few weeks. The bases I took one night after a tournament. We lost. I was the final out. On the drive home, he said, 'The only thing you're not a total embarrassment at is stealing bases. That's because you're never on base. Because you can never hit the goddamn ball.'"

Les resumed twirling the wire.

"So after he fell asleep, I went out to his truck and stole his bases." He did not smile. "I don't think he appreciated the joke."

Les's head cast ominous shadows that danced on the wall in the candlelight.

"Anyhow, unless there's a really big thunderstorm, we don't need to worry about being washed out," he continued. He reached into his pocket. I stepped back involuntarily before he offered, "Gum? I should warn you, it's the kind that *will* stick to most dental work. I use it mostly for hanging things."

I should have realized right then—Les was capable of some truly weird stuff.

But the more I absorbed it all, the more I saw the beauty in what he had built. It reminded me of *Star Survivors* Episode 36, the flaky one that originally aired on Halloween, where they are on the planet filled with Shakespearean characters and they have to make sure Juliet doesn't kill herself when she wakes up in the tomb. All we needed were some torches on the walls. And a race of psychokinetic spider-people.

"So, what do you do here?" I asked.

"Oh, you know," he said, trying to sound casual but obviously proud. "Some reading. I moved my surplus electronics gear here after my stepdad complained about the clutter at home. And some of my dad's old stuff that my mom was trying to throw out. I tried to wire the place up for electricity, but it turns out that car batteries are kind of heavy. And based on the experiments I ran on my stepdad's truck, they don't last as long as you would think. You can power a lamp for only a few hours before the charge gets so low that he can't even start the engine in the morning.

"That's only an average, based on several tests, of course." He almost—almost—smiled at that.

"But really, more often than not, I'm just passing through when I'm leaving Festus by the back door."

Back door? "What back door?"

Les pointed toward the ceiling. "See that shaft?" he said. I looked up into the narrow tube above us. It reminded me of the chambers on the *Fortitude* where Steele is always cross-circuiting the power in an emergency.

"That leads straight to the basement at the school. The maintenance room. Where the grate happens to be loose."

He looked at me with an excited glimmer in his eyes that had nothing to do with the candles. "Think 'Andromeda' again."

I looked up as I sought to grok his meaning. And this time I realized...

Rungs! A ladder! A wormhole—straight into Festus!

Which meant—an escape hatch straight OUT of Festus!

"This is why I never see you after school! This is why you're never getting beat up! This is why—"

"This is why I brought you here," he said. "You looked like you needed a break."

I was stunned. And elated. "What...when...how did you *find* this?"

"I found the pipe a couple of years ago while exploring the park. Actually, I was looking for shade while trying to avoid my stepdad during summer break. Anyhow, when I started at Festus, I had...incentive to avoid people after school. I was really desperate one day and ducked into the basement. I saw that big grate, did some quick reckoning and took a chance.

"I'm taking another chance by bringing you here," he said solemnly. "And especially by showing you this."

He handed me a piece of paper covered in lines and arrows and cross-hatching and strange symbols. At first I thought it was some kind of wiring schematic, until I recognized the shape: a giant *H*. With an extra line across the middle. With a boot-shaped box marked *office* on the lower right.

"I charted an entire wormhole network," he said. "The closets, the basement, a couple of air ducts, which I would avoid if you have allergies, because they'll really make the snot flow like a—"

He caught himself, and cleared his throat. "Anyhow, you can use it to go through the whole school without ever having to encounter another student. Which is how I usually prefer it."

If someone had used an actual pocket laser on me, I could not have been more stunned.

"So there's…like…even the gym?" I sputtered.

He smoothed out the paper against his chest, and then pointed to a set of neatly charted rectangles.

"Those are the bleachers," he said. "If you can get to the higher levels after Chambers has called roll, you can lie flat and hide for the rest of the hour. Nobody can see you from ground level. Don't think about what you're lying in, and it's kind of cozy."

I suddenly understood the elation the rebel leaders must have felt when they got the plans for the Death Star and found that nobody had remembered to put screens on the exhaust port. I didn't feel worthy.

"Why me, Les?" I spluttered.

He shrugged. "I figured we could, you know, watch out for each other. Sort of a Luke and Wedge thing. Wouldn't have to be around each other all the time, but maybe if one of us is caught in a crossfire, the other could, maybe, help."

I was speechless.

So I stole one of Captain Maxim's speeches. It was something he said at the climax of the pilot episode, the one where their uniforms are all the wrong colors, but who cares.

"'I don't know where we are. I don't know where we are headed. I don't know what we will find when we get there. All I can promise is, we will live, or perish, as one.'"

Les responded to me with the *Star Survivors* salute: two fingers touched his heart, and then, with his thumb extended and his elbow bent as if making a solemn oath, he pointed toward the stars.

Actually, he was pointing to the concrete ceiling. Both seemed filled with limitless potential today. And maybe, maybe, at least some of my problems were about to be solved.

5.02.01

There is a problem.

Les is complicated.

I mean, even for a guy who maps underground storm drains and charts secret passages through the school, he's complicated.

He'd already established why we couldn't be seen together, at all. But he then decided that being *not* seen together would be just as bad. Because people would get suspicious.

It is weird logic. But I agreed to a schedule: Mondays, Wednesdays and Fridays, I could use the escape hatch. Tuesdays and Thursdays, I could use other parts of the network but needed to stay above ground.

"We simply can't risk drawing attention," he explained, emphatically, when he surprised me in a corner of the library again.

"Can we talk? Or text?"

"No texting," he said. "I don't have my own phone."

"But you can call…?"

"Only on the landline, when nobody is around. Cell phones leave easily accessible call records. And they can be hacked, if someone knows how to install the right software."

I thought that *Webster's* might want to add a photo of him under *paranoia*. But given how grateful I was, agreeing to his rules seemed the least I could do.

How to describe the exhilaration of my first test "flight"? It was magnificent. I dashed out of Athletics, crossed the hall between the library and the cafeteria, looked both ways and slipped into the door marked MAINTENANCE.

I ran down a dark flight of stairs and into a dimly lighted basement. There, in front of the furnace, was the promised grate. I lifted it and slid it out of the way, slipped down the shaft, found my footing on the metal rungs and pulled the grate in place behind me. After descending through the darkness for what seemed like forever, I remembered to turn on the flashlight Les had instructed me to pack.

The final drop to the pavement was just a bit scary, but I landed in the Sanctuary, among all those beautiful books.

I paused and flipped through a tattered copy of *The Time Machine* before I headed down the long pipe toward Sand Creek Park, and home, smug in the knowledge that the entire Earth's crust was shielding me from my enemies.

True, I was still a frightened nerd walking through a

sewer because he was afraid to be seen in the daylight. But I reasoned: a brave man dies a single death; a coward lives a lot longer.

And I have decided to accept my fate. Some things in the universe are constant: Newton's laws, the speed of light in a vacuum, the level of miserable tedium and tedious misery in my life. These never change. And never will.

"I'm detecting signs of life, Captain . . . but it's like nothing we've encountered before."

—Commander Steele
Star Survivors Episode 61.
"Prick Me, Is My Blood Not Green?"

EXPEDITION LOG

ENTRY 6.01.01

The moment I walked into the ARC, I sensed something had changed.

Ms. Beacon was there as usual, doing paperwork behind the desk. The usual debris littered the tables—eraserless pencils, abandoned binders held together by decorative duct tape, math quizzes folded into triangle-shaped projectiles.

At the reference shelves in the middle of the room, the giant dictionary sat untouched on its rotating pedestal. On the walls, time-faded posters exhorted visitors to READ. As if you would do what in a library, EAT? Maybe JOG?

And at the table at the back of the room? A girl.

The black-haired girl.

The one who had been in the office.

And had disappeared from the cafeteria.

She looked at home. She had her own three-ring binder out—it was unbesmirched by tape or doodle—and she was engaged in a book. Maybe the posters worked?

I immediately shifted into stealth observation mode, cleverly cloaking myself by standing at a shelving cart at the front desk and pretending to survey the books there.

Her hair was long and straight, kept out of her eyes by bobby pins. She wore a dress that, once again, was slightly out of sync with basic Festus fashion trends. This one, like her previous outfits, had a lot of flowers. Little white ones. And what was she reading? I couldn't quite tell. Maybe if I moved—

"Mr. Sherman?"

I leapt as if I were under attack.

"Yes, Ms. Beacon?"

"Don't you have some reading to do?" She had not even looked up from her paperwork. Her powers were mighty.

"Yes, Ms. Beacon."

"You have no doubt noticed that you have company."

I looked at her. I looked at...her.

"I...no, I hadn't...I mean..." I didn't want to acknowledge how carefully I had been observing.

"Ms. Wah," she called. "Will you come here, please?"

The newcomer stood up, straightened her outfit, strode over in a deliberate, poised way and stood next to me. She was taller than I was. Most eighth-grade girls were. She was also lean. Exceptionally. I briefly thought of an episode where the *Fortitude* is trapped in the Second Dimension, and to escape they have to—

"Ms. Wah, this is Mr. Sherman. Up until now, he has been the lone student in my Independent Study session. Mr. Sherman, this is Ms. Wah. She is now your classmate. I understand that there were some difficulties in your previous fourth-hour class, Ms. Wah?"

"None for me," she said, brightly. "But my social studies teacher had some details wrong about contemporary European politics. I apparently was too direct in telling her. So it was decided that it would be better for both of us if I did independent study in the library. Thank you for having me." I thought she might curtsy.

"Ms. Wah," Ms. Beacon asked over the rim of her glasses,

"am I recalling correctly that last semester, you had a similar incident with another teacher, shortly before you were assigned to work as an office aide?"

The girl didn't flinch. "I don't recall any actual problems, Ms. Beacon. Except that some French teachers, it turns out, are maybe not as fluent as they should be and are perhaps insecure when corrected." Her brown eyes sparkled.

Ms. Beacon looked amused, in her own way.

"I doubt you and I will have similar problems, Ms. Wah. Now, for the next five minutes, I shall tolerate talking while Mr. Sherman explains the basic rules of our ARC. After that, I expect silence. Have I made myself clear?"

"Yes, Ms. Beacon."

She returned to her desk.

I looked at Ms. Wah.

She seemed supernaturally comfortable. Which made me slightly nervous. I was not quite sure I wanted a roommate in my ARC.

Her thin eyebrows arched, as if she were waiting for me to say something.

"Uh, I'm Clark," I said.

"Clark? That's not a name one hears a lot these days," she said.

Before I could sigh and explain, she added, "Are you named for the explorer by any chance?"

It was my turn to arch my eyebrows.

"You know, Lewis and...?" she asked.

My jaw dropped a bit.

"If you're not familiar with them, I can recommend a couple of books. I did a report last year. Actually, it was more on Sacagawea. Clark was clever enough, but it's kind of funny to think that he and Lewis would have been lost without a fourteen-year-old girl to guide them, isn't it?"

I eventually blinked, then looked around for hidden cameras. Maybe I was being set up for—

"Or is your name more of a Superman thing? Either way, my compliments to your parents."

Many seconds later, when I had remembered to breathe again, I began to work on my response.

One part of my brain told me, "She's awesome. This should be fun."

But another part said, "Every time you have attempted social interaction on this rock, some kind of bruising has followed." I rubbed my arm, reminding myself how much of that bruising was literal.

I could not take on another battlefront right now. So I diverted all power to my deflector shields.

"The rules," I said, pressing my palms against my forehead and focusing on Ms. Beacon's command to teach her the library rules. Problem was, I did not actually recall having been taught any rules.

Ms. Wah seemed slightly amused at my obvious frustration. Which irritated me even more. Who was she to come into my ARC, sit at one of my tables and force me to be sociable? I'd show her.

"You've been in a library before, right?" I asked. "Good. If you stay out of my way, I'll stay out of yours." And I turned to walk away.

"My name is Ricki," she said to my back, her voice now bright and cold as an icicle. I looked over my shoulder and saw that her chin was thrust forward, and her eyes had turned dark and angry. "It's a pleasure to meet you. Thank you for the kind welcome. Now if you'll excuse me, I have some reading to do."

And she walked away. Not as poised this time; her hands were balled up into fists, and she had a determined, bouncy stride.

The synapses in my brain fired as fast as they could to dial up some kind of retort, but all circuits were busy. Was I supposed to just let her go after she had spoken to me like that? A moment ago, that was exactly what I thought I had wanted. It was a big room; we had plenty of space to avoid one another.

But there was something in her voice...where had I heard that kind of sarcasm before? That kind of off-putting remark that sounds like a weapon, but is really a shield?

Oh yeah. I heard that voice in my own head. All the time.

I wished I could get a do-over on that exchange.

I watched as she made her way to her table, pulled her chair out, sat down and picked up that book she'd been reading.

It was green. I squinted. Something about that shade...

I gasped. Surely I was not seeing things clearly.

I started walking toward her.

I confirmed the initial visual scan even before I could make out the title. I knew that book's jacket well: the spaceship flying out of the exploding sun; the shadow of a marauding Vexon looming behind them; Steele and Maxim standing, side by side, ready to solve whatever problems came their way with a blast from a hand laser or a palm thrust and a shrill, "K'HAHHHHHHH!"

She was reading *Star Survivors: The Novel*.

I calculated the odds against seeing someone willing to make a public display of awareness of *Star Survivors* at less than 36,480 to 1, a number I came up with by estimating that I had crossed paths with the 912 students in this school five days a week for close to two months now and had not seen anyone willing to acknowledge their interest in public, until today.

I had so much to ask her. Where had she been? Were there others like her? Did she know the self-destruct sequence from Episode 17? 5-4A-1C? That is always the test of a true fan. Maybe we could—

"Mr. Sherman?" Ms. Beacon's stern voice halted me.

"Yes, Ms. Beacon?" my voice cracked. Did Ricki just snicker?

"Your five minutes are up. Find your way back to your table."

"Yes, Ms. Beacon. I just need to—"

"I will not have this period turn into a social hour, Mr. Sherman. Is that clear?"

"Yes, Ms. Beacon."

I knew better than to break a Beacon edict. But I kept standing, hoping to catch Ricki's eye. She finally looked up from the book just long enough for her to see me touch the two fingers of my right hand to my heart, and then raise my arm and point them toward the stars.

She beheld me as a curiosity. I could not tell whether she was confused, amused, bemused or even acknowledging me at all.

I returned to my seat and stared at the pages of the novel I had with me, but I didn't get a lot of reading done for the rest of that very, very long hour.

6.01.02

As soon as the bell rang, I went straight to Ricki, my head full of questions.

I suppose a smarter star explorer would have learned from

his experiences with Stephanie Spring that he had no business approaching females, but to be honest, I was so thrilled
at the prospect of having someone of my kind to talk to that I
forgot all of my fears.

So, of course, communicating is one thing she does not
want to do.

I dashed to her table before she had even put her books
away. "Can we talk?" I asked, breathlessly.

She glared coldly. "No."

"What?" I almost cried. Then I remembered how I had
behaved at the beginning of the hour. "I can explain—"

"Don't bother," she said.

"*Why?*"

"It's complicated," she said. Then she gave a saccharine
smile, pivoted and walked away in her bouncy gait.

What *is* it with this place?

But I was not going to let things with Ricki die that easily. First off, I was desperate. Second, what else did I have to
obsess about? Well, saving my skin. But Les's secret passages
had me feeling safe enough. Which made solving the Ricki
riddle my new primary mission.

My first theory was that she was disinclined to talk
because of Ms. Beacon's presence. So I resolved to find her
during lunch. But even though I almost ran to the cafeteria
the next day, she was nowhere to be found.

Next I thought I might try to find her after school. Then I
envisioned how this might transpire: Me, loitering around the
building at the end of the day. Ty, Jerry and Bubba approaching. Me doing the introductions: "Guys, meet Ricki. She's like
me, but a girl. Ricki, you can start running; I'll stay here and

slow everyone down by letting them beat me until my internal organs are oozing down the gutter."

I decided to skip straight to Plan C.

Plan C was to communicate by writing. This would be tricky. The phrasing of the message had to be exact, and the method of delivery would be a challenge.

I had no contact information for her, so I would have to create it old-media style, with pen and paper. Which made me nervous, given the number of times my personal papers ended up spinning across the floor between classes after a helpful nudge from Ty, Jerry or Bubba. I could just see my note being picked up off the floor and read aloud. The mere thought made me want to be vaporized.

So after dinner, I hunkered down at my communications center in my private bunker to choose my words.

An hour later I was still composing. No actual words were being printed, but I had done a thorough examination of the wall in front of me, of the tooth marks on my pen, and of the various ways a piece of paper could be aligned on a desk.

After another half hour of this, I decided to keep it simple.

R,
Why can't we talk?
Sincerely,
C

Which, I thought, was rather elegant in its functional simplicity, a real Bell X-1 of a missive that was quick, potent, powerful and certain to break barriers.

I folded it in half, slipped it in a notebook and stuck it in my Cosmos backpack.

The next day, I hugged every shadow on every wall to make extra sure I was not intercepted with my payload. I snuck past the hall monitor through the wormhole network to make sure I was the first one in the ARC after lunch. And I left the note at Ricki's usual spot.

I sat at my table across the room and waited.

She came in, ignored me as usual, took her seat, opened the note as if she had been expecting it, whipped out a pen, wrote something, set the pen down, pulled out her book, began to read.

The anguish of the subsequent wait is beyond my frail powers to describe. But when the bell finally rang for dismissal, she calmly rose, handed me the note with a smile and disappeared into the halls.

I kept my cool for maybe three seconds. Then I hurriedly unfolded the message.

It's complicated.
Cheers!

She also drew a smiley face.

I ran to the hall to try to track her, and on the way I nearly ran right over Les, who was coming in as I was going out.

I started to talk to him, saw the angry look reminding me that hailing frequencies were NOT open, rolled my eyes and stormed off.

The thought that this planet is just one giant asylum crossed my mind.

When I sat down in science class, something on my seat crinkled. I reached into the back pocket of my jeans and pulled out a piece of graph paper I didn't recall putting there.

Saturday
1100 hours
Usual coordinates

Les's handwriting was familiar. I thought: he might never steal a base properly, but he has excellent prospects as a pickpocket.

6.02.01

When I arrived in the Sanctuary, eager to get his thoughts on Ricki, Les was sitting in one of the old camp chairs and dressed in a yellow baseball uniform that was slightly too large for him.

I made the mistake of joking about how he was obviously getting ready for a day of joyful bonding activity with his dad.

"STEP-dad," he said, in a voice so cold that you'd have to measure it on the Kelvin scale.

"Sorry," I said. "I guess…I mean…" I should have known it was a touchy subject.

"Don't confuse the half-evolved primate my mom married with my dad," he said. "My dad would NOT have me in a baseball uniform. My dad would NOT be making me waste a weekend day doing batting practice."

I was suddenly fearful of being exiled.

"I'm sorry, Les. I just didn't know anything about...your dad."

Les held his breath for a moment, then exhaled and stared off down the pipe, looking at the light in the far distance.

"He was a musician," he said. "Or at least, he worked in a music store. He fixed amps. Did stuff with sound boards. I think. Mom once said it was painful to talk about him. So I don't bring him up."

He walked over to a shelf and picked up one of those gold-foil cassette tapes I had seen. "Which means I don't know much about him, actually. Except that he liked music." He held the tape up, examined it for a moment, then set it back down. "And he had a sense of humor. It was his idea to name me after a guitar."

"Your dad had a guitar named Les?"

Les turned around so I could see his look of disgust. "Les Paul. He played a *Gibson Les Paul*."

"Ah," I said.

Long silence.

"What happened?" I finally asked.

"Car crash, coming home late from a concert," he said matter-of-factly. "I was three years old. I remember the funeral. Not much else. There were lots of guys with beards. I can't even remember what his face looked like, actually, except from old pictures."

He set the tape down. "But I remember when my stepdad arrived. Ben. Ben and his boys. I was in third grade. Have you seen *The Lion King*?"

"Yeah."

"Well, imagine that after Mufasa died, Simba had been sent to be raised by Scar and the hyenas. That's pretty much my story."

I pondered this for a moment. I envisioned the howls of delight and the small tufts of yellow fur flying. It was not pretty.

"So they all live with you? Still?"

He looked down and drew a circle in the dust with his right shoe. "The older ones have moved out. There's just...no, not really, I don't see much of them. I wish I saw less. It's one of the reasons I need a hiding place, to get away from Ben and his frakking baseballs."

This was starting to feel like really heavy stuff, the kind of thing they would discuss on the *Fortitude* over a glass of blue liquid poured from an old perfume bottle.

"Have you ever asked him if you could, you know, just quit baseball?"

He snorted.

"What about your mom?"

"You don't know these people. Well..." He looked sideways, then back at me. "Put it this way. I remember how sad my mom was when I was little. And lonely, without my dad. And how happy she was at first when she met Ben. I could see that he made her feel secure. We both missed that."

He drew a breath. "I learned early on that she just wanted us to blend in with his family. Which meant we did things Ben's way.

"It wasn't so bad, the first couple of years. He was focused on his own sons then. Left me alone. Well, not entirely alone. There was some forced bonding over baseball. He'd put me on try to coach me. Tell me stories of playing baseball ...or college. Or he'd drag me to Coors Field, buy me a hot ..og and then spend most of the time flagging down the beer guy.

"But Ben got angrier over time. I don't know why. It comes out when he watches me play. A lot."

I pictured Les out at the diamond, stepdad yelling at him, mom wincing as he awkwardly stands at the plate, outfielders coming in and taunting, opposing parents laughing, then clapping as "Strike three!" is called against him.

"I'll bet they play a lot of baseball in hell," I said.

Les nodded grimly in agreement. "I wish it were a problem just at the baseball games. Or that I was the only one he took his anger out on."

I tried to imagine what he meant.

"Does he...?"

"Yeah. Sometimes. It's a good idea to not be around after he's had his third beer. Especially if the Cubs are losing. Or if...I don't know. Whenever one of us says the wrong thing at the wrong time...."

We were silent for a bit, staring at the candles, smelling the sweet aroma of molten crayon. I thought of being a little kid, back in grade school, when the biggest problem I faced was that the tip on the black crayon wore out faster than all the others, which made it hard to get the details on the *Millennium Falcon* correct. Watching those crayons go up in smoke made me feel...old. Maybe overwhelmed.

"I'm sorry, Les."

He went back to arranging some of his electronics gear. "It's OK," he said. "It's not like I can't handle it on my own.

It's like a math problem. They've thrown all these variables at me. I just sort of try to find ways to balance myself on the other end. You know—on the left is a wicked stepdad and a gang of thugs. On the right is me. x = survival. To solve for x, I spend a lot of time in out-of-the-way places looking at wiring diagrams."

I had thought I was good at math, but Les was doing advanced calculations that I could barely fathom.

"Yeah, well, Les, you know, count on me if I can help. I mean, by the transitive property, I think your problems are mine now."

That made him smile. "Thanks," he said. "I guess yours are mine too."

"Hey, I've got something maybe easier to solve that you can help with," I said, eager to get to a problem that seemed workable.

"Yeah?"

"There's this girl in my Independent Study hour," I said. "Her name is Ricki Wah. Do you know her?"

Les shook his head. "If you have any questions that involve the word *girl*, the answer involving me is 'no idea.'"

"Yeah, well, this is something different. She won't speak to me—well, that hardly makes her unique. But she reads. *Star Survivors* novels." I described her appearance, her fondness for floral prints, her walk, her hair.

"I have a high level of confidence that I would know of such a girl," he said. "Are you sure she's not a hologram?"

"Pretty sure."

He just shook his head. "Did you already look her up in the school directory?"

"School directory?"

"They print one out for the teachers. It lists all the students, their parents, their phone numbers. If you could find one, you could maybe call her or something."

Call her? Well, that was a novel idea. I'd tried talking in person, and sending notes, and pondered mental telepathy; a phone directory had not entered my mind.

"Thanks," I said. "I'll look into that."

"Just don't get ideas and call me," he said, his face suddenly tense. "Remember, we have to keep out of sight."

I sighed. "Yeah. I understand."

I didn't.

He lifted his cap. I thought it was some kind of parting gesture, but he surprised me by pulling out a folded piece of paper.

"This is for you," he said.

I accepted the paper gingerly, blew off some hair and flecks of—I don't really want to know—and found that he had charted out the entire neighborhood on graph paper. Festus was at the center. My house was marked with an x. The streets were neatly labeled in black ink, but strange dotted lines paralleled them, sometimes abruptly crossing the streets, eventually connecting back to my house, or the school, or our bunker. He had taken time to note several trees, a few hedgerows and the unnamed streets on the far limits of the subdivision, where new houses were being put in. Seemingly random numbers and red letters were scattered across the map.

"It's great," I said. I turned it around and around, trying to decipher it. "You really put some time into this."

"It's not perfect, but I thought it might help you find your way home," he said.

"I can find my street just fine, Les."

"I didn't do this to show you streets," he said. "Look at the dotted lines."

I squinted.

"If you want to stay out of sight, you can roam the neighborhood along these paths," he said.

"Paths? You mean, like hiking trails?"

"Not really. These are backyards that don't have fences, or have bushes that hide you from the owners. I've tested them for months. The numbers here"—he pointed—"indicate where you'll need to cross the street.

"For example," he continued, "if you follow this line from the mouth of our bunker, you'll end up in the yard at 1509 Sand Creek Circle. Stay in the yards that ring the park until you get here, at 1811 Aspen Crest Lane. Cut across the yard to the street, then—look both ways first—cross between the houses at 1812 and 1814. There's an old camper at 1812 that you can duck into if you think you're being followed. When it's safe, follow this line behind those houses until you get home.

"If you run into trouble, you can backtrack and take one of these alternate routes. Just avoid going near the red letters."

"What are they?" I asked, trying to drink it all in.

"The *H*, *S* and *P* are where Hunter, Sneeva and Pignarski live. You'll cut down on your encounters with them if you avoid being on the direct paths between the school and their houses. Also, between their houses and any baseball diamond. Also,"—he hesitated for just a moment—"you'll want to stay away from places like Sand Creek Lane, which has a long stretch of exposed sidewalk and a ready supply of ammo when the snow piles up. But then, you already are aware of that."

I looked up from the map, incredulous. "How did you know?"

He stared at the floor. "I overheard them talking," he said. "They made it sound like quite a party."

"Yeah, well, I apparently need to call up Commander Steele for a refresher course on the Omegan Fingers of Defibrillation."

Les looked up. "Huh?"

I retold the encounter, how they had closed in on me, how I had pushed my way through palm-first, how the iceball had hit just as I thought I had escaped.

"Wow," he said. "I didn't hear all *that*. I just heard about the throw, how Ty had nailed you from thirty yards out. You really tried the Omegan Fingers of Defibrillation on them? 'K'HAHHHHHHH!' and everything?"

"Yeah," I said.

He spoke in awe. "That's…that's…" He swallowed. "That's about the dorkiest thing I've ever heard." He started to laugh.

"It seemed like a good idea at the time," I said. And then I joined in the laughter. "Yeah, it was pretty dorky."

He sighed. "Survival: the first order of business."

I nodded in agreement with him and Maxim and studied the map awhile longer.

"Hey, you know where I live. Want to come over? Instead of hiding in a sewer?"

His face clouded. "I've told you, nobody can see us. You promised."

"Yeah, I did," I said. "It's just…it would be more…normal."

"For people like us, this is normal," he said harshly. "It always will be. Get used to it." He turned on the flashlight and blew out the candle. "I have to go. Give me five minutes so I can clear the park. I'll let you know when I can meet again."

I watched his light dance down the tube. Then I sat in the darkness for a bit. I suppose I could get used to living underground. But in the distance, I imagined I could hear the echoes of our laughter. It sounded like two normal guys having a normal weekend day.

Why did that have to be such a galactic challenge?

6.02.02

Back at the base, I have been investing a lot of effort in researching the effects of video games: how they speed up time and absorb the long, lonely hours; how they teach valuable skills about dealing with alien encounters. (Shoot first is a good strategy.)

Their application to the real world is somewhat limited. For example, I have never found any equivalent to the smart bomb, a magic button that would vaporize all my enemies at once, for the real world.

Also, although video games are good for working out frustration, they apparently can't mask it entirely.

I know this because my own frustration level has become critical enough that even my commanders have picked up on it. As indicated by the fact that the male commander just insisted on taking me on a trip to the hardware store.

Back at the home planet, he and I used to visit the hardware store a lot. He is not the handiest of guys, as the female commander likes to point out, so his purchases tended to be basic: tubes of caulk, cans of WD-40, a replacement bulb for the light inside the refrigerator, a second bulb when he realized he bought the wrong size.

But we would always walk down the aisles together to look at the cool tools—like leveling devices that employed actual lasers. And mountains of less fantastic but still important stuff, like space-ready work gloves, one-hundred-piece mechanic's tool sets, and way in the back, a small room devoted to model rocketry. Which my commander kept promising I could get into...later. For some reason, he seemed put off by all the DANGER: EXPLOSIVES signs.

Wandering the aisles amid all that stuff was the closest I ever came to living next to a junkyard, which I still hope to do someday. According to several books I have read, kids used to have regular access to junkyards, and they made the coolest things from stuff they found. Oh, what I could have made with the material from a real junkyard: A go-kart. A catapult. A robot. A robot-driven go-kart that had a catapult on the back!

The new hardware store is much less inspiring—just a big warehouse where everything is neat, orderly, orange and boring.

My commander was here to pick up some duct tape. But for old times' sake, I think, he walked me past the power tools. He stopped and reached out for a drill that was hanging off a couple of hooks. As if he knew how to use one.

"So, Clark," he asked me, casually examining the drill, maybe a little afraid of it. "How are things at school?"

Aha! Just as I had expected—he was trying to lure me into neutral territory and interrogate me! It's a good thing I had not let my guard down.

"Fine, I guess," I told him. I looked around at the tools, wishing to be somewhere he was not.

"You know, if you were having any problems, I'd be happy to try to help you," he said. He started to put the drill back on the display rack, but he missed the hooks, and it went crashing, loudly, to the counter.

As if I needed a reminder that he was not much good at fixing anything.

"I'm OK, Dad. Really."

He looked around to see whether anyone had watched him drop the drill, then walked on, with his hands thrust into the pockets of his old brown coat.

"Well, that's good," he said. "Because—you know, you could tell me if something were wrong."

Sure, I thought. But how could I tell him that *everything* was wrong? The teachers, the counselor, the principal, the lunchroom, the students, my weird friend from the underground pipe? How would Mr. Can't-Even-Hold-a-Drill fix any of that?

"I know," I said.

"Good," he said, turning the corner and looking lost, obviously disoriented in his quest for duct tape. "I'm sure this move hasn't been all that easy for you, Clark."

"It's been OK," I lied.

"And you'd let me know if you needed anything? Because it's OK to ask for help. Really."

He had passed three clerks while he looked up and down

the aisles, in vain, for the duct tape. He then walked past an entire end display full of the stuff.

"Tape's over here, Dad," I said, as he kept walking.

He turned, looked at me, confused, and then saw the shelf.

"Oh," he said. "Good eye."

As we drove home with the tape, the commander turned on the radio and tuned it to the all-sports station. "Hey, this reminds me," he said, listening to some kind of noisy chatter about drafts and salary caps, "I was getting coffee with one of the sportswriters at work, and when I told him where you go to school, he said something about you having a classmate who's already getting calls from college scouts. In eighth grade! Name was Hunker or Harper or something. Ever hear of him?"

"Doesn't ring a bell," I said, wondering if he would notice if I used a little duct tape to stop up my ears so I wouldn't have to listen to him anymore.

6.03.01

Somehow still feeling isolated despite my commander's outreach, and unable to maintain dependable communications with Les, I have redoubled my efforts to decipher Ricki Wah, who has a whole bookshelf's worth of mysteries surrounding her.

She is in the library every day but refuses to speak to me beyond repeating, "It's complicated." After class, she slips into the thick crowds and evades me. The one time I got close, she ducked into the girls' rest room.

I never see her in the cafeteria. And I can't find her in the school directory. I asked Ms. Beacon for this mystical document, claiming I was doing research of an unspecified nature. She had a bit of a smirk as she let me peruse her copy. But there was no listing for any Wah.

I suppose most people would have given up at this point. But one advantage to being an alien in a strange land is that you are not distracted by things such as a social life. For now, Ricki was the only hobby I had.

This was not some gauzy soft-focus obsession, like that thing between the long-haired yeoman and Captain Maxim from Season One. This is more like Episode 27, with the Invisible Girl who could walk through walls. I just wanted to know how she did it.

Also, what was the meaning of "It's complicated"? Did she think I was stupid? That I couldn't understand? I took this as a challenge. I mean, if I couldn't establish communications with a *Star Survivors* fan, how would I ever establish communications with *anyone*?

I was having an especially deep ponder on these matters, and was probably glaring across the room at Ricki, when Ms. Beacon called me up to her desk.

"Mr. Sherman," she said, "the office aide who collects attendance forms seems to have forgotten to visit our ARC this hour. I wouldn't want Principal Denton to think I had been derelict in my duties. Would you please run these to the office?"

I accepted the forms and grabbed the hall pass off her desk. These things were such a ridiculous waste of paper,

I thought as I made my way down the hall. But somebody needed the data. So there we were. *Sherman, Clark* and...

I looked at the form. Nobody named *Wah, Ricki*.

It was *Roy, Erika*.

I almost ran the rest of the way to the office. "Ms. Beacon said you needed these," I told the receptionist. "And, um, do you have a school directory handy? She wanted me to check something."

She pulled out a worn, photocopied list, stapled in the corner and with several names updated and initialed.

I flipped to the *R* page.

There it was: *Roy, Erika. Parents: Ana and Thierry.*

And a phone number marked *home*.

Which I copied onto my hand.

I practically skipped back to the ARC and smiled broadly at Ms. Roy-pronounced-Wah as I returned to my seat.

At last, a key mystery of Festus was being unraveled. By me!

6.03.02

I have known few pleasures in this universe, but the anticipation of triumph over someone who challenged you surely has to be one of the sweetest.

I vowed to test the number that very evening. I pondered what it would be like to talk to her, to say, "Well, I guess it wasn't too complicated to find YOU." Or maybe, "How's this for uncomplicated?" No, it should be more like, "Hello, Ricki. Do you know who this is? It's not so complicated."

Yes. That would work.

I waited until my command units were busy—one folding laundry while simultaneously watching the spawn and a basketball game, the other doing something with her cameras. I slipped into my quarters. I pulled out my phone. I savored the taste of pending victory.

I punched in the number.

The line clicked. In the moment before I heard the ring, I thought of Mercury and Apollo astronauts and that eternal wait people on Earth went through while the capsule was reentering the atmosphere, when the mission was at its most dangerous point but nobody could tell whether everything was proceeding according to the well-rehearsed plan or simply incinerating in an explosive, flaming disaster.

Ring! The call went through.

Ring! It rang a second time.

Ring! Well, maybe they weren't—

(Click.) "Hello?" It was a woman's voice. "Who is this? I do not recognize this number. We are on the 'Do Not Call' list, you know."

"Um, hi. I was trying to reach—"

"You sound like a child," she said, her words clipped, her tone cold. "Do you children in this country not know to treat an adult with respect?"

"Uh, yes ma'am. Sorry, ma'am. I was wondering whether Ricki—"

"Ricki? You mean Erika? "

"Uh, yes. Ma'am. She and I—" As my level of nervousness grew, so did the pitch of my voice.

"Are you one of those terrible girls who has been causing my daughter so many problems?"

"No, ma'am," I said. The pitch was climbing toward the range that only dogs could hear. "I have a class with Ricki, and I was just hoping to say—" At that moment, my voice cracked and squealed like a delicate vase being shattered against a chalkboard floor.

"My daughter has no time for boys."

I started to think that this was not going well.

"And if you don't respect me, then perhaps you will listen to Erika's father. THIERRY! THIERRY! COME GET THIS BOY OFF THE PHONE."

I did not feel disrespect. What I felt was...horrified. But I kept hanging on, as if I were a mere observer, wondering what would happen next.

What happened next is that I heard some shouting in the background, and then a voice that made me think of the bad guy in the first Indiana Jones movie.

"This is Erika's father, OK? And you will not call, OK?"

"Uh, yes sir."

He sighed.

There was some rustling on the line, and then the woman's voice again.

"And now, to show you that Erika has manners, I will allow her to tell you farewell herself."

More rustling.

A brief silence.

Ricki's voice, shaky: "With whom am I speaking?"

"It's me, Ricki. I mean, Clark. I mean—"

Her voice turned hoarse.

"I told you, it's *complicated*. Please do not call again. Thank you, and have a nice day."

Click.

She was right. It was complicated.

I envisioned a Mercury capsule making a fiery plunge into the sea, the scalded metal hissing as it sinks into the black and merciless depths where it would lie in dark solitude until the end of time.

I wished I had it so easy.

"The Omegan holy book on the art of war has a verse about our situation: *'Klavek turo; miktol tuvey; domini kla-tek; vin-tschu.'* The approximate Earth translation would be: 'We're up the creek, guys.'"

—Commander Steele
Star Survivors Episode 17.
"The Thanatos Gyre"

EXPEDITION LOG

ENTRY 7.01.01

Ricki was not in the ARC today.

7.02.01

Or today.

7.03.01

Or today. But neither was I, mostly. Because at the start of the hour, I was summoned by Principal Denton.

My walk down the hall should have come with a sound track—something with a lot of low brass and timpani. Music like that always plays before you meet a dark lord.

When I arrived in his office, he was rearranging things on his shelves.

"Ah, Sherman. I've been expecting you. Here, would you mind holding this for me, son? I'm just doing a little tidying up."

He handed me the framed case of his ribbons, dog tag and medals. In the middle was an engraved piece of metal that said GEORGE DENTON–SEMPER FI. That's when I remembered—we were supposed to be on the same team.

"So, how are things going, son?" he asked casually. He had his back turned to me as he ran a cloth along his shelf. I stood there, forced to stare down at his awards, while I pondered the possible responses to his question. The most honest would have been, "Considering I'm often being pursued by sadistic morons, that my only friend is too paranoid to acknowledge my existence, and I apparently just drove a girl into the Phantom Zone, I would say that things really stink for me. You?"

Instead I said, "As well as could be expected, sir."

"Good," he said, slowly circling back toward his seat. "Have there been any...problems in your Independent Study class?"

"None that I am aware of, sir." I kept holding the case, wondering what I was supposed to do with it.

"Are you sure?" he said, taking a seat and locking eyes with me. "Because I recently received a phone call from a disturbed parent. She's under the impression that her daughter is being picked on in that very class."

My mouth went dry as moon dust. And my hands must have started shaking, because I fumbled the case in a way that made the backing slip out, and everything rattled to the floor.

Denton's eyes flared with anger as I scrambled to pick up the pins that read RIFLE SHARPSHOOTER and PISTOL EXPERT and the dog tag stamped with his name.

"I'm so sorry, Mr. Denton, I was—OUCH!" I yelled as I felt a stabbing pain in my finger. I looked down and saw a tiny bead of blood oozing out where I had pricked myself on the bronze medal with the red, white and blue ribbon. I read the words SOLDIER'S MEDAL FOR VALOR on the back.

He rose halfway out of his chair and his forehead grew red as I hurriedly set everything on his desk, but he said nothing, just scooped it all into a desk drawer. Then he sat back down, exhaled and forced a smile.

"It's OK, son. That case was pretty old. And I've dealt with this particular parent before. She's a pretty high-strung…foreigner. Besides, I told you that you and I were a team. Semper fi, foxhole buddies—remember?"

I nodded, started breathing again and sucked on my finger for a moment before I realized that's probably gross.

"I really have just one question for you," he said. "If I made a note in my file that the problems in your Independent Study sessions were because of your instructor, would you agree?"

I stared blankly, not quite comprehending.

"You see," he said, leaning in toward me, his eyes cyborg-like, "I have to put something down as a likely cause of any parental complaint. I would like to say it was…'lax supervision' by the classroom instructor. Which it was. Right?"

"Lax…what?" I stammered. "Sir?"

He sat back a bit. "That's just what I thought."

I didn't want to agree, but I couldn't figure out how to disagree. All I could do was stare. Which was all he needed.

"Good," he said, making a note in a file, then closing it.

"Sherman, I knew all along I could count on you. A decorated combat veteran such as myself develops a sense of who he can trust in a bind. It's how one survives in the bush. And thrives in the dog-eat-dog world of business. So I've got your back, soldier. And this soldier is glad to know you've got mine. Semper fi."

I nodded my thanks—what for, I'm not sure—and walked out.

Back in the library, Ms. Beacon was at the checkout desk, filling out paperwork. She looked up as I came in, but I headed straight for my chair, sat down and tried to hide behind a book.

It worked, for most of the hour. But a few minutes before the bell rang, she called me to her desk.

"Clark," she asked, "have you seen your classmate, Ricki, lately?"

"No, not really," I said, staring at my shoes.

"Is that what Principal Denton wanted to discuss in his office?"

"Sort of." I felt a surge of guilt in my stomach and a rush of blood to my face.

She nodded, and studied me for a few seconds. "Did he ask some odd questions about my abilities as an educator?"

I raised my head just a little and gave a very slight nod.

"And did he also casually mention that he was a decorated combat veteran?"

I stood up straight. "How did you know?"

She smiled. "A lucky guess. I have been dancing with George Denton for many years, and I know his steps well."

Dancing? This did not compute at all.

"That's figurative," she explained.

Oh.

"Mr. Sherman, has anyone ever told you how George Denton became a principal here?"

I shook my head.

"Well, history is important. So here is a brief lesson. There are those in this community who think that what an educational institution needs is not professionals who understand education, but professionals who come from backgrounds that have nothing to do with education."

I tried to process this. "That doesn't make a lot of sense to me."

"Nor to me. But that was the will of the people. So several years ago, noneducators were recruited into this district's leadership positions, given cursory certification and turned loose on our schools. George Denton's exploits with a gun and his record as a business executive—he did mention that, I presume?"

I nodded.

"He is consistent in that way. In any case, his jargon so impressed the higher-ups that almost nobody here will challenge him. Even though the results of his blustering methods have shown what some of us predicted all along: he is an academic mediocrity."

Wow, I thought. Who knew that a history lesson that did not involve anybody flying a fighter plane could be so interesting?

But this background did not exactly make things easier for me. Like him or not, he *was* still a principal. And a war hero. And I was, technically, still a zero.

I ran the fingers of both hands through my hair until they met at the back of my neck. "I'm really confused, Ms. Beacon."

She huffed.

"And that is an abomination, Mr. Sherman. Because we are the people in your life who are supposed to be solving problems for you, not causing them."

She stared straight at me as she spoke. "I have no idea what Principal Denton has asked you to do. I suspect it is vile and reprehensible. And targeted at me."

She managed to add intensity to her voice without adding volume, something she probably learned in librarian school. "But you're not responsible for me, Clark. You are merely responsible for yourself. And for making correct choices on your own. Good choices.

"You can do that. I trust you."

Somehow, hearing those last three words did more for my morale than all of Denton's semper fi speeches put together.

7.03.02

Our conversation gave me a lot to think about. But I am not using that as an excuse for what happened next, because a star explorer is supposed to be ever-vigilant.

I wasn't. So what happened was entirely my own fault again.

It is almost officially spring, and marginally warmer weather means that the important lessons being conveyed in PE and Athletics have shifted from Throwing of Balls in Confined Spaces to the Mindless Circling of an Outdoor Pasture. Some people call it *track*.

On the one hand, being outside gives me more room to maneuver—and fewer projectiles to dodge. On the other, it requires even more precision timing than usual. If I want to avoid my predators in the locker room at the end of class, I must carefully keep them on the opposite side of the track. Failing that, I try to be surrounded by lots of people who can serve as a buffer.

But today, lost in thought about Ricki's disappearance, Denton's demands and Ms. Beacon's revelations, I made some critical errors.

First, I didn't see that Coach Chambers was actually monitoring us. And when he saw me walking what should have been my final lap, he made me do another. This threw off my timing considerably.

By the time I ran that extra lap, not only was I worn out, I was feeling a little sick. And I was so far behind the main pack of students that there was no hope of using them as a shield.

Staggering toward the school, I was hoping that this was a day when Ty's gang had some other urgent activity to get to, such as a kitten-drowning. But when I finally got to the locker room, sweaty and queasy in my baggy PROPERTY OF FESTUS gym shorts and T-shirt, I saw two things that froze me in place:

The rest of the class had already cleared out...

...Except for three people who were suiting up for a baseball practice.

You can guess which three. And you can guess what type of wooden baseball device they held as they stood there, grinning hungrily.

"Hey," said Jerry, calling me by a particularly terse anatomical nickname.

I looked behind me. Coach Chambers was out of earshot.

But I knew he was not far away. I couldn't run out past him in my gym clothes; he'd slap me with detention for violating his rule about wearing them only during class. But I hoped that his presence might quell any overt violence. So I needed to stall for time.

Then I remembered how, in Episode 14, Captain Maxim outwitted a squadron of Vexon destroyers by doing the unexpected: instead of fleeing, he charged straight at them. By the time the Vexons recovered and turned about, the hyperdrive had been fixed and the *Fortitude* got away.

So that is what I tried.

"Hi, guys," I said as I strolled nonchalantly through their midst and toward my locker. I bumped shoulders with Bubba as I passed.

It worked! They clearly had not expected that. Of course now they stood between me and the exit. I was counting on Coach Chambers walking in by the time I finished dressing. I quickly started pulling my street clothes on over my gym uniform.

But by the time I'd yanked my sweatshirt down and zipped my jeans up, he was nowhere in sight.

I tried to keep the bluff up, and my lunch down, as I grabbed my Cosmos backpack and strolled straight toward them, hoping that what had worked on the way in would work on the way out.

It didn't.

Ty stopped me with a full body check.

"What's the rush?" he asked.

We were deep in the locker room. The profanity he used in place of my name echoed off the concrete floor, against the cold metal lockers, through the mildewy air.

Retreat was not possible. Maybe one more feint forward?

"I don't want to make you late for practice, so I'll just get out of your way," I said, casting my eyes down as I tried to spin off of Ty and slip between him and Jerry.

It didn't work. Jerry jammed his shoulder into my side; I bounced from him into Ty, who pushed me forward. I held my backpack like a shield and faced them. This was the most dangerous situation I'd been in with them, but I was too afraid to be afraid. I felt…detached. I wasn't thinking about the wicked smiles on their faces or the heavy wooden bats in their hands. I was thinking about heads. And how the worst creatures in classic mythology always had three of them— Cerberus, the dog at the gates of hell; King Ghidorah, a match for Godzilla; the three-headed giant in that British film about Camelot that I tried to watch once. Why was it always three? Maybe because even the ancient people who wrote those classics knew that where a clever warrior could win any one-on-one encounter, and a strong man might defeat two, even a hero would be overwhelmed by three. Now, maybe if I had a lightsaber, I could—

Uh-oh, Ty was talking again.

"I don't think he heard you," Bubba said.

Ty pushed me, hard, toward the back wall.

"Are you awake now?" he asked, spitting out an angry combination of words that I had not actually heard before.

My wide eyes signaled, Yes, you have my attention.

"We've missed you," Ty said. "Where've you been?"

"Oh, out and about. You know me." The words were glib, but my voice—high, breathy—gave me away.

"Well, maybe we can make up for lost time by doing locker-room batting practice together." Jerry's and Bubba's smiles spread wide, as if someone had just told them Christmas had been moved up nine months.

I blinked rapidly. "Uh, thanks but no," I said. My tongue stuck to the roof of my dry mouth as I tried to form the words. "I wouldn't want to...to be in your way."

"Oh, you wouldn't be," he said, lifting his bat off his shoulder.

"Yeah, well, you know, um, I'm sure you could have plenty of, uh, fun practicing without me," I said.

Ty's smile became thinner and wider. "No," he said. "I think it would be extra fun *with* you." He grasped his bat and assumed a batting stance. "Locker room batting practice goes like this: One!" He swung mightily, and the bat carved an arc in front of him, backing me flat against the wall. "Two!" He took a step closer, and the bat missed me by less than a foot. "Three!" He swung a third time, and it missed me by a few inches.

I wanted to put up my arms to ward off the blow I was sure was coming, but I was afraid that any movement would throw off his timing.

Jerry spoke. "Pretty good. But a real power hitter looks like this." He demonstrated. I didn't actually see, because I had squeezed my eyes shut while I pressed my cheek against the cold cinderblock wall. I felt the bat graze my ear as it whipped past.

Jerry took about two innings' worth of powerful strikes. About half of them touched my ear. One brushed my cheek. Ty and Bubba kept the banter to a minimum. They were watching some precision work, and although I don't think they cared that much for the sanctity of my head, I do think they realized that their entertainment would be curtailed if my brains ended up splattered against the wall.

I wondered, If that happened, would I actually hear the

sound of my skull cracking? Would I feel it? Or would I just start walking down the long tunnel toward the light?

Finally, he declared himself out. "You're cleanup, Bubs," he said, passing the bat.

Bubba hesitated. "Uh, yeah," he said. And he stared at the bat. Was he doubting whether he had the same level of control as his friends?

I was. And I would like to say that I quickly calculated the odds of my survival against his bat versus the odds of surviving my alternate course of action. But that would be a lie. I acted out of terror. I pushed off that wall with every muscle in my frail, alien body, held my Cosmos backpack in front of me and gave a guttural yell—"GARRRRRRRRRRR!"—that bubbled up from somewhere in my churning stomach.

Eyes wide, teeth bared, I charged right at Bubba, and he took a step back in surprise. This gave me enough of a gap to slip between him and Jerry, and I raced toward the door. Whipping around the corner and toward freedom, I slammed right into Coach Chambers.

"What the...Sherman, what's your problem? Do I need to make you run another lap?"

I looked up at his scowling face, into those squinty brown eyes that sank in behind the sunburned lumps of his cheekbones. A gigantic sob was welling up inside my gut. I was determined not to appear weak in front of him, so I held it back. I held and held and held but it was no use. Out it came. With all the fear and frustration I had been keeping down. And also with my lunch.

SPLAT. It landed on his shoes.

He jumped.

And I ran.

7.03.03

I ran hard. I didn't care where. I ran toward the library, then realized it might already be closed, and even if it wasn't, I didn't want Ms. Beacon to see me like this. I turned and made for the front doors.

Then I heard squeals. It was the cheer squad, spreading through the halls as they decorated for Friday's pep rally. Sweating underneath my two layers of clothes, tears and puke staining my face, I did not want to be seen by them, either.

So I dove into the wormhole network.

I opened the nearest door, a seventh-grade science classroom. It was empty, but I ducked and began crawling on my hands and knees between the lab tables. I went into the supply closet, among the dusty boxes of prepared slides and pig fetuses in formaldehyde, then scrambled into the connected eighth-grade science classroom.

I crawled from room to room, in and out of closets and behind desks and anything else that could hide me, until I found myself in an English class.

The walls here were accordion-style partitions, so it was easy to part them and slip from one to another, except I forgot about the latch, which caught on my shirt, which suffered a greasy rip right across the middle.

I was now around the corner from the cafeteria and after that the maintenance room and the safety of the Sanctuary. Just one more section of exposed hallway to manage.

I stuck my head out the door and looked left. All clear. I

looked right. Equally clear. I crouched and prepared to lunge, when I heard:

"Ready, OK!"

A whole gaggle of cheerleaders had clustered in the cafeteria. I could not imagine a worse scenario.

A moment later, it got worse.

From far down the echoey hallway, I heard the clacking sound of heavy brown dress shoes. The sound made by only one pair of shoes in the school. The pair worn by Principal Denton.

He was looking for something. Possibly me. I pulled my head in as he rounded the corner. I heard him rattle the door on the adjacent room; he would be here in seconds.

What were my choices? I could try to walk out as if nothing were going on. I looked at my torn, stained shirt, wiped my sweaty forehead with a grimy hand, and decided to try something else:

Hide like the worthless coward I was.

Not that an English classroom had many options for this. The high-level kids were taught in an "open" environment, which meant chairs in a circle, lots of chances for expression, precious little cover.

Denton was closing in. I was about to crouch behind the bookshelf that held twenty-seven unopened copies of *Five-Paragraph Essays: The Intermediate Years* when I realized that the wall next to the teacher's desk, obscured by inspirational posters of rainbows and beaches, was actually a door. To a closet. I had no idea where it would lead. But I had no choice. I plunged in, closing the door behind me just as I heard Denton rattle the knob from the hallway.

Desperate for cover, I clawed my way through the darkness into the farthest corner.

"Ow!" said a voice.

And that is how I found Ricki.

7.03.04

Just enough light slipped through the crack under the door for me to see that she was sitting on the floor, wedged next to a roll of butcher paper and some extremely dusty toner cartridges, her knees pulled up to her chest.

She looked up fearfully. Then angrily, as she realized just who had shut himself in a closet with her. Then perplexedly, as she took in my disheveled appearance and look of panic.

"Shhh!" I told her, pointing a thumb at the door. "Denton!" At that she scrunched even further against the wall. I sat opposite her, atop a box of bubble sheets for a standardized test.

We heard the classroom door creak open. We didn't breathe.

I was shaking, and sweating, and would probably have thrown up again if Denton had found us.

He didn't. We heard the classroom door click shut; we heard footsteps taper off down the hall. We exhaled.

But we didn't speak. We just sat in silence while my pulse slowed, the sweat dried and the acid feeling in my throat began to melt. At that point, it did seem as if something needed to be said.

I was too tired for anything clever.

"This school is nuts," I said.

"You're telling me," she said.

"What are you hiding from?" I asked.

"Who says I'm hiding?" she replied defiantly.

It was difficult, in the darkness, to tell if she was joking. "This feels a lot like hiding to me," I said.

"It is not. I am taking control of the situation," she said.

I reflected on this for a bit. "You haven't, like, gotten oxygen-deprived in here, have you?"

"No, of course not."

"Then, if you don't mind my asking, do you have some other sort of brain damage? Because I'm really having trouble imagining how sitting in a closet can be seen as 'taking control.'"

"'A battle avoided is often a battle won,'" she said.

Right out of Maxim's logbook. Wow. But whom was she avoiding?

"Are you in trouble with a teacher?" I asked.

"Pffttt," she said. "Adults are easy."

"Then what's got you so...?"

I heard giggles in the hallway while the cheerleaders pranced past with their crepe paper and posterboards.

"Ahhhhh," I said, the situation suddenly clear as a Kryptonian crystal. "Is that...?"

"Yes," she whispered. "*Vexons with pom-poms.*"

"I understand," I said sympathetically.

"I doubt you could."

For a girl cowering on a closet floor in the dark, she could really stand her ground.

"Try me," I dared.

"You're not a girl."

I laughed. "Hunter and his friends would disagree."

"What does that mean?"

"Just that I've got my own Vexons to deal with."

"They're not the same," she said.

"How? What makes you so special? I'm the one who should be saying *you* wouldn't understand."

"You're just dealing with brute force. I have to deal with mind games."

"A few minutes ago, three guys were about to make a game out of knocking my mind out of my skull."

"That doesn't sound so bad."

"Compared with what?" I almost yelled.

She dropped her voice again.

"The wolf packs," she said.

"Wolf packs?"

"They move in threes," she said, her voice flat and hollow. "They're in every hall, in every class. Sometimes they ignore you, pretend you don't exist. Other times they wait until you pass, and then you hear mumbling, and laughter that you know is at your expense.

"Then sometimes, they take small bites by mocking little things. Maybe your clothes and how they came from the wrong store. Maybe something you said in class. Or didn't say. Maybe they send around a text about you. Or see that you're reading a book. About space. And tell you how stupid they think that is.

"And then, once in a while, they sink their teeth in and rip off a big chunk of flesh. They talk about your…chest. It's too flat. Or make jokes about the shape of your eyes. Or they talk in gibberish and ask you to translate. They call you…names.

"You can't fight back against that. Not when you're sur-rounded. The only logical option is to stay quiet. Avoid them. And everyone else. And at this moment, I am successfully not facing any of them.

"Hence," she summed up confidently, "I have taken control."

Her logic had an unassailable beauty to it.

"So...you hide here after school?" I asked.

"I just told you—it's not *hiding*," she said. "But I can isolate myself in lots of places. Sometimes after school, sometimes during. The bathrooms are good. If you find a clean stall and pull your legs up, nobody sees you. Certain closets work, if you know when the teachers are on break."

"How do you know that?"

"I have my ways."

"Do you go to class at all?"

"When I feel like it."

"Don't you get in trouble?"

"I have excuses."

"From your parents?"

She laughed. "They don't know a thing."

"Then how—"

"I'm an office aide second hour."

"And that means...?"

"Access to the attendance computer."

"Does that mean you can—"

"It takes about five seconds to erase an unexcused absence, if you know what you're doing."

"Don't your teachers...?"

"I told you, adults are easy to deal with. Unlike wolf packs, they aren't looking for trouble. Challenge them on facts, and the worst they'll do is make you transfer classes. If work shows up on their desk and you ace their tests, they never complain."

I exhaled a long, slow breath. "I was wrong."

"About what?"

"I was hoping we could be friends. But I think you're out

of my league." I was trying to show her how impressive I thought she was.

"Then why did you treat me the way you did when I first showed up in the library?"

Whoops. That didn't sound like an olive branch being accepted.

"I'm, uh, not so bright sometimes," was all the apology I could manage.

"Clearly," she said. She still sounded angry. But then she gave a worried sigh, as if she were reluctantly giving in to something. "But you're probably going to see everything fall apart today."

"How?"

"I ducked in here because after school is the worst. People sometimes ambush you if you're not careful, you know."

"Yeah," I said. "I know."

"It's best to lie low and let them pass. The halls are usually safe after about ten minutes. But I forgot it's a pep rally week. Wolf packs are everywhere. And Denton is prowling. If he sees me wandering the halls, I'll definitely get detention. My parents will, perhaps literally, explode. So I have to stay here until he leaves. Except if I don't leave now, my parents will kill me for being late. So either way, I'm dead."

I wiped my hands on my pants and swabbed my chin with a corner of my torn sweatshirt.

"Maybe I can help," I offered.

"I doubt it. Unless you can turn us invisible, or dig an escape tunnel."

I cleared my throat, then stood up straight—at least, as straight as I could without knocking something over in the crowded, dusty darkness.

"Princess," I declared, "I'm here to rescue you."

"I don't need a rescue," she replied curtly. Possibly able to see me as the scrawny, filthy, frail person I was, she added, "And I am not sure you are in a position to do much rescuing."

"No, really," I said. "I can help. If you trust me."

"Are you the person who called my house and made springs fly out of my parents' heads?"

"Umm…"

"And did you not just say that you are running from someone who wanted to liberate your brain from your skull?"

Silence.

"And does your plan for rescue involve leaping into the garbage compactor until R2-D2 can find the off switch?"

I fidgeted with the straps on my Cosmos backpack. "Kind of."

"I'll take my chances in the closet."

"OK," I said. "Go on and face Denton by yourself. And if you avoid him, you can march out right past the cheerleaders in the cafeteria, just you, squinting in the daylight, against them. All of them. If you can take that on—you're braver than I am.

"Me? I have a plan for getting out of here without being seen by *anyone*."

I let that sink in, then added: "It's risky. But so is doing nothing. And I know what Maxim would tell you."

"What's that?" she asked, urgently.

"'A no-win scenario just means you have nothing to lose with whatever course you choose.'"

At that moment, we heard chanting and shrieking in the distance. It made me think of witches. And human sacrifice.

"OK." She finally sighed. "I don't think you're that bright, but you're all I have. What's your plan?"

I felt my way to the door and opened it a crack. A beam of light shot in. I took a chestful of fresh air, blinked and looked around.

"Follow me," I said.

We scurried to the classroom door. I peeked through the rectangle of glass; nobody was nearby. But we could hear the laughter from the cheerleaders, who were still in the cafeteria, where all the doors were wide open. Nothing blocked the squad from seeing us if we tried to run past.

We really needed a cloaking device about now, but all I had to work with were a stack of chairs; a resin statue of a squirrel holding an apple sitting on the teacher's desk; and a TV cart, left over from the last substitute teacher.

Commander Steele could have turned these things into an invisibility ray, or a photon torpedo for that matter, but unlike him, I was not lucky enough to have been first in my class at the Galactic Science Academy.

But I *had* been on the sixth-grade audio/visual committee, and that gave me an idea.

I wheeled the cart out of the corner. It was a bulky, old-fashioned thing, and this one had a huge projector on it, the kind intended for use with a pull-down white screen but possibly large and bright enough to direct anti-aircraft fire at incoming bombers. Wired to it was an ancient VCR the size of a suitcase. It was quaint. But it would work.

Out of habit, I peeked at the little plastic VCR window to see how much tape was left. Sure enough, nobody had bothered to properly rewind the last movie shown. Some poor sub had merely turned off the film mid-showing and fled.

"Wait here until I tell you," I said. "When I signal, head straight for the door marked MAINTENANCE."

Ricki nodded.

I checked the hall one more time, then pushed the cart through the door. I was risking more than I let on to Ricki; our main goal was to avoid being seen by the cheerleaders, but we couldn't be caught pushing school property around without a teacher's note, either. We'd get detention for loitering, and probably charged with looting. Or attempted larceny. Or something.

I crouched behind the cart as I pushed it down the hall. I could hear the cheerleaders' chatter, but I wouldn't be exposed until I crossed the double doors of the cafeteria. I had thought that the cart would be bulky enough to screen us from view as we dashed past.

But I had to stop a few feet from the cafeteria entrance. From this angle, it was clear there was far too much hall for even that big old VCR and TV to hide us.

I began to retreat, but I again thought of Maxim: always move forward, he would say.

I spied an electrical outlet across the hall.

Quickly unspooling the power cord, I got down on my stomach and wormed my way across, commando-style. This was mostly for dramatic effect, but it made me feel braver.

I pushed the cart to the edge of what I thought would be the cheerleaders' field of vision and aimed the lens inside the cafeteria. I set the focus, raised my arm to signal Ricki and flipped the switch.

The VCR began to whir and hum, the tape spooled through and the powerful lamp flickered to life.

"Now!" I whispered. I turned the volume all the way up.

The cheerleaders instinctively turned toward the sound of the VCR, but the pulse of light blinded them. They then turned to the far wall, where a movie had suddenly appeared.

I marveled for a moment—it was one of my favorites, *Jason and the Argonauts*! It was right at the scene where the army of skeleton warriors rises from the soil, and even if the effects were primitive, it was still riveting. I had watched the film on many a Saturday afternoon, but never had I seen the grim, clanking soldiers of the earth elicit shrieks of disgust from a room full of cheerleaders. It was even better this way.

Ricki made it to my side.

"What now?" she asked.

"This way!" I said, and we ducked behind the door that led to the basement. I led her down the stairs, around the work-bench, past the shelves of cleaning supplies and to the furnace. I slid the grate out of the way and set my feet on the rungs.

"Down here," I urged. "Close the grate behind you."

Her mouth hung open in either disbelief or disgust.

We heard some kind of activity upstairs. "Trust me!" I said.

She looked behind her, then stared right at me. Her eyebrows were pressed together; her lips were tight.

After an eternity that lasted probably a second and a half, she huffed: "This is some rescue."

And down we went.

As we got nearer the bottom, I reached into my backpack for my flashlight. Then I realized—someone already had lights on down below.

We were not alone.

7.03.05

I thought of Maxim and kept moving forward.

From the bottom of the shaft, it was a ten-foot drop to the floor. There was no way to tell who or what I would find when I let go.

I let my backpack fall first, and it made a slapping sound as it hit the concrete floor. I landed next to it, in a clumsy Spider-Man-like stance. I looked up, and as my eyes adjusted to the light they fell on...

"Les!" I had totally forgotten that this was his day to use the Sanctuary. He wouldn't like that I had messed with the schedule.

Then I realized how much less he was going to like the surprise coming right behind me.

"What are you doing here?" he said, standing up from his chair and dropping his comic book.

"Um," I said. "We need to talk."

At that moment, a shoe fell on my head. A girl's shoe. Slip-on. Had Ricki been running in these things? She was more adept than I—

"Eeep!" she called. I jumped aside just as the other shoe, with Ricki's foot still inside, plunged down next to me.

I realized, too late, that I should have made some kind of effort to catch her. But there was no need; she landed gracefully, with one leg extended behind her, and made sort of a flourish with her arms.

"Tae kwon do?" I asked, impressed.

"Arabesque," she said. "Seven years of ballet, from six instructors. I always thought it was hundreds of hours down the drain. But I never knew I would be using it...down a drain."

In the yellow light of the crayon candles, I could see Les turning an alarming color. His lower lip was trembling. His eyes began to shine.

"I said you couldn't tell ANYONE!"

"Les, I–"

"I KNEW I shouldn't have trusted anyone!"

"Les! It was an emergency! Hunter and his goons nearly killed me!"

"So you decided to VIOLATE your word by bringing a frakking DATE down here?"

"Les, she's not a date!"

"She's a girl!"

"She's one of US," I said.

"I think I resent that," she said.

Her voice jarred Les out of his rage. It was as if he were surprised that she could speak.

"Les," I said. "This is Ricki Roy. Ricki, this is Les Martin. Keeper of the Fortress of Solitude."

They stared at each other. Les wiped his nose on his sleeve in a long, slow motion.

"I've seen you leaving his library class," he said.

"I've never seen you," she replied. "Just your name. On the attendance forms in the office."

He looked startled. "I keep a low profile," he said.

"I would too, if my brother was Ty Hunter," she said.

The chamber turned as quiet as deep space, as still as absolute zero.

"Your brother?" I whispered.

Les's face had gone from purple to red to white. His eyes were wide and fearful.

"Your *brother*?" I asked again, although it was clear that what Ricki asserted was true.

It wasn't exactly as shocking as learning the identity of Luke Skywalker's father, but to find out that my one friend had been hiding his family ties to my worst tormentor was akin to...to...something so infuriating that my mind would work only in staccato sputterings. Which is how Les spoke.

"Who said...Who told...How did you know?" he finally asked Ricki.

"I access the attendance database to excuse my absences," she said matter-of-factly. "I notice things. Like the fact that you have the same home address as Ty. And the same parents. I was just assuming you were related. I guess I was right."

It was my turn to rage. "Anything *else* you need to tell me, Les? Maybe you've heard a few good ones about me at the dinner table?"

"No, I—"

"Or maybe you didn't need to listen, because maybe you were hiding somewhere, after setting me up! Maybe you're one of THEM!" My head was spinning, and my insides had sort of a weightless feel.

"Clark! No!" he almost whimpered. "I was just trying to protect you! And me. And us."

I held my tongue. Not because I believed him, but because I didn't want to have a tear-streaked meltdown right in front of both of them. So I stood there, breathing hard. This gave Les a chance to speak some more.

"Ty is my *step*brother. I hardly even talk to him. In fact, he hates being seen with me. Which is why I stay out of his way. When he gets angry, he's a lot like his dad."

He let that sink in. I could see his logic, but still. "You couldn't have *told* me?"

"I'm sorry," he said. "I didn't...I don't know how..." He gulped a breath and looked up. "He's been hell on my friends in the past. And people don't stay friends with me for long because of it. I was afraid you wouldn't, you know, talk to me if you found out."

I could have pressed the "abort" button on our friendship right there.

But I did understand that loneliness makes a guy do desperate things.

Candles flickered as I thought about what to say next.

"You're a freak, Les," I finally told him. "I mean, everything I know about you is weird. Alien mutant-level weird." I let out a deep breath. "But everything I know about me is alien-level weird too."

"Yeah," he agreed, also exhaling. "Yeah."

"Is there anything else I need to know about you?"

He shook his head.

"Good. Because, um...," I looked over at Ricki, and down at my torn shirt, and back at Les. "Because I could really use your help right now."

His eyes stayed wide for just a moment. And then his expression faded into his usual look of controlled intensity.

"Yeah," he said. "You're a mess. How are you going to explain this to your parents?"

"Oh God, my parents," said Ricki. "If I'm not walking through my front door in a few minutes, everything comes unraveled. Everything."

Les scanned her. He was calculating something. "Can you make up some excuse for why you're late?"

"Sometimes I say I was meeting with my math teacher," she said. "But that doesn't cover me for long. I'm at least a half-hour's walk from home already. I think." She looked around. "I actually have no idea where I am."

"Where do you live?" he asked.

She hesitated, then said, "Pine Terrace condo village. Next to the college campus."

"That's like two miles away! You walk that every day?" he said.

"My mother says it builds character."

"I think it would build blisters," he said.

"It's also a break from her nagging," she added.

Les nodded approvingly and studied her in the dim light. "You have access to the attendance computer?"

"I have my ways."

"OK, here's the deal. I can get you home in eleven minutes if you do exactly what I say."

"How?" she asked.

"First, you have to swear that you will not tell anybody about this place. Or come here without permission."

"Agreed," she said.

Les pressed his watch. Its glowing face illuminated his in a ghostly way.

"Do you have any money?"

She shook her head. "I left my purse in my locker."

Les reached into his pocket and pulled out a couple of wadded-up dollar bills. "Here. You'll need this for fare."

"Fare?" she asked. She looked down the tunnel. "Is this a subway?"

"No. But Clark is going to escort you out of here, into Sand Creek Park. You'll walk quickly to the bus stop on Highland Boulevard, just south of here. A bus is due there in four minutes. If you walk fast, you can just make it. Ride it to Old Ranch Road. There's a stop in front of Pine Terrace."

She checked her own watch. "Let's go."

"OK," I said, and shined my light down the tunnel.

"Ricki!" he called, as we made our way toward the park.

She looked back.

He put two fingers to his heart, and then, thumb extended, pointed them skyward.

She rolled her eyes, but she also showed him just a hint of a smile. "You too?"

I led the way out with my flashlight. At the mouth of the tunnel, I showed her the steps, but I hung back; the world did not need to see us emerging together. We had enough to explain.

I thought there should be some kind of farewell scene, but Ricki had a bus to catch.

"See you in the library?" I asked.

"Maybe," she said. She stepped away from the pipe and out of my line of vision.

And that was that.

Except when she stepped back in long enough to say, "I still don't think you're that bright, and I was crazy to follow you, but I thank you for your support."

"Say hi to your folks for me."

She rolled her eyes once more and was gone.

7.03.06

How serious were things?

So serious that Les declared that he would call me at home later to come up with a plan.

"About 1900 hours. I can call from my basement; nobody will hear me." He was pacing. I thought about how much our hideout resembled a jail cell.

"I'll try to be free," I said, examining the greasy tear and other problematic stains on my shirt. "I've got a lot to explain to my mom."

"Take the north trail to the park rim," he said. "It's steep. You might fall and mess up your shirt. Get it all covered with dirt and who knows what else."

"Why would I want to...?"

He waited for me to catch up.

"Oh. Yeah. Great idea, Les. Thanks."

Sure enough, the command unit was waiting for me as soon as I walked in.

"There you are!" she said. "What on earth happened to you? I was starting to worry."

"Took a shortcut," I mumbled. "Slipped on a trail in the park."

"Oh no!" she cried. "Are you OK? Let me take a look."

As she examined my attire, the look on her face went from concerned to quizzical. "You're a mess!" she said. "This was all from falling in the park?"

"The trail is really steep," I said. I hoped that admitting to a fake, minor transgression might stave off a board of inquiry about my behavior. So I told her I had been exploring in the park instead of coming straight home, then had gotten turned around and been too embarrassed to call her and admit it.

It worked—I got off with a short lecture about not taking shortcuts and a reminder that I had been given a cell phone precisely so I *could* call when I needed her.

I promised I would and made a note to myself to be extra careful. The commanders were maybe paying a little more attention than I had realized. As if I needed one more thing to worry about.

7.03.07

Les called that night, right on time.

"Are you safe?" I asked.

"For a few minutes. They're watching basketball." His voice was low. "I need the whole story on what happened."

So I gave him a full report, starting with the baseball bats.

When I finished, he let out a long breath. "Ty does have a gift for that kind of thing. I think he worked with Hitler in his past life."

I nodded. "He must be…rough to live with."

Les's reply came haltingly.

"Yeah," he said. "He's like his dad…and he gets in my head. I get so I…I just…I will do *anything* to keep him out of my life. I'm sorry I couldn't tell you."

I nodded. "I get it."

"Every time I've made friends with someone, he's gone after them. And the people he goes after—weird things happen, Clark."

"Weird—like *torture*?" At this point, I wouldn't put anything past Ty.

"Not necessarily. What I mean is—" Les sighed. "Never mind. Right now we have to figure out what we're going to do about Denton."

"Why Denton?" I asked, still wanting to know the fate of those earlier friends.

"Because he called my stepdad this afternoon."

That focused my attention quickly. "About *us*?"

"I don't know. He's called here before, and even come by a couple of times…but, I don't know. Look, I'm used to just running and hiding and sorting things out on my own when things get complicated. And things are getting complicated. There's a lot of people to think about now. I mean, it's even getting crowded in the Sanctuary."

"I think we can trust Ricki, Les."

"It's not a matter of trust. Mistakes happen. Like, how do you know she closed the grate properly at the drain entrance? That she didn't drop a book with her name in it along the way? What if you left—"

An ancient projector running in the hallway? Near the door to our secret exit? On a day when I might have been seen running through the halls?

My masterful escape was looking a lot less brilliant.

"OK, I agree," I said. "We need to avoid the back door. I'm sorry. I didn't mean to be an idiot."

"I wouldn't have been able to do any better. And I could tell you'd had a bad day."

My stomach burbled at the memory. I was silent long enough for him to ask, "Clark? Are you still there?"

"Yeah," I said.

"I was just thinking...earlier, in the Sanctuary...did you call me an alien mutant?"

"Something like that."

"You know, I kind of like that," he said. "Because aliens and mutants, by thinking differently—they can have great power, can't they?"

"Yes," I decided. "Yes, they can."

"Of course, with great power comes great responsibility."

"So I've read."

"We should be careful. We might really turn life as we know it upside-down."

"Captain, it's clear that the antimatter inducer's implosion reversed the polarity on the time-space fabric and inverted us into an alternate existence."

"So—it's like Opposite Day, forever?"

"I believe that's what I just said."

—Commander Steele and Captain Maxim
Star Survivors Episode 46,
"A Broken Mirror"

EXPEDITION LOG

ENTRY 8.01.01

I went to school the next day expecting the worst, certain that Chambers would be all over me for spewing my lunch all over him. I also was certain that somebody would connect me with the wandering projector. And that Ty, Bubba and Jerry would be telling the whole school about how they'd made me cower until I barfed.

But when I showed up at first-hour PE class, all Chambers said was, "Feeling better today?"

Odder than that was how he almost seemed to be avoiding me. Not ignoring me—actively *avoiding* me. Maybe he was afraid that I'd unleash another puke-on torpedo at him? Funny. I'd never thought of my weak stomach as an asset before.

Oddest of all was that the Ty Hunter trio found me in a hallway and walked right on past without even saying a dirty word. They glanced at one another but didn't knock a book out of my hands, didn't make fun of my shoes, nothing.

I was puzzling over this behavior in English class when Denton summoned me to his office.

Well, I thought, this is it. Maybe I was about to find out what his call to Ty's stepdad was all about...but I probably wouldn't live to tell Les about it. I hoped that my execution would be merciful and quick.

I walked straight in. Denton closed the door behind him, then sat behind his desk. His Marine portrait and case of medals had been reunited on their shelf and gleamed even brighter than before.

"How are you today, Sherman?"

"Just fine, sir," I said, swallowing hard.

"Good, good." He picked up a pencil and started absentmindedly drumming his desk with the eraser end. "Nothing to report, then, I guess?" He sounded almost... worried.

"Uh, no, sir," I said. Was this some sort of mind game? A way to get me to confess to stealing school AV property before handing me the bill for Coach Chambers's shoes?

"Good, good," he said. "Well, if you think of anything, you'll be sure to come to me first, right?"

OK. It was clear that he knew *something* had happened. And there was a chance—just a chance—that he had meant what he said about us being a team. And there was a chance— just a chance—that if I let him know what was going on, he could put an end to it.

I stared over at the portrait of Marine Denton, standing tall in front of the American flag.

I decided I would try to trust him.

"Well, now that you mention it, I did have sort of an...incident yesterday."

His face looked stern.

"You did?"

"Yeah," I said. "There's these three guys? And, well, they had baseball bats. And they backed me up against the wall, and they..."

He held up his hand.

"Just a moment, Sherman," he said. "Did this incident involve any sort of physical harm to you?"

I thought for a moment: No, they never got around to actually hurting me, this time. They left no marks. They just came a couple of millimeters from knocking off my head, that's all.

"I guess not," I said.

He exhaled. "That's a relief. For you, I mean. Because if you had been hurt on school grounds, clearly, action would have to be taken. But you seem to have come out of it OK, yes?"

I nodded slowly.

"Glad to see that, Sherman. Remember, if you have any other problems, I've got your back. Think of me here, readying my sniper's gun, standing guard. You'll keep me posted on everything, right?"

I gave the slightest of nods.

"These are difficult times, Sherman. But sometimes you have to tough it out. Not complain to *anyone*. Why, I remember going through boot camp, and we were ordered to drop and freeze in the middle of a desert hike. Soldier next to me found himself on an anthill. He jumped up, and the drill sergeant had to throw him in the brig for disobeying a direct order. The Marine on his other side kept still, and today he commands his own brigade. So you see what I mean about the importance of keeping still and quiet?"

I told him I did.

"Good, I'm glad we got things cleared up."

Things were cleared up, all right.

I felt a little better when I arrived in the ARC and saw that Ricki had returned. She was in her usual spot, reading a book. She actually looked up when I walked in. I nodded at her. She nodded back.

I wanted to ask her how things had gone at home. But I decided not to press my luck; I surely had already used up a year's supply today.

I went to my own spot and discovered a carefully folded note on my chair.

Saturday, 12:15 P.M., *at the rec center?* it read. There was no signature, but a glance over at Ricki told me what I needed to know.

I pulled out my binder, ripped out a sheet of loose-leaf paper and drew a simple pattern on it: two circles, one stacked on top of the other, each surrounded by dashes, as if they were glowing lights. I slipped the paper in the front pocket of my binder and, without looking across the room, let the binder flip open and hang off the edge of the table.

Anyone walking by would have seen only a piece of paper with a meaningless doodle. But to a *Star Survivors* fan looking for an answer to a yes/no question, it could mean only one thing: "affirmative," transmitted in the style of former First Officer Elohim Prime, who had been paralyzed in a tragic incident involving a hyperbaric chamber and some genetically modified Betelgeusian jellyfish, and could communicate only by flashing a light attached to the respirator vest he wore—one flash for "no," two flashes for "yes."

I pulled out my social studies textbook, and over the pages, glanced across the room. Ricki nodded.

I tried to read, but my eyes kept rereading the same paragraphs. That Weird Al parody of the *Star Survivors* theme kept running through my head: "What a Difference a Stardate Makes!"

Yesterday, I was the fugitive king of barf. Today, I was master of my fate, a genius of stealth, a successful escape artist and…I had a date! Or at least a meeting with a fellow alien who happened to be female.

When the bell rang, Ricki disappeared into the halls just as Ms. Beacon asked me to step into her office.

"Mr. Sherman, do you happen to go past the seventh-grade English classrooms on the way to your next class?" she asked.

I told her I did.

"Good," she said. "Would you mind making a delivery for me?"

I told her I would not mind at all.

"Good," she said. "It's there in the corner."

I looked, and I froze as solid as someone dipped in carbonite.

In the corner sat a projector cart. With a suitcase-sized VCR that, I am guessing, held a tape of *Jason and the Argonauts*. "They'll be needing this for their discussion of Greek mythology in Ms. Weintraum's room later," Ms. Beacon said. "It's the strangest thing—the custodians told me they found this running in the hallway yesterday, abandoned. I do wish people would treat the audiovisual equipment with more respect. Some of it is quite old."

I nodded.

"I'm glad you concur. Now, you're sure you don't mind pushing it? I'm just assuming that you have some experience with this sort of thing."

I told her I thought I could manage.

"Good," she said, as she adjusted her glasses for a full-power scowl. "I am certain that the careless person who left it out in the open had a very good reason for doing so. But I am sure you would agree that person should have been more careful. If he had been caught on school grounds after hours without permission, possibly vandalizing school property, he would be beyond my help."

I blinked twice.

"I understand, Ms. Beacon."

I didn't, fully. But her warning tone could not have been clearer if it had been accompanied by a couple of klaxons and a robot shouting, "DANGER! DANGER!"

"A star explorer needs four things to survive: Determination, determination, determination and dumb luck. You can control only the first three. When you experience the fourth, be grateful."

—Captain Maxim
Stars in Alignment: A Star Survivors Novel

EXPEDITION LOG

ENTRY 9.01.01

For the rest of the week, Ty, Jerry and Bubba kept their distance from me.

I wasn't sure why. But I didn't ask. I needed the mental space to prepare for my Saturday meeting with Ricki.

Nothing in my training manuals covered such a moment—an actual, planned social encounter with a female human of my age. Granted, I had no idea whether our relationship was destined to be more Leia–Luke or Leia–Han. But even if we ended up being Jedi siblings separated at birth or something, I obviously had to show respect. And that meant proper protocol.

Full dress uniform was not in order, but I would need to look my best. Was there a guide on how to dress rec-center semiformal?

After a great deal of analysis, I decided that I would clad myself in my newest pair of red-tab jeans, my favorite shirt (a picture of Saturn with the words *I Need My Space*, which I'd found at a planetarium gift shop during a sixth-grade field trip) and a leather necklace with a pendant made of an actual bit of meteorite that my aunt from Arizona had sent to celebrate a solstice. It looked a little like a shark's tooth, and my aunt said it radiated positive energy. This seemed like a good opportunity to try it out.

This also seemed like a good opportunity to break in another Christmas gift I had hardly used: my new Trek bicycle, which had been intended as some kind of reward for enduring the move. With Les's map committed to memory, I had a safe route to the rec center all charted.

I decided I would also take the special provision of applying a small amount of scented fluid to my cheeks before I left the house. I had seen this act performed many times on television by men who had finished shaving and were about to encounter women.

So I found the small bottle from the Timber Peak gift set that I had been saving since my birthday. Timber Peak ads showed men in flannel shirts being smiled at by women in bearskin robes. I did not care for flannel, or for bear-women, but it would do.

9.02.01

Saturday arrived, sunny and clear and full of positive ions. The command units gave one another a look when I said I had decided to take my bike up to the rec center. They asked whether I was meeting anyone. I said no, I had just heard that they sold those red, white and blue Rocket Pops at the snack bar, and I was in the mood for one.

"But you just finished breakfast," the female commander said, puzzled.

I shrugged.

They looked at one another again. The female commander started to ask something, but the male commander gave her a look that probably said, "Hey, he needs the exercise." Then he wished me well, and I ducked out before they could think of more questions.

The ride to the rec center was only about a mile and a half. Which really is not that far on a bicycle. For a fit person. On flat ground.

But I hadn't been on a bike since...well, since before arrival on Planet Festus. And I had forgotten about gravity.

In space, it's never an issue. But here, it has to be contended with. Especially because the rec center was set on a hill at the top of my subdivision, and my base was near the bottom of that hill. So that mile and a half between the two included a vertical climb of, by my rough estimate, 10,000 feet. And the roundabout path that would enable me to avoid danger zones would add about a mile to my route.

I also had a few issues with the bike, which was more complicated than my previous model, in that it had more gears and newer brakes and other things that took time to sort out.

So when I arrived at the rec center, half an hour later than I had planned, I was not exactly the suave space stud I had been when I left home; I was a sweaty mess.

I chained my bike to the rack, spun the four rings on the lock and walked into the center. It was a large, brick facility, adjacent to a soccer/baseball field, with basketball courts, a pool, a weight room and an indoor running track. It also had a theater, where some kind of dance class was going on, several classrooms and—hey, a snack bar that sold Rocket Pops! I had overheard some people talking about them in the halls at school, but I didn't actually expect to find any. Cool.

I saw no sign of Ricki, but it was only 12:10, which meant I had five minutes to clean up. I stepped into the rest room to check my appearance. It was as bad as I expected—my face was flush, my hair was exploding off my head like a cheap Q-tip, my shirt's most eye-catching aspect was not the fine detail on the rings of Saturn but the stains spreading from my armpits. I splashed some water on my hands and tried to slick back my hair.

Moments later I no longer looked like a cheap, exploding Q-tip; I looked like a cheap, wet exploding Q-tip.

Giving up on the hair, I pondered the sweat stains. I thought maybe I could mask them if my whole shirt were slightly damp, so I splashed a little water from the tap. That made the shirt wet, all right. It also made me look an awful lot like someone who had thrown up on himself again.

I needed a paper towel, but this rest room had only air dryers. So I ran over to one and held my shirt in front until the surface of the planet felt as if it might bubble, at which point I said, "OW!" because my skin was starting to burn too. And possibly, my meteorite necklace was beginning to melt.

It was then that a rec center worker—an older guy, at least seventeen—walked in, looked at me and asked, "You OK, kid?"

"Never better," I replied. I pulled away from the hand dryer and made one last check in the mirror. It was not encouraging.

Well, at least I would smell nice. I had brought some Timber Peak along with me. Just to be safe. Because I'd expected I would need some freshening up. The Timber Peak came in a 1.25-ounce plastic bottle, shaped like a little pine tree, that had just barely fit in the front pocket of my crisp, new jeans. I reached for it. I pulled it out.

It was at this moment that a basic law of physics came into

play. Namely, one involving friction. Because while lodged in my jeans pocket, the bottle of Timber Peak had managed to invert itself. And when I extracted it, the top part of the little tree popped right off, and Timber Peak was suddenly dribbling into my pocket, soaking into my jeans and trickling down my leg.

If spilling water on my shirt made me look like I had thrown up on myself, this made me look like I had…a real problem.

I looked down at my pants—yes, I had a real problem. I looked at my hands—I was still holding the Timber Peak. I dropped it and looked in the mirror at the rec center worker, who was standing behind me, confused.

Then the smell hit him. "Phewwwww," he said, waving his hand in front of his face. "Dude, what's with the Pine-Sol? We cleaned the stalls just last night."

I stood frozen, then looked at my watch. 12:15! I had no time. I washed my hands furiously, wiped them on my jeans, shrugged at the rec center worker, and walked out. Maybe I would have a few moments to—

Nope. She was coming out of the theater. She scanned the lobby, immediately spotted me, then nodded toward the front door, signaling that I should follow.

She had been in that dance class. She was dressed identically to the other girls coming out, in black leotards with pink slippers, but she was taller and thinner than the rest. And when they gathered in little circles to chatter and give one another air-hugs, nobody bothered to say anything to her.

I followed her, ignoring the people who wrinkled their noses as I walked past.

Outside, benches lined the path to the entrance, and she sat on one. I sat on the same bench and hoped I was downwind.

"I think spring is on the way," she said, her eyes squinting in the bright sunlight. She took a deep breath of the cool air. "I can smell the flowers already. Although they smell kind of like Christmas trees, for some reason."

I wiped my hands on my pants again and tried to fold my legs in a way that hid the wet spot. "Yeah," I said.

"I only have fifteen minutes," she said abruptly. "My parents are coming to get me at 12:30."

"Oh," I said, hoping I didn't sound disappointed, though I was.

"I had some things I needed to tell you, and I wasn't comfortable saying them at school."

"Sure," I said, trying to radiate confidence and ease and praying that the wind did not shift.

"First, thank you for your help on Tuesday. It was...a bad day."

"I've had better myself," I said. Oddly, the memory of the shared disaster made me relax. Ricki had seen me at my worst already. I didn't have to pretend to be anything more than the hopeless loser I was.

"I've been in tough schools before, but this place is different. The girls are...they just...it's been bad."

There was so much I wanted to learn about her. But we only had fifteen minutes. And, well, her confessing to how bad things had been for her somehow brought every bad experience *I* had been through to the front of my brain. At once. Hearing someone else talk about them somehow made them very real. Something I was really living through, not just watching on TV.

"I know what you mean," I told her.

"Do you?" she asked. It was a challenge. "I mean, really?"

I thought back to our conversation in the closet, and all she had been through. And I compared that with the memory loops of all the things I had been called at Festus. My size, strength and clothes had been mocked. I had been given nicknames that equated to male and female body parts, as well as the excretions from those parts. Then I'd been challenged as to which parts, if any, I had. I had been hit by a door, hit by balls and hit by chunks of ice. I had been terrorized with baseball bats to the point that I threw up.

"Yeah," I said. "It feels like you're all alone. An outsider. The only one of your kind in the whole universe."

She sighed. "I knew you got it." Then she looked me in the eye. "That's why I had to tell you."

Oh wow. I focused all my attention on her. Because, well, we apparently were having A Moment.

I lowered all my defensive screens and smiled in a way that I hoped emulated a young Harrison Ford. "That...you wanted to see me?" I asked, my voice rising to a pitch that probably sounded more Wookiee than handsome rogue.

"No," she said. "That you're in great danger at school. And not from whom you think."

THUD. Well, that's what you get for lowering your defensive screens. But I would have to wait to consider whether this was what heartbreak felt like.

"What...you mean...someone besides Ty Hunter is out to get me?"

"Yes," she said.

"Who?"

She looked left, and she looked right. "Principal Denton."

I sniffed. "I had already kind of figured that—"

"*And* Ms. Beacon."

"*What?*" I pressed my hands to my temples, the way Captain Maxim does when trying to think his way out of a crisis. "You think—?"

"I know."

"But…how?"

"The office. I heard them."

"Heard them what?"

"Talking about you."

"Me? Are you sure?"

"You're Clark Sherman, right?" she said, annoyed.

"Yeah, but…what did they say?"

She gave a little frown. "I'm not exactly sure. I distinctly heard Beacon use your name and 'all kinds of trouble.' And then Denton said something about there being ways to get rid of such issues.

"I wanted to stay and listen to more, but I had to get to the attendance computer while nobody was looking. By the time I was back to my usual seat, Beacon was leaving the office, with a folder that said 'disciplinary' something, and she did not look happy."

"She never looks happy."

"She looked less happy than usual, then," Ricki snapped. "I'm telling you, it was something big, and you were the center of it."

"Then why—"

"I don't know anything else. I just wanted to tell you what I heard. You helped me. I'm trying to help back."

"Thank you," I said.

She looked off toward the parking lot.

"My parents are going to be here soon," Ricki said. "You need to pretend you don't know me. My mom would absolutely freak out if she knew I was talking to a boy. I think she invented the concept of 'overprotective.'"

"Your parents are...amazing," I said.

"I tell myself, 'Nature, not nurture' a lot," she said, shaking her head.

She replied to my puzzled look by saying, "I'll tell you about them someday."

"Do you want to call me?" I asked.

"Based on our prior experience, I think it is safe to assume that they would not want your voice in our home ever again."

"Is there some other way, then?"

She didn't say no right away. But when she opened her mouth to speak, she was cut off by the sound of distant thunder. I looked to the sky, expecting to see storm clouds. But it was just an old Volvo chugging up the hill and turning into the parking lot.

"My parents," said Ricki, sitting up straight. "Remember, you're not with me. I'm...I'm sorry it has to be so crazy."

I looked away from her. "'The only crazy people in this galaxy are the ones who expect it to be sane.'"

"Thanks, Captain Maxim," she said. "And be careful."

"You too. Find me if you need help." I stole a quick glance at her.

She turned toward me for just a moment, then back toward the approaching wagon. "Thank you," she said, and then, out of the corner of her mouth: "It's nice to not feel alone."

She stood and walked toward the car. As she did, a scowling blond woman rolled down the window and asked her something before casting an angry glance my way; next to her, I could see a pale man with a severe, angular face staring blankly ahead. Ricki got into the back seat, and they rumbled off.

As dates went, it had been...not much. But we had at least set a foundation for the next time. When perhaps we could work our way up to speaking for more than fifteen minutes and discussing something besides the imminent peril I apparently was in. Again.

The thought of peril led me to pay attention to my surroundings a little more. I watched the people coming and going into the rec center. I watched the little kids climbing on the monkey bars on the playground. I watched the players leaving the baseball game that had been taking place in the field beyond.

I squinted as some of them headed my way.

Three of them, in fact.

I ran to my bike.

9.02.02

I fumbled with the lock. I had made careful note of the combination before I left the house, but in my panic I couldn't remember—was it 5332, or 3552, or 5232, or...

Oh frak, they'd seen me.

Finally, at 3253, the lock slid open. Did I have enough of a head start?

Maybe I should just stand my ground. Steele would. Did I want the whole rec center to see me running like a coward? I quickly reminded myself—I was no Steele. Being seen running like a coward would be much better than being seen humiliated and abused and *then* running. ("Hey, did you see that new kid get the snot beat out of him at the rec center on Saturday?" "Yeah, it was ugly, but he sure smelled nice.")

I began to pedal away as quickly as I could. They reached the bike rack a few moments after I left, by which point I was across the parking lot. I looked back. They were staring at me but seemed in no hurry. I put my head down, shifted gears, nearly fell over when there was suddenly no resistance to my pedaling, shifted gears *properly* and headed out to the street at maximum speed.

I looked back again. All clear! They were still unlocking their bikes. All I had to do now was keep my balance, because it was all downhill from here—literally, for a change. Even I could make good speed on a 10,000-foot descent. Soon the wind was whipping through my hair as I cruised past Warp One to Warp Two and then Warp Three.

I followed the fastest downhill route, which took me a little east of home base. I would have to cut across Sand Creek Lane again, scene of the grimly remembered Battle of the Ice Clump, but with my pursuers so far to my rear, I felt confident. Let's hear it for the power of panic! I sat up in my seat and started riding hands-free. I felt that confident.

I turned onto Sand Creek Lane and had slowed to about Warp One when I entered the stretch that had only the "park" on either side of the road. The memory of what had happened the last time I passed through this quadrant made me nervous, and I turned around to look behind me, one more time.

Which is why I was totally surprised by the riders when they flew out of the park, practically E.T.-style, but with significantly less heartwarming charm.

They came over a knoll, across the sidewalk and directly into my path. "Yeee-hawww!" one yelled in midair.

(I don't like to stereotype, but that was probably Bubba.)

Out of reflex, I flung my right hand up to shield my face and grasped a brake handle with my left. As it turns out, this is the handle that controls the front brake—information I probably should have studied up on before I started flying around at warp speeds.

The good news is, those brand-new brakes were awfully effective at halting the rotation of my front wheel. It went from spinning at Warp One to a full stop in no time.

The bad news is that with the front wheel stopped, the rear wheel was sprung off the ground, and I was flung off my bike and onto the pavement, where my left shoulder became a braking mechanism for my body as it scraped along the ground at, well, just about Warp One.

As I slid to a stop, the riders surrounded me. They rode fat-tired mountain bikes, expertly, in the manner of people who had grown up in the neighborhood and knew, for example, shortcuts from the rec center that could be used to cut someone off.

"Hey look, it's Clark!" said Jerry. "We were worried we wouldn't get a chance to say hi."

"Yeah," snorted Bubba. "If Denton hadn't told us to back off, we—"

"Shut up." Ty glared at him, and he clammed up.

"Sorry if you got hurt," Ty said, turning to me. "We were just in a rush to get home and must not of seen you. Right, guys?" His henchmen nodded. "Jerry's right—we've missed you. And it might be a while before you hear from us, 'cause we've got a lot of baseball to play in the coming weeks, but"—he smiled his reptile smile—"we'll be back in touch right away after that."

With a nod, he directed the gang on down the street. But

he stayed and watched me writhe on the pavement, where I was clutching my shoulder, feeling the sticky blood soak my ripped shirt.

He sneered down at me before spitting on the ground next to my face. Then he rode off.

I stared at the sky for a few moments before trying to sit up. I was half hoping that a car would come along, not see me, and just put me out of my misery. But I had no such luck. I picked up my scraped body and battered bike and began walking at limp speed toward home. The smell of pine from my cologne-soaked pants filled my head, a reminder of the optimism I had greeted the day with. Man, how I hated that smell.

The command units went all medical on me when I got home. I told them I had swerved to avoid a kid on a trike. They were concerned about the bloody shoulder and kept using words like *infection* and *scar*. I just wanted to be left alone and frankly was more concerned about the loss of my shirt. Good dress shirts are hard to find, and I anticipated no planetarium field trips in my future. Just more confusion.

9.03.01

That evening, I could tell by the series of worried glances and closed-door conversations that the commanders were gearing up for another attempt at transgenerational communication.

Sure enough, the next afternoon, after I'd had a chance to rest and relax and allow the pain to spread from my shoulder throughout my entire body, the female commander declared that she and I should go clothes shopping.

I had no real desire to get new clothes, especially with a bandaged shoulder and a "Sci-Fi Sunday" doubleheader scheduled on Channel 31, but she insisted. I didn't fight too much. For one, there was no point. And two, maybe I would get lucky and find a replacement for that Saturn shirt.

Also, it would be nice to have the commander to myself, like in the olden days, without the spawn around. The spawn could be cute sometimes, but she did have a way of taking over the conversation.

So despite the fact that I would probably have to deflect a lot of questions about how school was going, I managed to get myself to the point of actually looking forward to this venture. It was then, of course, that the other command unit's phone rang.

When someone called for him, it was never good. Especially on a Sunday afternoon. Sure enough, I heard him argue, then gradually back down and reluctantly say, "OK, I'll be downtown shortly." This was followed by a weary look toward the first command unit. Her face sank as we heard the nap-skipping spawn squeal from her bedroom.

"But Clark and I were going to have a chance to *talk*," she said urgently.

"Sorry," the male commander said as he gathered up some papers. "It's an emergency."

"Another one?"

He gave both of us an apologetic look. "I'm really, really sorry," he said. Then he grabbed his coat and ran out the door.

She sighed and looked over at me. "Well, Clark, we'll just make the best of it. Give me a minute to get Gwen ready."

Forty-five minutes later, the spawn was changed, fed, cleaned, led into the car, given a sniff test, removed from the car, changed again, cleaned again and led back into the car. I was ready to call it a day, but the commander had a look of grim determination on her face. I knew better than to cross her.

As we drove down to the Forest Park Crossing Mall, she attempted to engage in conversation. It went something like this:

COMMANDER: "So, I never really heard how your ride went yesterday. I mean, before the accident. Did you see anyone you knew at the rec center?"

ME (swallowing): "Well I—"

SPAWN: "SCREEEEEEE!"

COMMANDER: "Gwen, hush! Sorry, Clark, it's as if she knows when I'm trying to—"

SPAWN: "Mah mah mah mah mah mah SCREEEEEEE-EEEEEEEE!"

ME: "It's OK, I'm sort of used to it now."

COMMANDER: "Maybe she'll settle down once she's in her stroller."

Once in her stroller, she did settle down. For about the amount of time it took to get from the car to the mall's interior, where we were confronted with a terrifying sight. Not terrifying to me—I had nothing against the Easter Bunny, who was being led by two bunny-elf assistants to greet a throng of happy children. But the toddler had a different viewpoint.

"Mah! Mah! MAH!...

SCRREEEEEEE! SCREEEEEEEEEEEEEEEE!...

URRRRRRRRPPPPPPPP."

The *urp* was whatever green thing she had eaten for lunch

coming back for a repeat appearance. Apparently, regurgitation in moments of panic was a family tradition.

The commander looked down at the flailing mix of chewed food and squirming terror. Her voice dropped into its lowest register. "Clark, I'm gonna need time." She reached into her purse, grabbed some cash and handed it to me. "Go find a game store or something. I'll meet you at the food court in, I don't know, half an hour?"

I probably should have said thanks to the toddler. But I didn't want to get that close. So I took the money and walked off.

I was tempted by the prospect of a new video game, but I had seen something potentially more engaging as we had circled the parking lot on the way in. I walked the length of the mall and exited the far side, near the movie theater. Across the parking lot, clinging to the periphery of the main mall like a barnacle, was a thin, rectangular building of glass and tan bricks that appeared to be several decades older than the rest of the development.

It held only three businesses. Two were defunct, or purveyors of FOR LEASE posters. But in between them, I had spied a hand-painted sign that read:

SOUND 'N' VISION
BOOKS AND MUSIC
USED, BOUGHT AND SOLD

I checked my watch and trotted across the broken pavement, around the black puddles of snowmelt that were rainbow-streaked with motor-oil drippings, and past the single vehicle parked in front of the shop: a small pickup with a rear window plastered in stickers referencing a dozen bands I had not heard of.

As I placed my hand on the cold aluminum handle of the glass door, I paused to admire the window display—a stack of paperbacks and a fading homemade poster that said CELEBRATE BANNED BOOKS WEEK.

I pulled on the door and stepped inside.

The store was a jumble of shelves, each marked with a wooden sign that I suspect someone's grandfather had cut with a jigsaw an eon ago: FICTION/LITERATURE. HISTORY/BIOGRAPHY. CHILDREN'S. And then I spied tall, magnificent stacks marked FANTASY and SCIENCE FICTION/ETC.

If I had seen enough spare floor space to unroll a sleeping bag, I might have asked to move in on the spot.

Off to my right, a bearded man sat behind a glass case, carefully sorting a stack of vinyl discs that were even older than my parents. He nodded in my direction. Behind him, I could see a room jammed with record bins that filled what used to be one of the adjacent storefronts. But I, of course, made straight for SCIENCE FICTION/ETC.

As I strolled, I ran my finger lightly along the spines of coarse hardcovers missing their jackets; squat paperbacks, titles marred by the vertical lines that indicated a well-read copy; and the occasional oddity such as the battered box that held a game called *[smudged] Fleet Battles*.

So many familiar names on that deliciously long aisle. So many yet to explore. The row ended at *V*, right in the middle of *Vonnegut*. I rounded the corner, eager to see what other surprises might await—

—and nearly plowed into Stephanie Spring.

OVERLOAD

OVERLOAD

DOES NOT COMPUTE

I had postulated that maybe on the weekends, girls like Stephanie wore old T-shirts, didn't comb their hair, allowed themselves to look...human. But Stephanie apparently was superhuman. She had on a perfect black sweater, her hair was tied back perfectly, and she looked—

"Oh wow. Hi, Clark," she said, wide-eyed.

—perfect.

"Stephanie?" I asked, as if she were some ghostly projection from another dimension. Because clearly, this had to be Alternate Stephanie, the one from the universe where I was cool and handsome and she was a girl who would hang out in used bookstores.

She smiled, meekly, as she took out her fancy earbuds. "I didn't expect to see *you* here."

"Uh, I think I could say the same." Which might have been the truest statement I had ever spoken.

We stood there, frozen. With great effort, I strung together enough words to form a sentence:

"Do you, uh, come here a lot?" I did not say it was a particularly *good* sentence.

Her eyes grew wider. "Oh no. Not at all. Usually. Really. You?"

"My first time," I said.

She nodded and bit her lower lip.

"Seems nice enough," I said, looking around. I noticed that the ceiling tiles had a bunch of blotchy brown stains.

"It has its charms," she said, inspecting a bit of worn carpet.

"I sort of left my mom back at the mall," I said, gesturing

with my thumb, desperately trying to think of something we might have in common.

"Really?" she said. This somehow got her attention. "I had to sneak away from mine, too."

"Sneak away?"

"Yeah," she said. "She thinks I'm shoe shopping."

"She'd rather have you trying on shoes than reading books?" I was so dumbfounded that I forgot to be flustered.

"Well, no. Well, sort of," Stephanie said. "She *does* like shoes. And dressing me up. I mean—shopping for me. We have a mother-daughter dinner at church tonight. She's looking for an outfit to coordinate with mine right now." She winced. "But she's not opposed to *books*, you know? It's just certain *kinds* of books."

"Like what?" I asked.

She looked at me as if deciding whether to elaborate. Finally, she said, "Let's just say she thinks that any book with a dragon on the cover was probably written by Satan himself."

"Ah," I said.

She looked the aisle up and down wistfully.

I set aside the shock of hearing Stephanie imply that she was a fellow admirer of great literature, because I was still thinking about how horrible it would be to love a book and be kept from it.

"You know she's wrong, right?"

She took her eyes off the books and met my gaze.

"Yeah, well, I'm not the one who's going to say that to Mrs. Cindy Spring," she said bitterly. "But it's fun to imagine."

I shook my head. "You have it tough, I guess."

"Oh, it's not so bad." She shrugged. Her face said otherwise.

I thought about how lost I would be without my books.

"Maybe she'd approve of something postapocalyptic? You don't find a lot of dragons in atomic rubble." I scanned the shelf and pulled out a familiar title that happened to star a teenage girl. It showed a mushroom cloud on the cover, but the girl was modestly clad in a radiation suit. "Here," I said, handing it over. "This one's a favorite of mine."

Her face brightened. "Oh, I *love* this. I've checked it out from the library, like, three times."

"So your mom's OK with that?"

"No. She has no clue."

"So it's a secret between you and...the Kaitlins, then?"

Stephanie smiled grimly. She looked down at the book, then gently slid it back in place on the shelf, letting a perfectly manicured pink fingernail stroke the spine as she let it go.

"Kaitlin, Kaitlyn and Katelyn and I have been friends since preschool, and our moms have been friends even longer," she said. "We share a lot of things. But when it comes to books, or music that's not just some stupid boy band of the moment, I'm sort of on my own. Well, my dad helps me with my audio gear."

"Audio gear?"

"Yeah. I'd been asking him about some of his equipment, and he'd been showing me with some of his old records how—" She stopped suddenly. "Anyway. It's sort of a thing I do. For him, mostly. But the Kaitlins—no, I couldn't talk to them about this."

"Why?"

She gave me an incredulous look. "Clark, there are some things you just can't share if you want to—"

And then her phone buzzed. She glanced at it to see who

was calling. "My mom's about to come looking for me," she said. "I have to go."

"See you at school, then," I said, as she turned away. "And, um, if you need help with any books, you know, just ask. I have connections."

She laughed, a bit sadly. "Thanks. See you around."

As she headed toward the door, the clerk hailed her, "Hey, that Bowie rerelease you were asking about—the 180-gram blue vinyl version? It should be in Tuesday. Should I set one aside?"

"Yes, please," she said. She turned back to me, slightly panicked, and added, "For my dad!" And then, much more softly, she asked, "Clark? You won't tell anyone you saw me here, right?"

Before I could respond, she glanced at her phone, spun away, and was gone.

9.03.02

I pondered our encounter once I was back in the minivan, where the spawn had fallen asleep and the commander had a defeated, sunken-eyed look as she drove in silence.

I thought about what it would be like to be friends with Stephanie. We seemed to have a lot in common—books and an admiration for her general appearance, just for starters. And I thought about what that friendship might mean for my present situation. After all, a supportive word from her could probably end most of my troubles. She had that kind of power over classmates. Boys and girls alike.

And then I thought, What would the cost be? Would being friends with her mean I would have to give up my own books?

What if I started hanging out with her, and the Kaitlins started to make fun of Ricki? Would I have to just stand by and let that happen? Could I?

No, I thought. I couldn't.

As I stared out the window and watched the split-level ranch homes roll past, I found myself thinking about solar systems. And gravity. The bigger the star, the heavier its pull. But every star orbits something too—another star, or the bright cluster of them at the core of a galaxy, which might have, at its heart, a black hole.

Maybe it was better to be an insignificant space fleck way out in some gravitational dead zone.

Nobody can see us, true.

But at least we can read what we want.

"Know thy enemy. And
through knowledge,
thou shalt find victory,
and satisfaction that he
whom thou confronteth
verily deserveth thy wrath."

—Commander Steele, quoting from *The Omegan Art of War*
Star Survivors Episode 53,
"Omegans Amok"

EXPEDITION LOG

ENTRY 10.01.01

At school on Monday, I didn't expect Stephanie to have time to chat with me.

And the way she avoided eye contact when I tried to say hi in the halls made it clear she did not.

If I'd had time, I might have been worried about her. But I had my own problems to deal with.

Ricki thought that Ms. Beacon might be out to get me. In my head, I knew that Ricki would not report false information. In my heart, I knew I could trust Ms. Beacon. How to resolve this?

I got my answer in the ARC.

After Ricki and I exchanged nods and I set my Cosmos backpack down, I walked toward Ms. Beacon's doorway and stood while she wrote at her desk. I wasn't sure what I was going to say, so I just scanned for clues.

I saw a shelf full of binders with dates and acronyms on them—references to budgets and book purchases. I saw wire baskets, filled with paper and envelopes, marked MAIL TO OFFICE and MAIL FROM OFFICE. I saw a file cabinet with labels such as SCHOOL BOARD MINUTES and PARENTAL CHALLENGES. I saw a framed photo of a smiling Ms. Beacon standing atop a mountain with another smiling woman, both of them sunburned and clearly pleased with themselves. A figurine of a football player, number seven, from the local franchise.

And then, on her desk, I saw a large brown envelope. DISCIPLINARY TRIBUNAL, it said. CONFIDENTIAL.

So Ricki had been right!

"Can I help you, Mr. Sherman?" Ms. Beacon asked.

"Uh," I said, "did you need any help shelving today? Because I'm, uh, mostly caught up on my homework."

"And I'm mostly caught up on my shelving today. You may read, Mr. Sherman."

"Uh, sure." I pretended to just notice the envelope on her desk. "Hey! Disciplinary Tribunal? What's that? I sure hope I'm not involved!" I forced a smile that I hoped conveyed a zany, carefree, I'm-not-actually-trying-to-find-out-what's-in-that-envelope attitude.

She put down her pen. She stared at me. Intensely. Which made me extremely uncomfortable.

"Mr. Sherman, I sit on the school's Disciplinary Tribunal. Do you know what that is?"

My silence indicated I did not.

"You should read your student handbook. The Disciplinary Tribunal is made up of the principal, a counselor and a senior faculty member, which is me. We review student infractions and recommend severe disciplinary action for students whose behavior warrants it."

It sounded intimidating. "Like...like a military tribunal? Or a court martial?"

"I suppose that is what Principal Denton had in mind when he invented it. When we vote on a course of action, the majority rules, so Principal Denton needs one other tribunal member to endorse his recommendations for him to get his way."

I thought about how every adult at Festus—except Ms. Beacon—acted whenever Denton was around. "I guess he gets his way a lot, huh."

Ms. Beacon put on her glasses again so she could stare over the rims. "Mr. Sherman, have you done anything to warrant the attention of the tribunal?"

My stomach squirmed some more. "Uh, I don't really think so, Ms. Beacon."

"Good. Neither do I. Beyond that, I cannot discuss tribunal matters or voting records with students. The rules regarding our proceedings are arcane and rigorously enforced." She gazed at me evenly. "I will say this, however: I managed to get myself on the tribunal only because no other teacher would volunteer—and there is often not much I can do for those whom Denton sets his sights on.

"So Mr. Sherman, I will emphasize to you: *Be extremely careful.*"

I nodded and backed out under her stern gaze.

Ricki's eyes followed me as I made my way to my table. I sat down, pulled a book out of my backpack and, while I was setting the backpack on the floor, flashed her an "OK" sign.

I figured that a little bit of attitude could only help. But I still had a lot of questions.

After school I took a roundabout route to the bridge, made sure nobody could see me and ducked inside the drain pipe. Les was waiting with his flashlight. He'd received the coded message I'd left in his locker.

"I can't stay long," he said. "What's the emergency?"

"What do you know about the Disciplinary Tribunal?" I asked.

"It's a bureaucratic thing for when they're planning to

expel someone. The principal, the counselor and a teacher. Denton's in charge of it."

"You sound like an expert."

"You forget who my family is."

"Oh. Yeah." I guess he *would* be an expert.

"Ty has been up for discipline more times than I can remember," he said bitterly. "He was regularly getting slapped with detentions in elementary school. But at Festus, he's always managed to get off with a scolding. Time after time."

I imagined what this must have been like for Les. "That could make a guy crazy, I suppose."

He picked at a glob of dried candle wax that had spilled onto one of the milk crates, rolled it around in his fingers, then flicked it away. "In the beginning, no. When my mom and I first moved in with his family, he just confused me. I mean, he was supposed to be a brother, right? But he was angry from the start. Angry at my mom. Angry at me. And I guess I was the one he could take it out on.

"But I still *tried* to make it function. And if I had ever seen even one *moment* where he acted decent, or even halfway human, if he'd ever attempted to apologize, even once, maybe we could have worked something out. But he would *never* let his guard down that much with me. It's like he wanted to see how far he could take things before his dad would pay attention to *anything* besides baseball and the velocity of his fastball. And he never found that limit.

"And then he started homing in on my friends and making life hell for them too. That was when I just about..." His voice trailed off, and he stared down the long, cold pipe that led to the park.

"Anyhow, then I found the Sanctuary. And I started using

the wormhole network. To avoid him. It's a lot easier—on everyone." He flicked away another ball of wax.

"Your mom never tried to help?"

"I don't blame her. She and I both know that her stepping in would have just made things worse."

"That must be—"

"Let's get back to your problems," he said abruptly. "Why do you care about the Disciplinary Tribunal?" I set aside my questions about him and related what Ricki had heard. "Do you think they're coming after me? Because of the projector thing?"

His brow furrowed. "No. That's hardly tribunal material."

"What is?"

"Big stuff. Drugs. Fighting. Making fun of your teacher's butt."

"They could expel you for that?"

"Probably."

"But I haven't done anything that bad."

He paused. "No, but Ty has."

"What does that have to do with me?"

He started to speak, then stopped himself. "Look, I can speculate all I want. But it won't matter unless we can see inside that envelope."

"Too bad we can't," I sighed.

He stared at me. "You could just take it."

"That would be stealing!"

"How can it be stealing when it's your information? Probably."

He had a point.

"How would we do it?"

"We? I think this is going to have to be all you. I mean, I'll give it some thought. But I'm in deep if I don't get home fast. Baseball season."

"You want me to break a kneecap for you, so you can sit out?"

His face brightened at the prospect, then fell. "Nah, he'd just tell me to walk it off." And Les exited down the pipe.

As I waited for my turn to go, part of me was terrified. Would I really try espionage? Risk turning my life upside-down?

Heck yeah.

10.01.02

That night, at the home base, all four occupants took ritual nourishment together again. So I used the opportunity to probe my commanders for useful data. They deserved a chance to not be totally useless.

"Dad," I asked, while the spawn was distracted by small chunks of meatball, "have you ever had to steal important documents from someone? For your job, I mean."

He nearly choked on his spaghetti. "Why on earth would you ask that?"

I had anticipated this. "I've just been thinking about what you do, and it's sounding interesting to me. Being a journalist and all."

This had an unusual effect on the commander. He looked at his co-commander, who pursed her lips in a suppressed smile. Then he began to give off low-level radiation that was not actually visible but could still be described as glowing.

"Well, I'm happy to talk, Clark. The short answer is, no, I have never stolen documents for any of my investigations. Although there was a time once, back when I was a cub reporter, that I…"

I have noticed that whenever the commander begins something by saying, "The short answer is," he always follows it with a long, dull story that I can mostly ignore. This one was about some kind of corruption or something in a politician's office. Or maybe he said police officer. Anyhow, the story involved some piece of paper he needed and a locked file cabinet and him making small talk with a secretary about her favorite band for a week until she let him copy some notes from that file cabinet. Or something.

"So the lesson is," he said, and this was the only part I was interested in, "don't be afraid to get help. You can get a lot more done in a pack than as a lone wolf."

Wolves? He hadn't said anything about wolves. Much less a pack.

He just kept talking. "I mean, look at John Lennon and Paul McCartney. Classic example."

I was puzzled. "Was Lennon the old guy with the funny lips whose band you saw in Los Angeles when I was in fifth grade?"

Now his expression looked pained for some reason. "No, Clark, you're thinking of Mick Jagger, of The Rolling—never mind. The point is, Lennon and McCartney were never as good solo as they were when they were together. "

"They were a band too, then?"

The female commander laughed. The male commander

looked skyward, as if praying to be relieved of a great pain, then simply said, "Yes."

I nodded—"Thanks, Dad"—and excused myself.

He was so obtuse.

10.02.01

Given the lack of help I was receiving from Les and my commanders, Ricki—the only one of us who regularly observed Principal Denton in his lair—seemed my best hope for answers. She was adamant about not being seen with me, but through a series of notes, whispers, hand-drawn maps and occasionally violent hand gestures, we came up with a plan. Which was: I would meet with her while she walked home.

I rode my bike to school. After Athletics, I dashed out the back to throw off anybody trying to tail me, then circled to the front, unchained my bike and took a roundabout route to the rendezvous.

It was on a street that was intersected by a narrow, paved path that ran east from Festus. Ricki was coming up the path as I arrived. She clutched her books across her chest like a shield and kept her eyes fixed straight ahead as she passed me, then paused as she prepared to cross the street. I rolled my bike behind her and dismounted.

"Follow me, but don't *look* like you're following me," she murmured.

I let her walk ahead, then grabbed my handlebars and began pushing.

The trail—apparently intended for people who liked to exercise, which was probably why I had not seen it before—wound behind the rows of houses, most of which separated themselves from the path with low fences of chain link. I followed Ricki and her determined, bouncy stride for another half block, when suddenly the fences fell away and the trail opened up onto a small, well-used playground. It was empty; the grade school would not be released for another fifteen minutes, and the aging equipment here was primarily targeted at such children.

Among the structures was one inviting work of art: the twenty-five-foot-tall framework of a Buck Rogers–era rocket, made of metal pipes, with a ladder up the interior, a slide coming out of what would be the second stage and an observation deck of sorts in the nose cone.

Ricki was ducking inside it.

I pushed my bike down the path a bit, chained it to a bench, looked around to make sure the coast was clear, and ran back across the play area. The pea-sized pebbles crunched as I scrambled toward the ladder.

Ricki was sitting cross-legged in the nose cone when I poked my head up.

"I have maybe ten minutes," she said.

I pulled myself in, tried to stand up, hit my head on the top of the rocket and plopped down across from her, not quite Gemini-style, but we could save historical accuracy for another day.

"I need help," I said.

"Try ice for your head, and maybe the mall for new shoes."

I looked at my feet, worried. "What's wrong with my shoes?"

"Nothing," she said. "It was a joke."

Her sense of humor was odd, I thought.

"I think your sense of humor is odd," I said.

"It probably is. My life is odd. It's actually dangerous for me to be up here with you."

"Really?" I didn't think of myself as dangerous.

"Yes. But that's OK. I kind of like it. What's your urgent need that led you to lure me here?"

I scrutinized her, trying to grok what she was really all about. I thought of this video game I once played that had a target inside a layer of rotating shields that was inside a layer of rotating shields that was inside a layer of rotating shields. Only when everything lined up exactly right did you have a clear path to the heart of the fortress. Ricki reminded me of that.

Why were we here? Oh, yeah. "Ricki, I need to find out what's inside Ms. Beacon's Disciplinary Tribunal file."

"Then you're in trouble."

I frowned. "You don't have access?"

"Nope."

"But I thought you could do anything in that office! I mean, you get on the attendance computer...."

"That's easy. When the receptionist is on the phone, I slip in, do my thing and slip out. I can't get to your envelope so simply. If it's not in Beacon's office, it's either with Denton or on Blethins's desk."

"So you know where it's kept?"

"No."

"Then how do you—"

"They pass it back and forth a lot. He leaves it in Blethins's in-box. She has to sign it or something before returning it to him."

"Other than that time, it's locked in a file somewhere?"

"Yes. Probably in his desk. And no, I do not have the key."

I stared out between the bars, over the sea of rooftops, and could see Festus uphill in the distance, a sight that always made me feel slightly ill.

Which gave me an idea.

"Ricki, if you were working in the office, would you have a way of getting a message to me?"

"Maybe," she said. "Why?"

"If you saw that folder on Blethins's desk, could you signal me quickly?"

"Yes," she said, her eyes narrowing. "Yes, I could do that. You'd be in Lopez's class second hour, right?"

"Yeah." I sat up straight. "How did you know?"

"I have my ways." She was fighting a smile. She might even have blushed.

She looked at her watch. "I am also going to have to leave in three minutes. Is there anything else you'd like to...discuss?"

She arched one eyebrow and still seemed to be fighting a smile.

We sat across from each other in our little space capsule, cut off from the rest of the world, a cool spring breeze blowing through the bars.

I leaned in toward her.

"Yes," I said.

She waited, expectantly.

"Tell me: how did you become a *Star Survivors* fan?"

The question seemed to surprise her, and she tilted her head to one side, as if to ask, "Seriously?"

"No, I really want to know," I said. It was the most personal question I could think of. Aside from asking whether she preferred Maxim or Steele.

She shook her head and laughed.

"You *really* like that show, don't you?"

"Don't *you*?"

"Well, yes. It has a few flaws—the women's uniforms are much too tight to be practical, and I think *I* could have navigated the ship back to Earth by the middle of Season Two using some simple triangulation techniques that Steele surely could have computed, but it's a pleasant diversion. Perhaps even inspiring. And I happen to like that it annoys my parents."

I overlooked her criticism because I wanted to hear about her parents. "They aren't fans?"

"HA! They think television is for weak minds. I'm not supposed to watch."

"So how...?"

"My father is always off at his lab, and my mother works part-time on campus. When she's out, I can turn on the TV and get caught up. Without them knowing I'm being corrupted. And lecturing me about how they expect better from me."

"Your parents are even more intense than I thought."

She folded her arms across her chest and scowled. "They get freaked out so easily," she fumed.

"So I've seen," I said.

"Tip of the iceberg," she said.

"Mine are mostly clueless," I offered. "I mean, the stuff

they don't notice....They're totally unobservant. Sometimes I wonder if we're even related."

She gave me a funny look, as if she were about to say something, but stopped.

"What?" I asked.

"It's complicated. Or it is for you, apparently."

"Please," I said. "It's just—parents. How can your situation be that much more complicated than anyone else's?"

"Clark," she said, speaking slowly. "You've seen my parents, right?"

I thought back to the stern, blond woman and the tired-looking man in the Volvo. "Yeah, so?"

She waited, both eyebrows now arched above her brown eyes.

Hold on...

"Ricki," I asked, putting it all together, "are you—"

"Adopted?" she said, impatiently. *"Yes.* And if your main complaint about your own parents is that they are not observant, it is clear that you may be more like them than you think."

"Well, I've had a lot on my mind," I said defensively. "It's not like I've been sitting around, pondering your family situation or something!"

We were silent for as long as I could stand before I asked, "So, uh, did you want to tell me about your family situation?"

"Oh, we're just your normal, everyday American family," she said brightly. "I mean, lots of people are adopted, right? For lots of different reasons? At least, that's what the pamphlet said. The one my mom gave me last time I brought up the subject."

"She gave you a *pamphlet*? To talk about—"

"No, there's no talking, Clark. Not when a trifold piece of paper can do all the communicating for you. Which is funny, considering my mom is technically quite capable of communication. She was born in Sweden and speaks several languages."

"She's from Sweden? But your dad sounded—"

"French? He's from Quebec. It's a long story that ends with them meeting in a lab at MIT and getting married and adopting me from Seoul."

I tried to add it all up. "So you're...French Canadian-Swedish-Korean-American?"

She sighed, unfolded her arms and let her hands fall to her lap. "More like, 'None of the above.'"

"OK. You win. That's complicated," I said. The expression on her face was not triumphant, though. "And I'm sorry I asked."

"I actually don't mind explaining it," she said. "I don't get a lot of chances. I *do* get a lot of people asking, 'Where are you from?' And then angry stares when I tell them, 'Boston.' And then they ask, 'No, where are you *originally* from.' And when we finally get to 'South Korea,' they start with the insults."

"OK, good," I said, relieved. "I mean, that you aren't upset with me. Not good about the insults. And that you don't get to talk about it. If you want to talk about it. I mean..." What did I mean? "I'm just sorry. You deserve...better."

She looked as if she didn't quite believe me. "I think the insults just go with the whole...*outsider* thing," she said. "I mean, Festus is bad. But not unique."

"Well, do your parents—"

"My parents don't get it. They seem to fit in wherever they find work. Montreal. Los Alamos. Here. They're good at enrolling me in activities and making sure I do my homework but have no clue what it's like to always be the new kid, much less the one who doesn't look like everyone else, and not even like her parents. They've never dealt with the jokes, never heard the Kaitlins make fun of—"

The thought of the Kaitlins made her draw her shoulders in and bow her head, as if she were trying to make herself less visible.

"Anyhow, my parents…I suppose they mean well. But I…I don't think they know what to do with me. Besides try to shelter me from everything. Lock me up, like Rapunzel or something. And they just don't know what that's like… to feel like you were hatched on another planet or something." She looked up. "You know?"

I nodded slowly. I most definitely *did* know. But as I struggled to find the right words to explain that, we heard the bell from the elementary school ring in the distance.

"I have to go," she said, and she began to gather her backpack.

Why was it that the people I wanted to talk to were always running away just when things got interesting?

"Wait—Ricki, I—I—" I stammered as she began to climb down hurriedly.

"Superman," I blurted, as I suddenly remembered something from a comic book the male commander had given me a long time ago.

She paused at the top of the ladder, then flashed an angry look. "You are a very random and disturbed person, did you know that?"

"He's adopted too. Also an alien. You two probably have a lot in common."

Her look indicated that she thought I had just displayed the intelligence and insight one might expect from a fungus. "I think he's got more than a few advantages over me, Clark."

"Yeah, but you know, Ricki, you've got your own skills. From what I've seen, at least."

She stayed there, holding on to the top rung, and tilted her head as she thought that over.

"I suppose your brain *is* interesting sometimes," she finally said. "I didn't know it held much more than *Star Survivors* quotes. I thought you were going to ask me whether I preferred Maxim or Steele."

"Well, actually, I *was* kind of wondering...."

Which earned me an eye roll. "I'll think about giving you an answer the next time we get together."

That was promising, at least. "And you'll signal me if you spot the envelope?"

"For whatever good it will do you."

"Thanks for the vote of confidence."

"I said I would help. I didn't say I thought you were all that bright." She steadied herself on the ladder. "But you *are* mildly amusing."

She descended, looked up and down the path, and started toward her home.

I waited a few minutes, enjoying the vibe in the air, until a cool wind out of the west made me shudder.

Then I climbed down and rode home, half my brain filled with Ricki-related thoughts, the other half trying to figure out how I would get that folder out of the office, if I ever got the chance.

10.03.01

My chance came the next morning, during second hour.

Mr. Lopez had us reading silently out of the lang arts textbook. I have never understood how this type of assignment is considered "teaching." "Teaching" is supposed to be a verb, implying action, correct? This was merely "boring." As in, "boring me and the rest of the class to death."

So I was left to amuse myself by staring intensely at the pages and seeing whether I could cause any to ignite with my heretofore untapped telekinetic powers. I failed. But while I stared, the intercom did erupt with a loud electronic tone. This was what happened when the office receptionist was about to summon someone. I expected to hear her next.

But the voice was a girl's: "Um…oops! Wrong…hailing frequency." And then a click.

Mr. Lopez shrugged it off; the intercom system was old and full of quirks, and the office staff was not known for its machinelike efficiency.

But I knew a coded signal when I heard one. Ricki had spotted the envelope, and it was time for me to take it.

I hadn't formulated a full plan, just the first phase. But I knew this might be my only chance. So while I sat at my desk, I put the operation into action: I held my breath, pursed my lips, and tried to force air out of my eyeballs.

I knew this wouldn't actually cause my tear ducts to bubble—but it did make my face purplish and my breathing came in odd gasps afterward.

I stood up and approached Mr. Lopez, who was reading

the sports section of the newspaper. "I don't feel so well," I said with a moan. "Can I go see the nurse?"

He took one look at me, widened his eyes, scrawled out a pass and told me to hurry. Maybe my reputation was helping me for a change.

I staggered away.

Once around the corner from his classroom, I slowed my pace. Fooling a teacher like Mr. Lopez is easy; fooling the nurse would be something else. And then what would I do? This would merely put me in the office. How was I going to get that envelope?

My stomach flipped. Yes. That, unfortunately, was the only answer.

I took a detour to my locker for supplies. In this case, a plastic bottle. The one I'd stuffed in my lunch bag. The one I'd carried out of the cafeteria last week when I'd seen my enemies blocking the path to the recycling bin. The one I had then shoved in my locker.

I opened my locker, and then the bottle. The days-old milk smelled of death, or as close to it as I ever hope to come. I peered inside to see how much was left. It was just enough. I swirled the chunky remnants around, closed my eyes, put the bottle to my lips and gulped them down. Just barely.

Then I set off for the office. Slowly, because I needed time to work my nerves into a real frenzy. So as my mouth began to feel as if a rancid slug had slithered across my tongue and down my throat, I started thinking about how afraid I was of getting caught. I thought about Hunter, Pignarski and Sneeva. I thought about maggots. I thought some more about Hunter, Pignarski and Sneeva. I thought about this mysterious cease-fire and how it was going to end at some point. I thought about the pent-up rage they would have.

I thought about my future on this planet—how there was no hope for rescue, how there was no hope for relief, how I was likely to spend the rest of my life as the new guy, the scrawny guy, the zero, the last-place runner, the kid who plays with his friends in a sewer pipe.

I thought of aliens, how we are always aliens, always surrounded by people better and cooler and more coordinated and smarter and stronger than we are, how they want to bruise us and chase us into corners and laugh at our clothes and our hair and our eyes and our skin and swing baseball bats within an inch of our sanity.

And then I was in the office, staring at the receptionist.

"Nurse McDowdy, please," I said, weakly waving my hall pass. I was shaking. Ricki was in a far corner, collating papers at a seat next to the intercom controls. She did not look up. Which was good, because I didn't want her to see what was about to happen.

I was allowed behind the reception desk, to the little hallway where the offices for the principal, counselor and nurse were. The nurse's office was directly across from the counselor's. Blethins's door was open. She was not there, but I could see the envelope on top of her in-box.

I was almost ready. I felt clammy; my chest was tight; my stomach was churning with fear and humiliation and despair and more fear and sour milk chunks.

"You again?" Nurse McDowdy stood in the doorway to her chambers and sneered. As her lip twisted, I stared at the small mole there, the one with three dark hairs. That helped.

"Well, what is it?" she asked.

I looked at her, and down the hall I saw Principal Denton, boring into me with his inhuman eyes. And with that, I was ready.

"Ralph!" I said.

Out of politeness, I had intended to speak into a waste-basket; my only goal had been to establish a reason why I should be loitering in the office area. But Nurse McDowdy had blocked access to any convenient receptacles. And I spoke with such vigor that my argument was soon spelled out not only on her open-toed shoes but was splattering all over the hallway.

It was a rather pointed statement, I thought.

"Ew!" she shrieked. She grabbed for a paper towel from her office dispenser, but finding none, ran toward the rest room.

Principal Denton puffed out his cheeks, pivoted on his heels, and walked back the way he came.

I was alone in the hallway and would be for several minutes, I figured. I almost smiled. Who knew that fear and a weak stomach could be a hidden superpower?

I stumbled into the chair in Counselor Blethins's office. I grabbed a couple of tissues to wipe my mouth. And then I grabbed the envelope, gently slid the papers out and began to read:

Loretta T. Festus Middle School
Disciplinary Tribunal Report

Attending: George Denton, principal
Nancy Blethins, counselor
Edna Beacon, ARC coordinator and faculty
representative

It is the majority opinion of this tribunal that
no out-of-school disciplinary measures are

warranted against the students mentioned in report 14220 and that the measures enacted thus far are sufficient in regard to the situation.

Signed,
George Denton
Nancy Blethins

BACKGROUND INFORMATION
Disciplinary Action Plan 14220

Counselor's report

Student Name	ID	Grade
Hunter, Ty	311967	8

The student was referred to me over an incident related to bullying. *(The last four words were crossed out, and someone had written in the margins,* Change to "alleged encounter with another student."/GD) Ty is a student who has been referred to this office for such incidents before. *(That line also was struck, again with the initials GD.)* Ty is established as an athlete at this school, and he has been warned that misbehavior could cost him his place on the baseball team. *(A little* v *was written here, followed by,* This warning has been sufficient to bring noticeable improvement in his behavior.)

Ty's history of problems probably relates to...

I heard footsteps coming, so I quickly thrust the papers back into the envelope. And then, feeling panicky, I jammed the envelope into my Cosmos backpack and slouched back in the chair.

Counselor Blethins peered into her office, surveyed the situation, and said, "Oh my."

My heart was racing, and for a moment I was afraid I was going to be ill again, involuntarily this time. But I took a deep breath and decided—no, I could keep control.

"Clark!" she said. "What happened?"

I lifted my head, gazed at her with upturned eyes and weakly shook my head.

"Oh dear. Oh dear," she said, looking up and down the hall. "Has anyone alerted Nurse McDowdy?"

"I'm pretty sure she's aware," I croaked.

I would be fine, I thought, if I just had a toothbrush—and a few more minutes to finish reading that packet.

"You poor thing," she said. "I'll keep you company until she shows up."

I gave her a feeble smile and tried not to look at my Cosmos backpack. She walked around behind her desk and began nervously to arrange some papers. I had to get her out of there. Maybe I could ask her to get me something, a glass of water perhaps....

"There you are. Here, drink this," said an exceptionally agitated Nurse McDowdy, thrusting a Styrofoam cup of tap water into my hands so forcefully that it almost cracked. "I'm not allowed to give you anything without a note from a doctor. You'd better call home." Satisfied with her work, she went into her office, grabbed her purse, and walked away again in the direction of the faculty lounge.

Counselors who can't counsel. Nurses who can't nurture. Someone *really* needed to investigate whether the polarity of this place was inverted.

In any case, I was stuck in the counselor's office with a full audience, which soon included the custodial staff (a kind man named Ed, who was quietly dealing with my work) and a secretary, who was asking whether they should be calling my mother or my father.

"Actually," I said, "my dad is out of town, and my mom had to take the baby to the doctor today, I think." It might have been true. I hadn't really been paying attention. "And to tell you the truth, I think it was just something I ate. I'll probably be OK in a few minutes."

Counselor Blethins smiled, said, "That's good," and found some more papers to shuffle.

After a while, when it became clear that she wasn't going anywhere, I declared myself well and asked for a pass to return to class.

"Are you sure you'll be OK, Clark?" There was genuine worry in her voice. I appreciated that.

"I'll be fine," I said, standing. "Except…" I had a thought and sat back down, quickly. "You know, I'm just a little bit wobbly. Do you think an aide could escort me back to class, just in case…you know?"

Counselor Blethins smiled. "Oh, sure. We can have the student assistant help you. Ricki? Could you come here please?"

Ricki arrived a moment later, staring with vacant cheerfulness.

"Ricki, would you mind walking with Clark on his way back to class, just to make sure he's OK?"

"Yes, Ms. Blethins." She nodded and turned away. I stood,

zipped my backpack tight, and thanked Ms. Blethins for her concern. I followed Ricki into the reception area, where she was tearing off a presigned hall pass for us to use.

Once we were a few steps from the office, she spoke without looking at me.

"That was too gross for words."

"I stole the envelope," I said.

"And that's just too stupid for words."

"I couldn't finish reading it. Not enough time."

"You should have plenty of time when they *expel* you."

"Maybe I can sneak back and return it later without them noticing."

"And maybe I'll just sneak onto the cheer squad without them noticing."

I turned and looked at her. "I could use a little moral support right now."

"You could use a breath mint too."

I clamped my lips and looked at the ground.

"Sorry. I'm being honest," she said. "It's a flaw."

I winced at this. "Jeez, Ricki. Honesty is hardly a flaw. I mean, it's one of the reasons I like you."

Did I just say that? "I mean, as a friend. You're one of the only people I can trust right now. No, really. So, yeah. And do you have any gum?"

She reached into the little purse she carried and pulled out a mint.

"Thanks," I said.

"You too," she said.

"For what?"

"I mean, I like you too. As a f-friend. And… And…" She was stammering now. "And I trust you. I don't know how to help. This has gotten very, very complicated. But if I come up with anything, I'll let you know."

"Thanks," I said. We were at my classroom.

She held the hall pass in her hands. "You might be able to use this," she said.

I looked at the pass. "Won't you need that to get back to the office?"

"No," she said. "I mean this."

She slid her fingers together while pinching the pass. A second piece of paper slipped into her hand.

"I took two. This one is presigned but undated. You'll have to forge that. Be careful."

"I'm glad you're on my side," I said.

"If you get caught, I never knew you," she said, then turned and walked away.

10.03.02

I should have kept that folder in my backpack until I was safely off campus, but the need to know was too great. So after an agonizingly long hour in math, instead of going to lunch, I slipped into a closet, and by the light of my flashlight, continued to read.

> Ty's history of problems probably relates
> to unresolved grief, control issues, anger
> and guilt stemming from the absence of his

mother, who has not been present in his life for many years. His father has resisted suggestions of therapy on the grounds that it might somehow weaken his son's competitive edge. His stepmother deferred decisions to Mr. Hunter. (His stepbrother, Lester Paul Martin Hunter, has been sought for sessions, but the student aides sent with the summons never seem to be able to find him.)

In one-on-one sessions, Ty has shown signs of repressed hurt but refuses to acknowledge them. He expresses few ambitions beyond playing baseball. His father has suggested that any child who had a problem with his son's behavior should probably learn to stand up and take it like a man.

It is the opinion of this counselor that Ty's combination of low self-esteem, low parental emotional engagement, high physical development and a peer group that encourages acting-out behavior make it highly unlikely that intervention at anything less than the highest level will have much effect. *(This last line was crossed out by GD.)*

Amazing! This was more revealing than an Omegan Mind Siphon! But then I turned the page.

BACKGROUND INFORMATION
Disciplinary Action Plan 14220

Counselor's report

Student Name	ID	Grade
Sherman, Clark	6270712	8

Clark Sherman moved to Festus in the middle of this school year. He is a student of apparently average academic standing who has not caused discipline issues independently of his encounters with Ty Hunter and friends. *Again, the little v, followed by:* (Although he has not distinguished himself academically or in any other way, he was the subject of a parental complaint that he was harassing a fellow student in the Independent Study sessions set up to accommodate his learning needs.—GD)

Clark has had several sessions in Principal George Denton's office, in lieu of formal counseling sessions with Counselor Blethins, at Principal Denton's request. *(GD drew a line through that last part.)* Principal Denton reports that Clark has not made any complaint about his treatment by any other student. (Add: His primary concern was some of the unorthodox teaching of his Independent Study advisor, Edna Beacon.—GD) Edna Beacon has reported signs that Clark is fearful of some unnamed fellow students. (But he did not single out anyone nor lodge a formal complaint, which would be required before any action were initiated, *GD adds.)*

District policy calls for parents to be alerted if their child is subject to disciplinary or counseling action, but the actions taken by staff at this point have not reached that level, so no parental engagement is mandated.

BACKGROUND INFORMATION
Disciplinary Action Plan 14220

Supplemental teacher report
Jack Chambers
Physical Education

Both of the student's involved in this report have been in my class. I would call the behavior I have seen as "typical boy" and "mild roughhousing." As students, Ty Hunter is a real "leader." I would call Clark Sherman more of a follower. I suspect this will cause him difficulty being as he is small.

Hunter's deserves credit for his athletics as well. I would point out that he is undefeated as a pitcher this year, is on course to set a district record in K's and stands an excellent chance of bringing the school and district much success this year and in the future as we continue to coach and develop him, which we could not if he were not

allowed to remain a student athlete. I have
fielded six phone calls from colleges asking
to see his video, and if that doesn't say what
quality is, then I don't know.

JC

BACKGROUND INFORMATION
Disciplinary Action Plan 14220

Prior incident summary:

DAP No. 13724—Student Ty Hunter accused
in bullying incident. Plan terminated after
accuser changed schools and declined
formal complaint.

DAP No. 14161—Student Ty Hunter accused
in bullying incident. Plan terminated after
accuser changed schools and declined
formal complaint.

DAP 14200—Student Ty Hunter accused
in bullying incident. Plan terminated after
accuser rescinded complaint, then changed
schools.

My hands shook as I pawed over several other forms and legal
documents, and then, at the end, one more note, typed on
school letterhead:

I dissent from this report, which I consider a travesty.

Ty Hunter's involvement in incidents like these has reached a level that mandates the most severe disciplinary action, as per district policy. But it is clear that the objective of this administration is to use loopholes and technicalities to protect its pet interests, while using innocent students as pawns. Shamelessly.

I most strongly recommend that district administrators examine the issues fully: Ty Hunter is being protected only because of his athletic ability. He is a bully and should be treated as such. For the sake of Ty, his victims, this school and common decency.

Edna Beacon,
ARC Coordinator
Faculty Representative, Disciplinary Tribunal

I switched off the flashlight and sat in the dark. Then, in my head, came a vision right out of Episode 68, the one with the showdown against the Vexon Battle Star: Torpedoes were loaded into firing tubes. Weapons banks were charged. Fighters were readied. Jaws were set.

I was—gods of Omega, hear my vow—going to war.

Just as soon as I found a way to sneak this envelope back to the office.

10.03.03

I sat in the closet through the lunch hour. When the bell signaled the class change, I slipped out and headed to the ARC. On the way I actually passed Les in the hall, and he made eye contact with me. He looked worried, or frightened, or afraid. In other words, normal.

In the ARC, Ricki looked tense as well. I suppose it's because she knew what I was carrying.

Me? I was beyond fear. It's amazing what carrying a satchel of top-secret documents can do for your focus. I felt alert, engaged with the world and on the verge of doing something heroic. I just needed to execute my newest plan—once I had one—and bring down my enemies.

One of whom, it turns out, was in the ARC.

Principal Denton was standing over Ms. Beacon at her desk. "The file was due this morning, and I will not tolerate excuses," he was saying.

"I left it with Nancy, right on time, and *I* will not tolerate your bluster, George," she said.

They glared at each other. It was matter meeting antimatter, and I fretted for the safety of the galaxy.

Denton blinked first. "If you don't hand over the envelope today, I will be forced to put another insubordination notice in your file. You know that the rules on such matters are quite explicit."

"When you find it, I will demand another apology from you, but I will not actually expect to receive one."

Denton huffed out, giving me an odd sideways glance as

he left. Maybe he was worried about his shoes. Given the turmoil in my stomach, he had good reason to be.

I could only assume that the missing file he was after was the one in my Cosmos backpack. Which meant I had to get it back to him at light speed. I closed my eyes and took a deep breath. The situation called for calm. Calm and ingenuity. Ingenuity and courage. Courage and control. I had all these things, I told myself. I could make this work, I told myself.

"Mr. Sherman," Ms. Beacon said in her sternest voice.

I opened my eyes. "Uh, yes?"

"Is there a reason you are standing in the middle of my library with such an odd look on your face?"

I had forgotten to sit down. "Uh, no," I said. I turned toward my table.

This was definitely a no-win scenario. I was much too conspicuous to make a second appearance in the office today. I couldn't endanger Ricki by asking her to slip the file back in place. And I couldn't endanger Ms. Beacon by holding on to it.

Things were so bad that I saw Ricki, usually a model of good posture and stoic behavior, chewing on a pencil eraser. I wanted to hide. Like the stowaway in the engine room on yesterday's *Star Survivors*. Hidden among some innocuous cargo and riding around the galaxy. That sounded good.

And—as I saw an aide walking through, pushing a small cart full of interoffice mail—inspirational.

I set my backpack on the table and unzipped it, then adjusted things so that the envelope was right on top. I waited nervously while the aide, a girl I did not know, walked into Ms. Beacon's office, picked up several folders and some mail, and walked out.

As she did, I sprang toward the desk. "Oh, Ms. Beacon!" I called. "I had a homework question I was hoping you..."

I "accidentally" tripped over the cart; folders went flying; I dropped my backpack with a thud.

"Hey!" the aide barked. "What are you *doing?*"

"I'm so sorry!" I told her. "Here, let me help you pick things up." I did so, and while she was gathering stray envelopes from the floor, I reached into my backpack, pulled out the folder, and slipped it onto her cart.

The aide gathered up the rest of the mail, gave me a withering look and pushed the cart out of the ARC and down the hall.

My sigh of relief was interrupted by a very stern, "*Mr. Sherman.*"

I timidly walked to Ms. Beacon's desk.

"Yes?"

"I do not know where your head is today, but mine is on some very important reports. Would you *please* stop acting like a small child and behave in the manner I have come to expect from you?"

"I'm sorry, Ms. Beacon." I had never seen her this annoyed before.

Then she grimaced, shook her head and pressed her fingers to her temples.

"Forgive me, Mr. Sherman. I am having a particularly challenging week. I don't mean to take it out on you. Nevertheless," she added in a low voice, "you *must* use extreme caution and not draw attention to yourself, Clark."

Wait—did she just use my first name?

"Excuse me, Ms. Beacon?"

She looked across the room at Ricki, whose nose was

buried in a book. "Please come with me." She motioned me out the door and into the hallway. We were alone except for the office aide, who was wheeling her cart around the corner far down the hall. When she disappeared, Ms. Beacon turned to me.

"I'm going to tell you some things in confidence, Mr. Sherman. I can trust you, yes?"

I nodded. My pulse raced.

"I cannot discuss other students' records with you," she continued softly. "But perhaps you know one or two who have crossed the lines of decent, acceptable behavior?"

I nodded again, more vigorously.

"They should have been dealt with long ago. But Principal Denton is a powerful man inside this building. He can protect the people he wants to protect. Do you understand?"

"Yes," I told her.

"He is also well known in the community. And he has friends on the school board. He is not to be trifled with.

"But even a decorated combat veteran and experienced business executive has standards to meet. And even if he— well, I've never been able to prove my suspicions about him, so I'll spare you those details. But I am hoping that soon, I can get some key people to listen to me about his lack of competence."

"Like, Counselor Blethins?" I blurted out.

She raised an eyebrow in surprise at my suggestion.

"She could be helpful, yes," she said. "But she's fearful, and I've never quite been able to persuade her to..." She seemed on the verge of saying more, then halted herself again. "It comes down to this: Principal Denton is in a precarious position. He knows that if enough voices make themselves heard, his situation will become untenable. That might make him desperate. And desperate, petty men are capable of ugly things. So please, for the sake of both of us—"

I nodded. "I'll be careful, Ms. Beacon. I'm—I'm sorry."

"No need to apologize. But again, don't get caught up in any...shenanigans. Stay out of trouble, and with luck, we might see the resolution of multiple problems that have been disturbing both of us. Now, return to your seat, please."

This time, I did.

Of course, I didn't get a whole lot of reading done. I stared blankly at Ricki until I processed what had just happened.

The folder was out of my hands, safely headed back to its proper home.

Nobody would know it had been missing.

Everyone would be safe.

All systems were nominal.

And Denton was in a precarious position!

Ricki looked at me questioningly and I broke into a grin and gave her a Chuck Yeager–caliber thumbs-up.

Maybe I would take on a new nickname. People could call me "The Captain." Because I was totally in command.

10.03.04

Ms. Beacon had warned me to be careful. And I had intended to do just that. But when I had to walk past Ty in the locker room before Athletics, he pretended to be swinging a bat at me. This made Jerry and Bubba laugh.

And that made me burn with determination to get rid of him.

As I understood the tribunal file, Ty was right on the border of serious trouble. Beacon thought he had crossed the line already. Surely I could push him totally over the edge, make him do something that would force Blethins and even Denton to act.

But what?

Les would help me figure it out. I had to tell him what I had learned, and fast. But he was nowhere to be seen. I'd have to try to catch him in the Sanctuary.

When the last bell finally sounded, I made a quick dash from the gym to the park to the drainpipe.

I had hoped to catch him passing through on his way home. I did, but not in the way I expected.

"What are you DOING in here?" he said, when I found him in the chamber, where he apparently had been for a while. "Didn't you get my message?"

"Uh, what message?" I asked.

"In the usual spot! On your math desk!"

"I was—a little distracted this morning."

"I wrote FORBIDDEN ZONE! I drew a radiation symbol!"

"Les, if I'd seen it, I'm not even sure I'd have…"

"Stuff is happening, Clark! That's why I passed you in the hall today! To make sure you knew to be on alert!"

"Les, I guess if you need me to understand something, you're going to have to speak in a language besides Advanced Nerd next time. Look, I need to ask you—"

But Les wasn't listening. His teeth were clenched. His body was curled and tense, as if he were about to pounce on something. "Leave. NOW," he said.

"Huh?"

"Just…just go, Clark. I can't have you here!"

"Les, is this about breaking the rule about whose day it is? I'm sorry, but I really need—"

"GO, Clark. I mean it."

"Don't you want to hear what was in the envelope? It's—"

"Clark!" He kept looking around, frantic.

"OK, OK, I'll go!" I said. "But answer one question: Do you know anything that Ty has done that would have him on the verge of being kicked out of school? Or why—?"

I was cut off by a loud series of whoops from the tunnel entrance.

"I guess you can ask him yourself in a few seconds," Les said flatly.

My blood turned to liquid methane. Which, if you don't know, is really, really cold.

"I must have been followed."

"No," Les said. "This my fault."

I didn't have time to figure out what he meant; I needed to flee. I looked up at the ladder that led to the school above. The lowest rung was out of my reach. I could try to hide behind the wall of milk crates that Les had stuffed with old paperbacks and electronic bits—but for all its functional beauty, it wouldn't conceal me at all.

That left the small drain pipes that flowed into this chamber; they were unexplored and barely big enough for me to lie down in.

They were all I had.

I pulled myself in feet-first, rolled over on my stomach and scooted backward. "Jam one of those crates in here," I told Les. "One with lots of books."

Les analyzed what I was doing, nodded, then did as I had asked. As he shoved the camouflage in place, he gave me a furious stare and said, "No matter what you see, *don't say a word.*"

As he turned around, Ty emerged into the main chamber. I lay flat against the dusty concrete and hoped the books would protect me. I could see Ty stand up, look around and smile.

Jerry and Bubba came behind him. Bubba looked slightly unnerved. Jerry looked right in his element in an underground den, weasel that he was.

"Pretty cool," said Ty. His voice had an odd ring to it. It was...sincerity. I had no idea he could speak that way.

"Gives me the creeps," I heard Bubba say. "I'll bet there are spiders."

"Don't be such a wuss," Jerry said.

Their banter was relaxed, and crudely friendly. I had forgotten that Les had to live in their world every day. Maybe he had learned some sort of survival skill that enabled him to blend in.

"Yeah, don't be a such a worthless wuss, Bubba," said Ty. "Les is playing designated worthless wuss for the rest of the season. Aren't you, Les?"

Or maybe not.

"If I'm worthless, then why did you come?" Les said. "Perhaps you're worried I'll stop doing your homework?"

They responded with angry silence. Nice one, Les!

"So talk, *little brother.*" Ty's voice had an edge again, like a switchblade. "You've got nowhere to hide now, so this had better be good."

"I brought you here to show you that I didn't need anywhere to hide now. That I'm serious when I say it's time for a new deal."

"I like things just the way they are, where you do my homework, and I don't beat the crap out of you whenever I feel like it," Ty said. The others laughed.

"I'm sure you do," Les said, his voice cold and steady, the way it had been with me the day he rolled out from the bottom shelf of the library. "But I heard your dad talking the other night. About school. About how you're one mistake away from being kicked out. And how that would ruin your baseball career. That makes me think that I have a lot more power over you than you have over me."

"Dad will beat the hell out of you if he thinks you're screwing with me and baseball," Ty warned.

"I can handle him on my own," Les said. "Can you say the same about algebra?"

Jerry and Bubba stared at Ty, awaiting cues, while he folded his arms and sneered.

"What do you want?" he finally asked.

"To be left alone," Les said.

"Whatever. I don't like to be seen with you anyhow."

"That goes for me *and* my friends."

"Double easy," Ty said, laughing. "Since when do you have friends?"

"I'm talking about Clark Sherman."

Wow. Did he just say that?

There was a long silence, followed by a trio of guffaws. "So you're friends with Clark Sherman himself?" Ty asked, although instead of "Clark Sherman" he used a term that would indicate a person with a severe urological deformity. "It figures."

"Yeah, Sherman's the only person in the school who's a bigger wuss than *you*," Jerry added. "Such a wuss that he needs *you* for protection! What a total−"

"Actually, Ty," Les said, cutting him off, "I'm trying to protect *you* from *him*."

Ty snorted. "What, are you gonna tell him not to puke on me?" More laughter.

"No," said Les. "But I'll make sure he doesn't discover exactly how much he can hurt you right now."

I could see Ty's eyes narrow in the candlelight. "What do you mean?"

"I mean, it's not just your grades that are a problem. We both know that your disciplinary record is full of near-misses. If a formal complaint made it up to the district level, you'd be history. All Clark would have to do is go to Denton, or even Blethins. If he reported everything you've been doing to him, even they would have to act."

"I've been threatened before. I've always managed."

"Only because your victims ran when Denton pressured them. But I know Clark. He's not afraid. They'll punish you *and* ban you from sports. They'll *have* to. Denton knows that. So does your dad. It's why they told you to stay totally clear of him, to not even look at him."

Ty growled through bared teeth. "How did you−"

"I heard them talking on the phone. Every single word."

On the phone? How in the name of the Great Bird of the Galaxy had Les managed to−

"If you've been hacking his phone again, Dad's going to kill you."

Oh. That's how.

"I don't care. If he's raging at me, that doesn't change my

life a bit. Yours will change an awful lot, though, if you're sent to alternative school."

"That'll never happen. Denton says we're a team—and we can stay a team all through high school."

"Did he tell you that?"

"No. Dad did. He says he's been talking to the principal at the high school. Told him he was trying to decide whether to enroll me there or at St. Andrew's Prep."

"You wouldn't last a week at St. Andrew's, and you know it."

"The high school principal doesn't. And he and the baseball coach want me. Bad. So Dad says maybe we might cut a deal—the high school could hire Denton as like, deputy principal in charge of discipline or something. And Chambers as an athletic director.

"They'd all get nice new jobs. And when they do, they can keep watching out for me. Me and my arm. I'm set for the next four years."

Ty—shielded by Denton and Chambers—for *four more years*? I would have clawed through the concrete until my fingers were bloody shafts of bone to get away from that prospect. And I might have started trying, if Les hadn't spoken.

"But if you're expelled, you lose it all, Ty. Nobody would touch you. Not the baseball scouts. Not St. Andrew's. Nobody wants a head case with a criminal record. Especially if he's failing half his classes. And once you're out of baseball, you're as good as dead to your dad. Look what happened to your brothers."

Ty's fists were still clenched, but his voice was dead calm. "That's B.S. You don't know all that."

"Maybe your dad didn't spell it out to you as clearly as I

just did," Les said. "But he talks a lot when he's drunk. I hear everything."

It was amazing to watch: Ty had been boxed in, backed into a corner, checkmated. If Les proposed his deal again—that Ty back off of me in exchange for continued homework help—Ty would have had no choice but to accept.

But Les wasn't done.

He folded his arms, looked over his shoulder and sent a warning glance toward my hiding place. And then he let his last arrow fly:

"You know, Ty, even with your arm, you're quite a disappointment to him," he said. "No wonder he blames you for driving your mom off. How old were you when you figured out that she left because she was sick of taking care of kids—right away? Or did you hear it in one of your dad's rages?

"Either way, both of you losing her to some Harley-riding guy from Alaska—does that sting much?"

Ty, in a verb, lost it.

His thin lips curled into a snarl, his hands turned into angry claws, and he pounced on Les ferociously. Ty went straight for Les's throat and wrapped his fingers around it. Les tried to squirm away but looked, for all his effort, like a tiny mouse in the clutches of a raptor.

Ty spun Les around and twisted his arms behind him. Les gasped. I could see his face. His eyes were screwed tight and his lips peeled back as he writhed.

Just when I thought his head was going to pop, Ty pushed Les into Bubba, who jabbed him in the stomach, then pushed his hunched body into Jerry, who swept his ankle and flung him to the floor.

"How do you like this deal?" screamed Ty as he kicked

him in the side. "Maybe it's a disappointment, huh?" Another kick. "AND LEAVE MY MOM OUT OF THIS!" An extra-hard kick. "NEVER, NEVER, MENTION MY MOM!" Another kick. And another.

Les had told me not to say anything, no matter what I saw. But surely, he hadn't expected to be used as a mop on the sewer floor. But how could I defend him?

Suddenly, I was living what I had read in a book about test pilots. How their minds focus on the problem in front of them, and time seems to slow as they calmly go through the options, even as their craft plummets toward the earth in a flat spin. The ones who get out of it go on to become astronauts. The ones who don't…

I pushed that thought aside and focused on my options.

I could lie here, hide, wait for them to leave, help Les when the coast was clear.

Les could be dead by then.

I could push the crate full of books out of the way, crawl forward, leap to the ground, and, using the element of surprise, immobilize them with some precisely administered Omegan Fingers of Defibrillation.

Yeah, right.

I could improvise using available tools. This had worked for Commander Steele in Episode 21, where he's able to build a lithium cannon out of a broken communicator, the frame of an old bicycle and a jar of pickle juice. But I didn't have any of those things. I had a milk crate, some paperback books, a flashlight and…

A box of matches. The ones I used to light the candles.

Les's moans and his attackers' laughter concealed the sound as I unzipped my backpack and felt around for the matchbox. I grabbed it and pulled out my English reading list as well.

I struck a match, fearful that the sound would reveal my hiding spot too soon. It took a moment for the reading list to ignite. But eventually, a flame started turning the gray words into white smoke and brown ash.

I slipped the burning paper through the back of the milk crate and waited for the books to light. I said a silent apology to Ray Bradbury in particular; I hoped he would understand.

As the corners of those old paperbacks began to glow orange, then blacken and curl, I realized the first flaw in my strategy: I was getting a face full of smoke and was going to be blind and choking in about five seconds. This would be a serious impediment to the rest of my plan, which, as usual, I did not know yet.

I waited as long as I could, then pushed hard and dumped the crate to the floor. My hopes were pinned on two things: surprise, and...well, one thing. Surprise was about all I had. So to help with that angle, I accompanied the crash of the crate with a shout, in my deepest voice.

"FIRE!" I yelled. "EVERYBODY GET OUT! FIRE!" And I started hacking and coughing, which was not in the plan, but which enhanced the mood nicely.

As the crate crashed to the ground, pages from several of the older books came unbound and were consumed in bright yellow flames. It wasn't quite an explosion, but it was close enough.

Ty, Jerry and Bubba let go of Les. Nobody could see me; I was too far back in the pipe. The gang could hear me, though; the acoustics had the effect of amplifying what I said and making it sound as if it were coming from multiple directions.

And they could see the smoke that had started to fill the chamber and the rising bonfire in front of them.

Bubba bolted toward the exit with a speed that was surprising for someone that large.

As the smoke thickened, Jerry, too decided to run.

That left Ty, who was staring down at Les. Ty watched the flames, then looked at his stepbrother, incapacitated from the beating he'd taken.

Then Ty did something shocking. He slowly bent down, touched Les's face and said, "Oh God. I'm sorry, man. I swear, I never meant for it to get this crazy. I swear to *God*. But when my mom just…and the way my dad never…and you're always such a…" He broke off.

The hate on Ty's face had melted away; his eyes were watering and he looked like a frightened, messed-up kid who was in over his head and unsure where to turn. It hit me—Les had finally found a way to make Ty act halfway human, and even offer an apology. Too bad he wasn't conscious to see it.

I expected Ty to run, like the others had. But as the smoke made it ever harder to see, he kept holding on to Les. Just as the smoke became thickest, he hoisted him on to his back, grunting under the burden, and carried him out, firefighter-style, crouching awkwardly so as not to scrape his brother against the low ceiling.

I watched them go. For a moment, I thought of Ty as a real human being.

The feeling passed quickly. But I can't deny it.

I coughed my way out of my hiding place, watched the flames turn the books into cinders that rose toward the school through the access tube, which was working like a chimney. I felt cool air being drawn in from the park. There was no real danger. I had known there wouldn't be. I congratulated myself and started to weigh my prospects as a test pilot.

I thanked the writers of the smoldering books for the way they had saved me. Then I took a look around the smoky Sanctuary. I knew this would be the last time I passed through. My battles would be out in the open now.

I grabbed my backpack, put the matches away and walked toward the light.

10.03.05

I was worried about how I would explain my smoky clothes to my commander—maybe she'd believe that the Boy Scouts had held a recruitment wiener roast after school and things had gotten slightly out of hand?

But as it turned out, moments before I got home, the spawn had discovered how to use a Marks-A-Lot. On the wall and herself. So the commander was elbow-deep in toddler and suds and didn't even see me come in. I dashed to my room, did a quick change and doused my clothes with Timber Peak body spray—enough to mask an entire forest fire—before shoving them to the bottom of the hamper.

When she was older, I would have to thank Gwen for being such an excellent diversion. She was really saving me from a lot of explaining lately.

I went back to my room and pretended to do homework while I wondered how Les was doing.

He called in the middle of *Star Survivors*.

"I'm OK," he said.

"You made it home?"

"Somehow," he said. "I woke up in the park, not far from our house. I got smacked in the head right after I heard you yell, 'FIRE.' It gets hazy for a bit after that, but I must have staggered into the park when the others ran."

I didn't tell him what I had seen—about the apologetic, frightened Ty—because I wasn't sure I believed it. Or if it had really happened, what to make of it.

"I was worried," was all I said. "Why are you breaking radio silence?"

"I'm done hiding from him," he said.

"Does that mean you're going to Denton?"

"No," Les said, reluctantly. "I–I can't. I want to. But if I ever did anything to mess with Ty, it would make Ben angry. Off-the-charts angry. I mean, me getting Ty kicked out of school *and* out of baseball? I–I couldn't do that to my mom."

"Your mom?"

"I mean, probably he'd direct all the rage at me. But he might turn on her after that. And it's my job to protect her. So I can't..." He paused for a moment, thinking. "No, I can't."

"But Les, didn't she see what Ty *did* to you? You looked...pretty bad." That was an understatement. A few more kicks and he would have been ready for a role in a zombie movie.

"Clark," Les said slowly, "my family has seen this all before."

He let that sink in.

"But while you and I were down there," he finally said, "I

realized you're the answer, Clark. Do you understand now? I can't turn him in...."

I got it. "But I can."

"Right," Les continued. "They can't stop *you*. The only problem, I realized, was that some authority might ask for proof that Ty was dangerous. That's why I set him off. To create evidence. You have all my bruises and scrapes to show them."

I felt humbled by Les's gift. And simultaneously, a little like Peter Parker must have felt the day after being bitten by the radioactive spider. Or young Kal-El when the first rays of a golden sun hit him.

I had a superpower, and it did not even involve vomit. This would have to be handled with courage, with foresight, with strategy, with—

"Clark! Are you there?"

"Yeah, sure," I said. "Let's do this."

"Revenge is a drink best served like cold Klattarian ale; pour it liberally, inhale it sweetly—and slam it down with great violence."

—Vexon Proverb
Star Survivors Episode 60.
"The Seven Tasks of Amontillado"

EXPEDITION LOG

ENTRY 11.01.01

As I strode into Festus the next day, I told myself: Ruining Ty's life will be so simple that even I couldn't screw it up. It could be done in a flash. Although I knew that Ty had to be thinking about how dangerous I was, and I wanted him to agonize a bit.

So, when to strike to maximize that anguish?

Not first hour. Too soon. Ty and his partners kept their distance in any case. I could see them whispering and looking at me from the far side of the track. Excellent.

But in the crowded halls on the way to second hour, I decided that proper dramatic structure required me to serve justice...during Athletics.

Yes. I would let them squirm all day, then release the Kraken on them, as it were. I would saunter into the office and make sure Denton was around. "Ms. Blethins," I would say, "I need to tell you something about a student who has been causing problems." She would have to send someone to fetch him from right under Coach Chambers's nose. Chambers would watch helplessly as the star of his precious baseball team was marched away, never to return.

Denton would be flustered, but the mechanical part of him would know—the law was the law. He would have to follow the rules. He was a Marine cyborg, after all.

After lunch I was so excited I could hardly contain myself as I walked into the ARC. Ms. Beacon would be almost as big a winner as I was. I reminded myself that I would have to stay humble and modest around her when she became effusive in her praise.

It was at this point that I was reminded of one big difference between real life and TV shows. On *Star Survivors*, every time danger looms, you can brace yourself for it by the musical cue. The sound starts low, with the basses vibrating nervously, then crescendos up to a series of panicky horn blasts and screeching violins as the peril reveals itself.

In real life, you just walk into a room, see your friend Ricki staring at you, wide-eyed, turn to look at your teacher and see—

"Are you Clark Sherman?"

He was a man in a dark suit, slightly better fitting than Denton's, but probably purchased off the same rack.

"Yes sir?"

"I'm Gerald Branigan, assistant superintendent for school security. Will you join me in your principal's office so I can ask a few questions?"

11.01.02

We sat in the office. The assistant superintendent, a balding man with sharp blue eyes, and I sat across from Denton, whose fingertips were making a tent and touching one another rhythmically.

"Clark," the assistant superintendent said, "there was an incident yesterday. Someone smelled smoke in the basement that was coming from the storm drain," he said. Things were arranged so that looking at him also meant looking at Denton's Marine portrait and the display case that held his Soldier's Medal for Valor.

"Oh," I said. I began to wonder how I was going to look in a jail jumpsuit.

"Some other students said they saw you playing near the entrance to the storm drain yesterday."

"Oh," I said.

"Clark," he asked, "did you see anything unusual yesterday?"

I thought for a moment. "Nothing out of the ordinary, really." Which was the truth.

He looked over at Denton, who nodded at him.

"Clark," the assistant superintendent said, "arson is a very serious crime."

"Yes," I said.

"The repercussions can be very severe," he said.

"I'm sure," I said. I wondered whether I would qualify for solitary confinement or if I would be left to be dismembered by the general prison population.

"It would be an awful thing for a young man to have on his permanent record," he said. "And it could, at the very least, get you sent to alternative school with the other juvenile delinquents."

I thought of being at a whole school full of Tys—only

bigger, stronger and meaner. I thought of the last time I had visited the zoo and witnessed feeding time at the lion cage.

The assistant superintendent looked up at Denton, who folded his hands and placed them on his desk.

"Mr. Branigan, maybe I have an answer for you. You and I have known each other quite some time, have we not?"

He nodded. "For quite some time, yes."

"So my recommendations would carry some weight with you, yes?"

Again he nodded. "Yes, certainly, George."

Denton fixed his gaze on me. "Jerry, this boy is OK. Leave him with me."

The assistant superintendent rose. "It's your school, George. I'm here to help." He opened his jacket to put his pen in his pocket, and I noticed that he had a tie tack that looked like a tiny baseball. I also caught a glimpse of a pair of hand-cuffs clipped to his belt.

"Thank you, Jerry. I'll call if there are developments to report."

The assistant superintendent looked at me, nodded knowingly at Denton and left.

As soon as the door clicked shut, Denton spoke in venomous tones.

"And there will *be* developments to report, Sherman, the instant you cause any sort of problems. For me or any fellow student. I will use paperwork to take you out of this school the way I would have used my gun to take out an enemy when I was a Marine: Quickly. Efficiently. Mercilessly. And if you try to go over my head to the district, the first person you'll have to deal with will be my friend Branigan. Who will make sure things go my way. Am I perfectly clear, son?"

It was way, way too clear: I was in over my head.

"It's clear, sir," I said.

"Excellent," he said.

I stood. "Shall I report back to Ms. Beacon now, sir?"

The grin on his face made me ill. "You may return to your class, but your instructor is no longer Ms. Beacon."

Blood drained from my face as his smile broadened. "W-w-why not?" I stammered.

His malicious tone could have been stolen right from the Vexon Praetor himself. "Because she has been placed on permanent administrative leave."

He let the news sink in, then explained.

"An important, confidential student file was lost while in her possession. It later surfaced in the regular interoffice mail. Failure to secure sensitive student records is a breach of district policy, if not federal law. Given that, and her record of lax supervision and conflict with her superiors, I had no choice but to begin termination proceedings.

"She was never much of a team player," he said, shaking his head. "I don't expect you'll be seeing her again."

11.01.03

I staggered back to the ARC.

When I got there, I saw that Ms. Beacon's office had been cleared of most of her photos and knickknacks.

I felt like Luke, watching the annihilation of Obi-Wan.

Except in this case, it's as if I had built the lightsaber myself, then handed it to Darth Vader.

A young, nervous substitute teacher sat at the desk.

"Are you Clark?" she said. "Mr. Denton—Principal Denton—told me you'd be by. When I asked him about a lesson plan, he said to assign you a book report. It's due next week."

She then looked around as if making sure nobody was watching. "I also found this note with your name on it." She slipped me a piece of official school stationery, folded in half. I opened it, and saw, in unfamiliar handwriting: *"Mr. Sherman—Colby 359.9."*

I recognized the reference to a Dewey decimal number and trudged to the shelf in a daze. The book I found was *Always Faithful, Always Ready: Real Stories of the United States Marine Corps.* Clearly, Denton had taken care of every insulting detail.

I pulled it off the shelf and stumbled back to my seat, avoiding eye contact with Ricki the whole hour. When the bell rang at the end of class, she ran over to me.

"What happened?" she asked. "Where's Beacon?"

I shook my head. "Gone."

"What? How?" she asked as she followed me out. The halls were crowded with students, but we didn't care.

"The envelope. I—they think she lost it, and they fired her."

"No!" cried Ricki. "That's not fair!"

She was right.

"What are you going to *do*?"

I shook my head. I didn't want to confess that I was powerless. That I had walked right into a trap. That I'd had failures of courage, of intellect, of...everything.

"Please, can we talk about it after school, at the rocket ship park?" she asked.

"Yeah," I said. "Sure."

Actually, the only thing that seemed sure to me was this: there could be no worse feeling than appearing so weak and dumb in front of Ricki.

Later, on the way to Athletics, I found out I was wrong even about that.

As I began the long walk down that hall, I lifted my head and saw Les coming toward me, out of the shadows. He was limping, and he wasn't holding his head perfectly straight, but with the blood cleaned off his face he didn't look that awful, and he was smiling.

"I've been waiting all day for this," he said. "I knew you'd want to do it during Athletics. It's too perfect."

I stopped. I looked him up and down.

"Yes, I still hurt," he said. "But I wouldn't miss your destroying them for the world. For a couple of worlds."

His ice-blue eyes sparkled. "Hey, I have an idea. Maybe you can do some big dramatic presentation about what they did to you, and then say, 'And if you want proof, just look at this!' And I can come staggering in, and—"

I opened my mouth to speak. The words caught in my throat. I could only shake my head.

His smile collapsed. "No," he said. "No, no, no. They didn't. You wouldn't."

I tried to tell him.

"It—I…they trapped me, Les. They threatened to kick me out of school."

"But you…you were the answer," he spluttered. "You were supposed to be smart. Not like the others. You were…"

He was sobbing now, and he flung a paper bag at my feet.

"You weren't supposed to be a STUPID COWARD!" he said. And limped off.

I couldn't watch him go. I just stared down at the bag he tossed. When he was out of sight, I picked it up, reached in and pulled out a hand-lettered note from Les—*To victory!*—and a small, clear plastic case.

I opened it. Inside was a set of trading cards. Hard-to-find trading cards. The complete set of trading cards from the rarely seen *Star Survivors and Friends* cartoon. Captain Maxim, looking wise and strong. Commander Steele, ready for action. The crew, standing together. Even in cartoon form, they looked determined, resolute, ready for the next challenge. They were survivors.

I was not.

I walked toward the gym, where I should have been suiting up. But I kept on going. Out the school's back doors, into the bright spring sunshine, away from everything. I had nothing to lose.

11.01.04

I had never gone AWOL before, but it was surprisingly easy. I just drifted away. Like a real spaceman.

I meandered into Sand Creek Park, walked the rim for a ways, then picked up one of the neighborhood trails. I did not look up from the rutted dirt and cracked asphalt.

The trail eventually led me to the rocketship park. I climbed into the capsule, lay on my back and stared up into the rusty nose cone.

In the distance I heard the bell signal the end of the school day. I thought back to my first moments at Festus—my smashed face, the mockery, the insults from the administration and students. Through all that, one thought kept me going: The idea that I could figure it out. And make it get better. Because, well, it had to, right?

I kept hoping that I would find evidence that I was indeed special. That at the crucial moment, Obi-Wan would speak into my headset, I would fire the torpedoes, personally destroy the Death Star and be revealed to have the secret, untapped power to redeem my universe.

I did not seem to be in that kind of movie.

I did not seem to be in any kind of movie.

Far off in the distance, the happy kids, the normal kids, the ones with lives and futures, were laughing and playing with each other as they spilled out of school.

I stayed on my back and studied the rust patterns. They looked like laughing monsters.

Ricki would be here soon, but I could not bear to face her again.

I left the plastic case with the trading cards Les had given me at the top of the ladder. I wrote my own note.

I'm sorry. For everything.

And I left.

I walked random streets until I was sure there was no chance of seeing Ricki. When I felt the wind pick up and saw thick, dark clouds churning in from over the mountains, I turned toward home. When I was about halfway there, a heavy rain started. I thought of the stormwater that would eventually make its way past Les's barrier and down the drain, flushing the remains of our sanctuary into the muddy creek. There would be no trace of us. It would be as if we had not existed.

11.01.05

At home there was a fresh box of snack cakes on the counter. And *Star Survivors* was on.

I walked to my room.

The command unit was complaining about the mess as she followed my wet footprints. She found me, still in my soaked clothes, lying on my bed.

She didn't say anything as she went to the linen closet, grabbed a towel, and brought it to me. She smiled as she patted around my face. It was a look she often gave the spawn but hadn't had time to give me lately.

"Long day, I'm guessing?" she said.

That was all it took. The terrestrial metaphor would be, "The dam burst." I am thinking that it would be more appropriate to describe the outpouring as, "The spacesuit ripped." Everything that had been under pressure all this time came gushing out. The isolation. The bullying. Denton. Beacon. In a messy torrent of tears and sniffles.

"Oh, Clark. Oh, Clark," was all she could say. She rubbed my back while sobs shook my body. When they finally slowed, she kissed the back of my head.

She sent me to the shower to get cleaned up.

I went.

11.01.06

The male commander was home even before dinner was ready, but I didn't speak during our meal. I felt emptied out, word-less. Even the baby seemed oddly quiet, unsure of what to do amid the tension. I retreated to my quarters afterward.

It was the male command unit who knocked on my door a few minutes later.

"Clark, can I come in?"

I didn't say no.

He entered and sat on the foot of the bed.

"Mom told me about...everything," he said. "And I want you to know, we'll be there for you. She and I are going to talk to the principal. Now that we know what's been going on, I'm sure we can fix—"

"NO!" I shouted. I bolted upright in the bed.

The commander sighed. "Clark, I know that nobody likes to have their parents meddle in their lives, but this is—"

"It was my war. I lost it, and I don't want to be reminded."

"Clark, it's not *war*, it's *middle school*, and I don't think you lost, I just think you—"

"Think I let down the only friends I had? Think I got my favorite teacher fired? Think there is nothing, NOTHING that talking to the principal is going to fix?"

The commander stared off into space. "Well, I'm sure you feel cornered. But Mom and I can talk to him, as adults, and—"

"He's not an *adult*, Dad. He's a *principal*. And he's too tough. He was a Marine. A decorated combat veteran. They gave him a Soldier's Medal for Valor and everything."

He looked confused. "How do you know?"

"I saw it, Dad. It's in his office. 'Soldier's Medal for Valor.'"

"For what?" Dad asked.

"Does it matter?"

He seemed confused, then shook his head and went on. "Clark, if you just let me help—maybe there's a teacher you know who can…"

"He *fired* the one teacher who could have done anything to stop him, Dad."

"The librarian Mom mentioned? Ms. Bacon?"

"*Beacon*, Dad."

He puzzled everything over for a moment, then said, "Well, maybe I could get someone else to talk to him. I know a guy, a Marine, maybe I could—"

"Haven't you done enough, Dad? This move is all your fault. You didn't—you didn't ask for my help when you were deciding whether to come to this stupid place. And I don't want your help now. Because…because if you and Mom get involved…"

I flopped back down on the bed, exhausted. "It would be just another sign of how stupid and weak I am."

Dad stared at me for a long time.

"You're right, Clark," he finally said. "You should have a say in how this is handled. I won't take that away from you."

I hadn't expected him to come around so quickly.

"You deserve better than you've gotten, Clark. From your school"—he paused to inhale—"and from me. I'm sorry I didn't do more. It's not that I didn't want to, but I had a lot of…" His voice sounded all tight as it trailed off.

"Anyhow, I'll let you call the shots here, for now. But in the meantime, I'm going to start looking into—well, just know I'll do whatever I can for you. You *do* know that, right?"

I nodded. And turned toward the wall so he couldn't see the return of my tears. I hated crying. It was confirmation of everything my enemies had said about my weakness.

Dad stood up and walked out.

I sobbed until I fell asleep.

"Your ship crash-landed.
There were no survivors."

—Final Screen
No-Win Scenario: The Star Survivors Video Game

EXPEDITION LOG

ENTRY 12.01.01

The next morning Mom signed a note to excuse my wandering away from campus. She made up a story about a sudden doctor's appointment. I'd never seen her lie before. I appreciated it.

"Are you going to be OK?" she asked.

"Yes, Mom."

"Are you sure you don't want a ride?

"No, Mom."

"Maybe you should stay home and rest today. I can tell them—"

"I'll be fine, Mom. Honest. I just want to get on with my life."

"And you don't want us to...?"

"Please, no. I know you want to help, but—can we let it go?"

She looked me over and said, "For now." Then she hugged me, ordered me to call if I needed her and kissed me goodbye.

I walked toward Festus under a bright sky. The air felt crisp after yesterday's rain. In Sand Creek Park, an actual creek flowed. I supposed the remnants of the Sanctuary were halfway to the ocean by now.

My heart felt similarly cleaned out. Unburdened. I didn't like where I stood in the world—but at least I knew my place.

I focused on my mission of the day: reconnoitering for the crew I had abandoned. I found them, believe it or not, at lunchtime in the cafeteria. Together. At a table by themselves in the back.

I took a seat next to them.

"I thought you'd be in deep hiding," I said.

"I thought you'd be enrolling at a new school," Les said.

I shrugged. "I've had enough of new schools for this year. Why are *you* out in the open?"

He shrugged. "I'm just tired of eating in closets."

"Or stairwells," Ricki added.

"Or air ducts," Les said.

"Bathrooms are the worst," she said, nodding.

"Except for—"

"It was time," Ricki said, cutting him off. "Time for all that to end."

Les nodded, and our table was silent as I pulled out my sandwich, fiddled with the seal on the plastic bag and tried to think of what to say.

"Look, both of you, I'm—"

"Don't," said Les.

"No, really, I'm sorry for—"

"Clark," said Ricki. "We understand."

"Ricki and I compared details and examined your alternatives," said Les.

"You have the details?"

"Between what I heard from my stepdad telling Ty about being off the hook again, and what Ricki learned in the office about Beacon getting fired, pretty much."

I stared down at the table. "I'm sorry I blew it. After all you did."

Les was peeling the crust off his sandwich in long strips, then ripping those into tiny squares. "You made the only logical choice."

"And nobody thinks your destiny should be a school full of criminals," Ricki said.

"No," Les said. "She's right."

Then he sighed glumly and propped his face against his palm. "Even though revenge would have been very, very sweet."

I bit into my sandwich. Feelings of failure kept gnawing at me, like one of those alien things that grows in your intestines and then explodes out, spectacularly.

"When did you two find time to talk?" I asked while I chewed.

They exchanged a glance.

"Um, it turns out we have a couple of classes together," Ricki said. "We just haven't been showing up at the same time."

"Or by the same door," Les added.

"But things have changed," Ricki said. "It feels slightly abnormal, being out here, but I'm sure we'll be OK. I mean, there's barely two months of classes left. And then high school. It'll be different there. Right?"

I might have agreed with her, but my thoughts were interrupted by an explosion of cornbread crumbs.

Someone had lobbed a corn muffin, expertly, from across the cafeteria. It landed smack in the middle of our table and blew up, showering the three of us in tiny bits of yellow shrapnel.

I turned in time to see Jerry slap Ty on the back. Ty was grinning smugly.

I asked myself, What would Maxim and Steele do?

And the answer was: Damn the corn muffins. Lock weapons on target. And move ahead. *Full power.*

I turned to my friends.

"We can still end this," I said quietly.

"It's hopeless," Les said.

"He's right," Ricki said. "You can't win."

"No, I can't win." Then I leaned in. "But what if I found a way to lose *my* way, instead of theirs?"

"Clark," Ricki said, her teeth clenched. "What are you talking about?"

"What I'm talking about is…" I took a deep breath. "Denton is basically blackmailing me. About the fire. If I try to tell any school officials about Ty, I'm toast. Denton expects me to keep quiet.

"But what if I'm not? What if I stick to the original plan—tell Blethins everything that Ty has done to me, and to Les? I'm pretty sure she'd have to do *something*. Put something on his record, get someone above Denton involved? And Ty would still end up ejected from the school, right?"

"Wrong," Ricki said. "Because the moment Denton sees you coming, he'll call his security friend and have you expelled—in handcuffs. To a school where the uniform is an orange jumpsuit."

"Yeah, but this way, Ty will end up right behind me. It's what I mean by losing *my* way."

"You say it like it's a game," Ricki said. "But you'll end up a prisoner."

"We're kind of Denton's prisoners already," Les said. "And will be, for another four years, if Ty is around."

"Exactly," I said. "Could getting hauled off to alternative school be so much worse than staying here, having to deal with this?" I said, flicking away a cornbread chunk.

"It's a pawn sacrifice," Les said, stroking his chin. "And you're the pawn."

"A pointless sacrifice," said Ricki. "And anyway, what makes you think Blethins will suddenly stand up to Denton? Or anyone else?"

I thought about how helpful and efficient Blethins had been all year. And how she sometimes trembled at the mere thought of Denton's presence.

"You have a point," I said dejectedly. As secret weapons went, Blethins would be as helpful as a paper towel tube in a lightsaber fight. She couldn't help me; nobody at this school could help me. I ran my fingers through my hair in frustration.

Then I thought, It was true. Nobody could help me.

But maybe *everybody* could.

"I have another idea," I said.

Ricki and Les leaned in.

"Les," I said urgently, "could you make a diversion? Something loud enough to draw people out of the office, toward the flagpole? Here," I said, fishing in my backpack for the blank hall pass that Ricki had stolen for me. "This might help."

"Loud noises and forged papers? I'm comfortable in this element."

"Ricki, could you teach me how to work the intercom?"

"Not complicated," she said. "But what are you thinking, Clark?"

I lowered my voice to be barely audible. "You're going to help me turn the office into a broadcast studio. While the staff flees because of the diversion Les creates, I'm going to rush in, lock the door, grab the microphone and tell everyone *everything*. It's one thing if only Blethins hears it, but once I tell *the whole school...*"

Ricki frowned.

So did Les.

"What?" I said. "You think it's too daring?"

"No, it's not that," Ricki said. "It's just that I...well, it won't work."

"What do you mean?"

"I mean, it's a screwy plan. A *diversion*? That's going to make everyone in the office get up and leave? These people work at a middle school, Clark; they do not scare easily. And if they *were* diverted, how would they hear your little broadcast?"

"I don't know," I said testily. "Do you have something better, Admiral Ackbar?"

"I didn't say I did," Ricki snapped. "I just thought you would want to know that your plan had some flaws."

"Actually, it could work," Les said.

"Really?" Ricki asked, disbelieving.

"Really?" I echoed. "You can create a diversion while I storm the office and—"

"No, that plan's screwy," he said. "But I could help you do a schoolwide broadcast. If you got me a microphone. The wireless kind. And an old FM radio. And gave me a day to find the right patch cord. And to get back down into the basement. Maybe two days."

"What for?" I asked.

"To tap into the intercom wiring again."

"Again?" Ricki asked.

Les shrugged. "I was taking a shortcut between classes

last year, one that passes through the basement, and I found all these wires. I started fiddling around to see whether I could, you know, tap them. If the need ever arose."

I let this sink in. "I would say it has, Les."

"OK, then it'll be a piece of cake."

"Where are we going to find all that stuff?" I asked.

"I actually have most of it lying around," he said. "Except the microphone."

"Well, where are we going to find—?"

"You can use mine," Ricki said.

Les and I looked at her disbelievingly.

"It's from a karaoke set. My aunt thought it would encourage me to spend more time practicing piano," she said plainly.

I stared at her, and back at Les, and back at her. "I'm really going to miss you guys."

Ricki looked at me as if I had just revived a painful memory.

"Then let's drop it," she said. "It's a complicated and unnecessary action. I mean, there's only seven weeks of school left. And..." She coughed a little cough. "I like having you here. It's, uh..." She looked to either side and back at me. "It's nice to have someone to have lunch with."

I agreed. With all my heart. But more than lunch was at stake. I quoted Spartacan, from the climax of that *Star Survivors* episode with the Centaurian Megaworm. A Centaurian Megaworm consumes everything in its path and is impervious to attack from the outside. But Spartacan figures it can be blown up from within—and uses himself as both bait and bomb-delivery device.

"'It is a far, far better thing that I do, than I have ever done; it is a far, far better space that I go to than I have ever known,'" I said. It was the last transmission he gave before he was digested. Les and Ricki nodded in recognition. "Getting kicked out of middle school is probably not as noble as being eaten by a space worm, but…it's something. You know? And I owe it to Beacon. I owe it to you." *And to myself,* I thought.

The bell rang. Around us, trays clattered, chairs screeched. Far away, I could see Stephanie Spring surrounded by Kaitlins, who were hooting at a passing boy in a football jersey. At the band table, a cluster of percussionists did an impromptu show, using the tables as drumheads. Musicians laughed in approval.

Here at the alien table, my friends sat quietly and stared at me.

"Can we do it quickly, before I lose my nerve?" I asked.

They nodded.

12.01.02

Ricki handed Les the microphone at lunch the next day. He turned it over in his hands and smiled. "I'll make the adjustments at home tonight. Meet me at the Sand Creek bridge in the morning," he told me. As the bell rang, he moved with confidence and energy. This really was his element.

Ricki and I headed toward the now-dreadful ARC.

"You really think this is the right thing? And that you can do it?" she asked.

"If I can stay motivated, yeah."

"What's motivating you?"

"Telling myself that if Luke can leave Yoda and confront Vader for the sake of his friends, I can face Denton for mine."

"That didn't work out so well for Luke," Ricki said, opening and closing her fist in my face.

"That's a great reminder, Ricki," I said.

"You said you liked honesty."

"Well, what I'd really like is a real-life example of a weak person overcoming pure evil. Maybe you could come up with something along those lines?"

It was supposed to be a rhetorical question, but that's when Kaitlin, Kaitlyn and Katelyn came around the corner. Their cheer uniforms were identical, except for the names on their skirts. Their silver, black and blue hair ribbons swung in unison, and the bells on their shoes jingled as they walked.

"Hey, look! It's Ricki!"

"I didn't know they let you out during the daylight."

"Who's your friend? Did you hire a translator?"

Giggles.

I kept my head down as we walked past. But something made Ricki whip around toward Kaitlin, Kaitlyn and Katelyn. Man, I thought, those ballerinas know how to spin.

"I have had enough of you," she said.

She wasn't just spinning; she was snapping.

"Ricki," I whispered. "I don't think—"

"Hush," she told me. Her voice was low and resolute. I stepped back.

The Kaitlins looked at her, and their shiny, lip-glossed mouths formed little O-shapes.

"Oh my God I am like, so shocked to hear you speak, and so ready for you to shut up already," Kaitlin said.

"What's going to happen? Are you going to have your little boyfriend protect you?" said Kaitlyn.

"I'm so *scared*," said Katelyn. "Maybe he'll throw up on us!"

More giggles.

"Leave him out of this," Ricki said. "And if you choose combat with me, I will give it back, to the finish."

Whoa! She was using the Omegan Death Challenge! Once given, nobody can leave the arena, except in victory—or in pieces!

She had assumed a position. Maybe it was first position, or maybe it was some type of combat stance she learned from studying Commander Steele. But she stood in perfect balance, her feet forming a *T*, her chin out, her long arms behind her back. She looked strong. I almost thought to warn them, "Never cross paths with a determined Omegan!"

But it was too late. A crowd was gathering. Combat commenced.

Kaitlin put one hand on her hip and looked down her nose. "Are you really choosing a fight with *us*?" She punctuated her remark with a particularly nasty one-word insult.

Ricki stayed calm. "I'm merely suggesting that you need to leave him alone. And me. Us. Today. And from now on. As I said, I've had enough of you. So you can stop now. Or else." Her voice was slowly gaining volume, with that spookily bright, cheerful tone she used with me when she was about to reveal exactly how complicated she could be.

Kaitlyn scoffed. "As if."

Katelyn rolled her eyes. "For real."

Kaitlin sneered. "*Or. Else. What.*"

Ricki absorbed the death beams from their eyes. "Or else I talk."

Kaitlin laughed. "Like, what could you say that would matter to us?"

"You're insignificant," Katelyn said.

"Up until today, you barely knew *how* to talk, unless you were sucking up to a teacher," Kaitlin said. "So why should we worry about what you have to say now?"

They stood in their triangle of doom, and I waited for them to pounce and rend my friend into Ricki McNuggets.

She held her ground. And smiled. And spoke.

"Because I could say which one of you mocks people who can't afford designer perfumes—but who sprays herself with bottles of Walmart knockoffs when she thinks nobody is watching. And I could let the cheer sponsor know which one of you snuck away with a sophomore during your church ski trip—and what you boasted about doing with him in the hot tub during personal prayer time. Possibly while wearing her purity ring.

"Or I could even say which one of you is on that trendy raw-food detox diet that's giving you such digestive issues that you're probably wearing an adult diaper right now out of fear that your tumbling runs might lead to...actual runs. Your outfits provide barely enough cover for your problem. I am under no obligation to do so."

There were gasps. There were *Whoas!*

And here I'd thought there was no such thing as a real-life smart bomb.

The Kaitlins' crumbled facades crashed to the floor. Cheeks flamed. Skirts were nervously adjusted. Panicked glances were exchanged.

They hurried away, jingling, without saying another word.

Ricki did a graceful bow to the crowd, which started murmuring, then laughing out loud. She then glanced at me and, with a nod, indicated it was time to get to class.

I looked at her with the kind of awe I usually reserved for photos taken by NASA probes.

"Uh, Ricki...how did you even..."

"...know? It's not that complicated. It's amazing what you see and hear when you hide in a stall in the girls rest room with your feet pulled up for several hours a day."

She was smiling at me, but her lower lip was trembling. She lowered her voice, which sounded shaky.

"You said you needed a role model in how to face pure evil. How'd I do?"

I opened and closed my hand, then gave her a thumbs-up. "Better than Luke, that's for sure."

She looked pleased. And I felt ready.

12.01.03

But that night, in the cold solitude of my bunk, I was not so sure.

I kept picking up and putting down my most militaristic books for guidance on how to comport myself in a combat situation, although I wasn't sure how lessons in, say, lobbing nuclear bombs from the moon or blasting alien insect hives really applied here.

I even found myself going over *Always Faithful, Always*

Ready, the Marine history book Denton had told me to do a report on the day he fired Beacon. Which got me to thinking—books had done little to help me in the real world of late. Except when I'd set them on fire. And this book was one of the worst ever, full of jargony writing about tradition and protocol and not a lot of actual cool Marine stories. By the time I got to the charts of medals and decorations at the end, I wasn't sure whether to be extra fearful of Denton or just extra angry at him.

As I stared at the charts, mind kept drifting back to Ricki. How brave she had been. It was odd to learn that reality can be almost as inspiring as science fiction, sometimes.

"Would it offend your Omegan virtues if, before we die, I hugged you and told you that I was glad you were my friend?"

"Yes."

"Well, I guess we'd better not die, then. Fire when ready."

—Captain Maxim and First Officer Steele
Star Survivors Episode 68.
"The Final Battle"

EXPEDITION LOG

ENTRY 13.01.01

This was it.

I went over the battle plan in my head. Energized deflector screens. Locked S-foils in attack position.

Ran into Dad in the kitchen as he was scrambling to get out the door.

"You're up early," he said, surprised.

"You too," I said. I pushed aside my guilty feelings about not telling him what I had planned and for the shame I would be bringing him when I was expelled.

"I, um, need to compare some notes with a friend before work. You want a ride? You might find this story interesting."

Hearing Dad talk was the *last* thing I needed this morning. I declined.

He started to say something, then headed to his car. I headed to the park, where Les was waiting at the bridge.

"Is it set?" I asked, as he handed over the microphone, which was now wrapped in duct tape and had a few extra wires hanging out of the end.

"Yes," he said. "It was easy. The polarity was clearly marked. All I had to do was—"

"Les," I said, "I don't really care about that right now. I just need to know—"

"Right. How it works. It's pretty basic technology. The microphone has a miniature FM transmitter that broadcasts to a fixed frequency. I wired the receiver into the intercom system. Just stand within about fifty feet of that receiver, turn the microphone on, and you should be good."

"Great. Where do I need to stand?"

"Anywhere in that fifty-foot range. I hardwired the receiver into the junction box. Once you start transmitting, the whole school will hear everything."

"So, I should be in the basement?"

"No. Too risky this time of day. But if you're on the floor right above, anywhere in that 50-foot range, you should be fine. I adapted the mic so that it draws power from a nine-volt battery instead of a double-A cell. And I replaced the antenna coil so that—"

"Les!" I asked impatiently, *"Where do I need to stand?"*

"Oh," he said. "Well, I drew a map." He reached into his windbreaker pocket.

Once again he had a graph-paper rendition of the school, this time with a series of concentric circles, like a target, centered on the ARC.

"I'm supposed to stand *here*?" I pointed.

He nodded.

"Les, this is the quietest spot in the whole school!"

"I can't guarantee it will work anywhere else. Just stay inconspicuous."

"I'm going to be pretty conspicuous standing in the middle of the ARC holding a microphone!"

He shook his head. "Use my reading room."

My blank look told him he needed to explain.

"Go to the farthest corner of the ARC, where the nonfiction books start. There's a double-doored gray cabinet labeled MATH CLUB WORKSHEETS. Nobody ever looks inside. Besides me. If you have a flashlight, you can sit and read for hours without anybody seeing you. Or hearing you. You'll be inconspicuous enough."

I shook my head in wonder. "You amaze me, Les."

He shrugged. "It's amazing what you can accomplish when your brain doesn't bother to make room for things like knowing how to catch a ball."

Any other day I might have laughed. But as I looked up the hill and saw the school towering above, I felt no mirth. Once this was over, I might not see Les again.

I tucked the microphone deep into my Cosmos backpack and zipped it up.

"Well," I said, hoisting the pack over my shoulder, "here goes nothing."

"I'll be behind you, all the way."

"Thanks," I said. "I really need that, Les."

I took a few steps, then paused and waited for him to join me. I was looking forward to walking in together, just this once. But he didn't budge.

I looked back expectantly.

"No, I meant it," he said. "I'll be behind you all the way. At least a hundred feet. I don't think we should be seen together today."

"Les, are you kidding me? I thought you were over–"

I stopped when I saw his face. His jaw was set. His eyes burned fiercely.

"I can't be a suspect," he said. "My stepdad will be going

nuts as it is. I'm sorry. That I have to let you pull the trigger alone. I mean, 'We live, or perish, as one.' And…"

He blinked and swallowed. "And—thanks, Clark."

I nodded. "I understand. I'll try my best, Les."

"Try not," he said. "Just—good luck, OK?"

Minutes later, as I walked through the sadistic doors of the meanest school in the universe, I was thinking: I will not miss anything about this place. Not one single thing. Not one scuffed floor tile, not one flickering fluorescent tube, not a single cinderblock marked with tiny brown spots of adhesive from annoying, lying posters about pride and spirit. None of it.

I went to check my locker one more time. I opened the door, saw nothing I would miss, slammed it and saw Ricki standing next to me.

OK, *there's* something I will miss.

"I wanted to say good luck," she said. "And good bye. If you're really going through with this, I mean."

"What do you mean, 'if'? It's decided." I paused. "No, *I* decided."

"I know." She had a funny look on her face. "You're not doing this just to impress me, right? You shouldn't try to impress me. I'm not impressible. I mean, not that you're not being impressive. But, um…"

"Ricki," I said, "of all your terrible pep talks, this is the worst yet."

She looked at the floor. Then looked up. She was smiling. Sadly.

"You're just not that bright," she said. "And your plan is stupid. But I'd—I'd jump down a drain with you again."

"Call me sometime," I said, clearing my throat and forcing myself to think about the mission.

We started walking. "I'll be in the office second hour," she said. "I'll do what I can. But I think you're alone from here out."

"Yeah," I said, taking a deep breath and exhaling. "I know the feeling."

We parted.

My plan had been to slip into the ARC before the bell and camp out in Les's cabinet for first hour, then make my speech during second, when Ricki might be able to see Denton's reaction. It would be fun to have her tell me about it in a letter someday. I would need reading material in my cell, I was sure.

Waiting until second hour would also give me time to think about what I wanted to say. I had tried writing it all out, but in the end I decided to speak from the heart. I had my key talking points, of course: I would curse the Ty Triplets, Chambers and, especially, Denton. I would expose their secret evils and make the point that the weaklings would indeed someday inherit the earth and that apparently, today was that day.

I would laugh maniacally. Should it be more of a *"HEH HEH HEH!"* or a *"BWAH HAH HAH?"* I wondered. Such details matter.

It should have been easy to slip into the ARC amid the morning buzz of activity there—people rushing to get last-minute homework done, teachers trying to find a book they needed for that day's lesson. But talking to Ricki put me a little behind schedule. And then, of all things, I ran into Stephanie Spring just as I was preparing to slip inside. She was nervously stuffing some thick books into her gym bag, and I was awkwardly looking for a way past her. It took an eternal moment to sort out.

By the time I got around her, I had just seconds to spare. But through the safety glass, I could see no crowd to get lost in. Just the substitute librarian. She was standing and nodding to someone I could not see. I waited and waited for her to turn away. She finally did, just as the bell rang. I dashed in—

—and smacked into none other than Principal Denton, whose coffee mug fell to the ground and shattered.

"Uh, s-sorry?" I stammered.

The principal looked at the shards of mug, then at me. Something told me that tactical puking was not going to get me out of this one.

He studied me for a long moment, then slowly turned to the substitute librarian. "Did you witness what Sherman just did, Miss Willow?" he asked.

She nodded nervously.

He looked back down at me. "Running indoors is against the rules, Sherman. That's earned you one detention."

I started to protest, and he held up his right hand to silence me. Then he looked at his watch. "Tardiness is also an infraction. That's a second detention."

"But I—"

"Shut it, Sherman," he said. The look on his face told me he was just warming up. And sure enough, as he took a handkerchief out of his pocket and dabbed a possibly imaginary coffee stain off his shirt, he said, "Intentionally assaulting a teacher or administrator is not only a third infraction, it is an expellable offense. Given your other disciplinary issues, Sherman, I think it's time we discuss your future at a different educational institution. Starting today. Follow me to the office. Now."

What could I do?

Nothing.

There would be no broadcast. No triumphant laughter. No justice.

Denton had struck preemptively. He'd probably made the same calculations I had about how easy it would be for me to ruin his plans. Or maybe he was just worried that in the end, I was too tempting a target for Ty, who would eventually, some-day, come after me in a way that Denton couldn't cover up.

I knew I had never been his foxhole buddy. But he'd just put me right in his crosshairs and pulled the trigger.

I had no backup plan. I felt beyond defeated.

I thought, when a meteor falls to earth through the awe-some heights of the upper atmosphere, it leaves a vivid trail in its wake. Something everyone can see. Even a sand-sized speck of space dust can light up the night sky.

I was more insignificant than that, apparently.

I was bird poop, falling unseen straight to earth, landing with a watery plop.

No, even bird poop makes a mark on the world. I was lower than that.

I was nothing.

I hung my head and followed Denton down the hall.

13.01.02

We went directly to the main office. He confiscated my Cos-mos backpack and handed it to a surprised Counselor Blethins.

"This student attempted to assault me," he said. "So we are

initiating the disciplinary plan I told you about. Summon his parents and finalize the paperwork."

For a moment I thought she actually was going to resist. "Really, Principal Denton, I doubt that Clark–"

"Counselor," he said in a low voice, "I have a faculty witness in the ARC who will tell you that she saw things *exactly* as I describe them. And I would remind you that *she* replaced a faculty member who was not willing to act according to my wishes on a *very similar* matter. I would not want to have to terminate a second employee over this. But I will. You know I can always find a way."

Her eyes darted between him and me. Then she bowed her head and turned away.

He led me into his office and closed the door.

He had won.

Absolutely.

I thought it would be nice if, like the supervillain at the end of a movie, he explained exactly what he had been up to–why he'd declared war on me. Why he allied with Ty. And what he hoped to gain from it all. But he just sat at his desk, writing out notes, just another day at the office for him. One final reminder that my life was not a movie at all. There would be no clever tagline for me. I would just be X'd out with the stroke of his pen.

I sat for what was probably most of an hour. I couldn't really tell you how long; I felt so empty that I maybe was not existing in normal time. Eventually, Counselor Blethins came in and placed a folder on his desk. "His parents will be here as soon as they can, they said." She looked at me, looked away and left.

I remained silent for as long as I could take it.

"Mr. Denton?" I finally asked.

He didn't look up.

"What did you have against me?"

The room was quiet, but for the usual random popping noises coming from the intercom.

He paused in his writing and looked me over. "There's a military term I'm fond of: *Target of opportunity*," he finally said. "Ty saw you as such—by which I mean, you crossed paths with him on your very first day and incited him. That made you an instant enemy to me.

"You see Sherman, we—that is, Ty and I—we're part of a team. A *real* team. We're each destined for great things, but it is only through each other's success that we will achieve them. And when you're destined for great things like we are, you can't let anyone get in your way. Like the others over the past two years who have distracted him. And been foolish enough to challenge me."

He picked up his pen and returned to his memo. "It's nothing personal, son. Which is why I don't mind letting you know. Middle school—all of life—is about survival of the fittest. The weak get culled out, tossed aside. The true leaders emerge. Even a 'zero' should be able to grasp that."

That made me angry.

"But I'm not a zero," I said, standing. "I never was. That was your stupid computer's fault!"

"Yes, that was a shame for you," he said. "But it worked well for me. Keeping you in low-level classes maybe made you a little easier to isolate and control."

I froze. "You're telling me—"

"I'm not telling you anything," he said. "And if I did tell

you something, you could never prove it. But really, don't you think I could have fixed your scheduling problems if I'd wanted to? I'm the principal, after all."

I slumped back down in shock.

"No," he said casually, "you nerdy kids—you sometimes get ideas when you band together. It was much better to keep you culled out from the herd, where I could keep an eye on you. And keep you from getting ideas about challenging me. Or Ty."

My mouth felt dry. My mind raced. Maybe I *should* have asked my dad for help. Maybe he could still—

"Incidentally, if you are thinking of telling your parents about any of this conversation, it will do no good. No teacher will support you, and the district head of security will support *me*. I have paperwork that shows you were harassing other students, a constant nuisance to the counselor, a possible arsonist and, finally, became physically out of control. So don't waste your time trying to find a way to escape."

I stared at the floor. "Ms. Beacon was right. You're dangerous."

At the mention of her name, he snarled. "That *woman* was too stuck in her old-school, obstructionist and possibly Marxist ways to understand what I was trying to accomplish here. She made herself an enemy. I'd been building a case against her for years." He smiled coldly. "Thank you, son, for diverting that envelope and giving me a way to terminate her at last."

I gasped. "You *knew?*"

"I guessed. *She* would never have been so careless with such an important file. But when I saw it ride into the office with the rest of the mail from the ARC, it was as good as seeing a termination order from the superintendent herself. It was truly a gift."

Getting punched in the stomach would have been more pleasant than watching his smug grin spread as he continued to write.

"And this is all because of... Ty?"

He stopped smiling, put his pen down and stared at me. "Ty Hunter is the single greatest athlete to ever come through this school, if not this district," he said. "I sensed an opportunity the moment the college scouts started calling. He's going to go far. And the people around him—we're going to go far too. For me, it may only be to a secure, new job at the high school. That is all I need. At the moment.

"But he needs some help. He attracts... trouble. Frail students who bring out his rough side. Teachers who emphasize current grades over his future potential. I've had to clear a path for him. Make issues disappear. Issues such as you, Sherman. He couldn't see the harm you could cause. I could. Which is why he and I make a great team."

He shook his head in pity. "Like I said, it's not personal. So here is some life advice, son. Next time, get help. Maybe if you'd been on a team of some kind, it would have stood up for you. And maybe if you had fought back harder and faster, you would have survived. Like they taught me in the Corps, 'Naked force has settled more issues in history than has any other factor.' They were talking about war. But it applies to eighth grade as well, doesn't it?"

He laughed at his own cleverness and went back to filling out my death warrant.

My failure was complete. I felt as helpless as I had on my

first day here. I had let absolutely everyone down: My friends. My family. Myself.

When I turned my head in disgust, I had to stare at that stupid portrait of Denton as a Marine. The young, confident man in front of the flag, looming over the display case holding his awards. I had an urge to knock them off the shelf, scatter them to the floor, the way I had by accident before. I thought of the way I'd been pricked by his stupid medal that day. How a man this evil could have done anything to deserve a medal for valor would never make sense to me.

That made me think of all the conversations we'd had about his Marine years. All the little lectures he kept repeating.

And then I thought of something from a book. The Marines book. The one he made me read. The one I had been studying for inspiration.

I rose and walked over to the display case.

"Soldier's Medal for Valor," I said, remembering the words I had read.

Denton kept writing.

"Mr. Denton, did you ever tell me what the Marines gave you that medal for?"

He stopped without looking up at me. "Sherman, this is not the time to discuss anything other than your impending expulsion."

I nodded.

"I'm just—it's just that in the *Always Faithful* book I've been reading, there's a chart with all the medals given by the Marine Corps, and I don't remember seeing that one."

"Maybe you didn't look closely enough," he mumbled.

"Maybe," I said.

I waited for him to return to his writing before I continued.

"But I did read the chapter about Marine traditions. The one that says Marines really hate being called *soldiers*."

The pen stopped moving again.

"It also said that Marines are picky about some stuff. Like calling their weapons *rifles,* not *guns.* But I've heard you talk about guns lots of times. Marines don't like the term *foxholes,* either. Although you sure do."

He put the pen down, quietly.

"And you know, I'm pretty sure that line you just used about naked force came right out of *Starship Troopers.* In fact, now that I think about it, a whole lot of what you've told me about your Marine experience could have come right out of *Starship Troopers.* I'm wondering if you even know what *semper fi* means."

If I thought I had seen him give me a cyborg stare before, it was nothing like what I was seeing now. He spoke in a voice with a James Earl Jones rumble to it.

He rose slowly, menacingly.

"Is there a point you're trying to make, young man?"

"No," I said, trembling inside as I looked him right in the eye and told him what was slowly dawning on me: "Except that it doesn't make sense that a Marine hero would go to war against kid like me. For any reason. Unless, maybe, you're not a Marine hero. Maybe the medal is a fake. Maybe you're not even a Marine. And maybe you're just...a desperate, petty man."

He didn't move for a moment. But then he strode around his desk and stood next to me. I had to bend my head back to keep my eyes locked on his. But I did.

"I don't know what crazy ideas you have developed in

the last five minutes," he said, "but let's say you think you've caught me doing something wrong. First, you haven't. Government records will confirm my Marine enlistment. Second, let's say you think you're smart by bringing up that medal. I assure you, it will be gone long before anybody else gets a chance to study it. So even if you tried to tell someone, it would be the words of a respected school principal against the words of an eighth-grade zero.

"So—think carefully. Is there anything you want to say to me?"

I did think carefully. I thought of Maxim, Steele and Vexons, and Luke and Vader. And mostly, about Les and his dad, and Ricki and her wolf packs.

"Yes, there is, sir." I took a deep breath.

"You win. I accept that. And I'll get over it. I mean, I've got my whole life ahead of me. But this—being a, a...a *dictator* over a bunch of kids and teachers—this is a high point for you, isn't it? And that's...that's pathetic, isn't it?

"I mean, wherever you send me, I can feel pretty good, knowing that for the rest of my life, I'll be getting stronger, and you'll be...fading. You can be buddies with Ty for a few years, but he's going to move on, right? Maybe he'll get you tickets to a pro baseball game someday. Maybe not. He might just forget you. Or end up in jail."

"Me? Well, it can't get much worse than today. But I've survived you. I've survived Ty. I'll survive wherever you send me. I might face your kind again...and next time, I might outsmart you all."

I thought for one more moment, then added, "You know, I've been called a lot of names this year. I should probably direct a few of them at you. You deserve them all.

"But when it comes right down to it, you're not worth the spit."

Denton was silent. In the distance I could hear whooping from students throughout the school. Must be lunchtime, I thought. I hoped Les and Ricki were enjoying the start of their lives without me.

A knock on the door made Denton unlock his death gaze from me. "Nice speech, Sherman," he hissed. "But this ends now. Come in!"

Counselor Blethins entered the room, leading my father and a large man in a rumpled blue suit. "Clark's people are here, Mr. Denton," she announced as she set a fresh stack of papers in front of him. I was momentarily alarmed at the arrival of my dad, who was going to be really angry with me. But of all things, he was smiling. The poor, clueless man.

"Principal Denton? I'm Clark's dad. And this is Pete Manaia. He's my—"

"Mr. Sherman, there was no need to bring an attorney," Denton said, coolly. My dad and the stranger exchanged surprised glances, nodded and let him continue.

"This should be fairly quick," he said. "It is not a matter for due process, it's a simple matter of facts. Your son's actions leave me no choice but to expel him, as these documents will show...."

He picked up the papers that Blethins had just left, and a puzzled look crossed his face.

"Counselor, you've brought the wrong documents," he said.

"No," she replied, her voice sounding not at all mousy for once. "I've brought the right ones."

"Counselor, this is an expulsion order. But it's for...Ty Hunter."

"Oh yes. I thought you might be needing that, Mr. Denton, since I'm not going to lift a finger to help you punish Clark."

"What are you talking about, counselor?" he growled.

"Well, even after I called Clark's parents, I just couldn't imagine that he deserved expulsion. I was staring at the blank form, wondering what to do—and then I heard the discussion you were having with him here. And I thought I would go ahead and use my pending authority as head of the Disciplinary Tribunal to do something right for a change."

"Head of the Disciplinary Tribunal?" Denton asked, bemused. Then he seemed to realize something, and his voice became very low. "Counselor, what do you mean, you heard our discussion?"

She smiled. "Oh, didn't you know? Somebody seems to have been playing a prank with the intercom. Everything you two have said has been broadcast to the whole school. I suspect they're listening still."

There was another schoolwide round of whooping.

Denton's entire frame locked up. "The whole...school?"

"Yes," she said. "And then some. Because halfway through, I put it on conference call with the district headquarters. Some people Edna Beacon had been urging me to talk to. Some people who are going to be very upset. The superintendent herself might even be calling you later today. Shortly before your leave of absence begins."

The phone on Denton's desk buzzed urgently. Blethins glanced at the caller ID. "Oh, there she is now. I guess she's more efficient than I gave her credit for."

The whole building began to vibrate with a frenzied roar that came from every classroom.

"You...you don't have anything," Denton stammered. "I-I have paperwork that will show—"

"Actually," my father interrupted, "I came here today to talk about paperwork. Specifically, your résumé, which was on file with the school board, and your military release papers, which a source at the Pentagon read to me just yesterday. One implies you're a decorated combat veteran. The other says something very different.

"I have a colleague at the newspaper looking into this, by the way. So be ready to answer some questions from him too."

Denton fell back into his chair.

"Along those lines," my father continued lightly, "Pete here would like to speak with you in private. He's an *actual* Marine veteran. I'm sure you two have a lot to discuss."

The bulky man in the blue suit glared at Denton in a way that made me think, Oh. *That's* what a real Marine looks like.

And for a moment, Principal Denton's skin did take on a tone that absolutely, positively made him look like an alien.

My mind was on overload trying to process how everything had happened. Who could have found a way to broadcast Denton's words to the whole school?

Then I heard a loud pop of static from the intercom.

And I knew.

Denton had tried to tell me I didn't have a team. But I had the best: Beacon. My family. Even, it turns out, Ms. Blethins.

And, obviously, the ones who had made it all happen: Ricki and Les.

"Never cross paths with a determined nerd," I told Denton, and I followed my dad out of the room.

13.01.03

Dad and I went to wait, just the two of us, in Blethins's office, as a million things seemed to happen at once.

I could hear Pete Manaia, the guy in the blue suit, start to say some things to Denton about what it means to be a Marine and what kind of lowlife would lie about it. Denton was saved—if you could call it that—by an office worker saying that the superintendent was waiting for him to pick up the phone. I would like to have heard that conversation, but that's when someone finally cut off the intercom.

I peeked around the corner and saw Manaia, whom the worker had escorted out, standing near Denton's closed door, appearing to take notes; he must have been interested in that conversation too.

All the time, Blethins was moving as if tossed about by a hurricane—pulling files, summoning Ty from his classroom, calling Ty's father and telling him to get here quickly.

"We're ending this, and ending it now," she said as she placed the phone in its cradle. She was no longer the least bit gerbil-like. "George Denton has done too much damage to this school for any of his... his *wrongness* to last even a moment longer. I should have tried to stop him a long time ago, but he scared me. He scared me. All that war-hero bluster. All that talk of discipline and order and obeying superiors. The way he managed to 'disappear' everyone who—"

She paused and looked at me. "Clark, I'm sorry. Edna Beacon had been trying to persuade me to help her do something about him for years. Her dismissal terrified me. *Terrified.* But when I heard you standing up to him in there, I realized what a coward I had been. George Denton is not going to hurt *any* of us *ever again.*" She stood and gathered a stack of files from her desk.

"We're going to prove that by sending a message—and getting rid of this school's Number One Problem, Ty Hunter. Do you know how many children like you have suffered, Clark? Just for getting in Ty's way? And even before Ty arrived, how many teachers and students Denton made examples of just to intimidate the rest of us? Too many, too many." She was a blur of filing and form-filling.

When Ty was summoned from class, they made him sit in the nurse's office. He tried to glare at me from across the hall, but I could tell he was afraid. While I stared at him, my dad put a hand on my shoulder.

"I'm sorry, again, that I was so late to see everything you were up against, Clark," he said.

"It's OK," I said. Pete Manaia and the stuff about the Pentagon had come out of nowhere, but Dad had really helped save the day. "I didn't even know we *had* an attorney."

Dad cleared his throat and looked around furtively, then mumbled, "I never said we had an attorney."

Huh?

"Pete is the cops reporter at the paper. I tried to tell you about him. He really *was* a Marine. Sorry, *is* a Marine. Once a Marine, always a Marine, they say."

"So I've read."

"Anyhow, after you mentioned that medal, he and I started making some calls."

"Dad!" I cried. "I asked you not to get involved!"

He raised his eyebrows. "Clark," he said, "I'm your dad. You didn't really think I was going to make you fight this alone, did you?"

I didn't say anything.

"Although I'll give you credit—you were making all the right friends. Ms. Beacon told me—"

"You talked to Beacon?"

"After you mentioned that she had some kind of information about Denton, yes, I tracked her down. She's a pretty sharp woman."

"I *know*."

"She had a hunch. But she didn't have access to the right records. Pete had a friend at the Pentagon who did."

"So the stuff about Denton's record—my hunch was right?"

"Your hunch was excellent. Denton *was* a Marine—for three weeks. He wasn't lying when he said he enlisted. But he dropped out of boot camp. He just couldn't keep up physically, and that was it. He's been lying about his service for years, and nobody bothered to challenge him before now."

I tried to absorb this. "So basically, he flunked PE with the Marines?"

"I—I guess so," Dad said, blinking a few times. "I guess so."

That was so beautiful I actually felt tingly inside. "I wonder how he got that medal?"

"Well, he certainly didn't win it for his combat exploits. I looked it up—you have to do something heroic *not* during battle, for the *Army*, to win one. He probably liked the way it looked and picked it up at surplus store or something."

"Was he lying about being a business executive too?"

"I haven't figured that part out—except that he listed only one company on his résumé, and the owner of record was his mother. My guess is he was no better at being a business executive than he was at being a Marine."

Flunked by the Marines and fired by his mom. And he called *me* a zero.

"But here's a question for you, Clark: When did *you* become an expert on Marine traditions?"

I was going to tell him about *Always Faithful, Always Ready*, but just shrugged. "I can read."

Dad nodded approvingly. "Better than Denton, at least. Your books served you well."

It was at that moment that Ty's father—a large, paunchy man in a green polo shirt with a logo from the cable TV company—stormed up to the reception desk. "Where the hell is he?" he demanded.

I jumped; I thought he was coming for me. Instead, he stomped into the nurse's office, and I saw him grab Ty by the shoulders before he kicked the door shut.

Words like *idiot* and a few that were new to me could be heard. I heard a strange gasping sound, and I realized that it was the sound of Ty sobbing. Sobbing! He was being treated even worse than he had treated me. And he finally, finally was getting what he deserved. And then some.

It felt...not as good as you would think.

As the shouting increased, Counselor Blethins stood up from her desk, smoothed her dress and prepared to walk in.

"Clark, it's all set. All you have to do is sign a piece of paper that says what Ty did, and I can get him sent away. The problem will be over."

That sounded so good. So, so good.

And yet, I found myself thinking about what I had read about Ty in his permanent file. The part about his mom. He probably could have used her now, as his dad amped up his screaming.

Then I recalled Ty in the Sanctuary, amid the smoke. The way he had looked like a frightened, confused kid. That kid probably was hurting a lot right now.

I related to that kid.

I thought, if he gets kicked out of school, yeah, the problem would be over...for me.

But against all that was rational, I found myself asking, *What about him?*

"Counselor Blethins?" I said. "Can I ask you something?"

She anxiously looked toward the nurse's office, where the shouting and sobbing were concurrent. "Yes, Clark?"

"What does Ty need right now? I mean, what would fix him?"

"Fix him?" She gave me a puzzled look, then said, "That's a complicated question, Clark. He and his family have a long road ahead. I'm going to have to alert some authorities. Ty himself probably needs a lot of help."

"Will he get any at the alternative school?"

She stared off down the hall. "That's not really what they specialize in there, I'm afraid. It's more of a place to keep students from hurting one another until they graduate or drop out."

"But if he stayed *here*, would you be able to, you know, help?"

She gave me a sad smile. "It's what I would prefer to do, instead of adjusting class schedules and signing paperwork."

"So you could, like, counsel him, right?"

Across the hall Ty's dad was pounding a counter, and I thought of Les. Even though I'd been the one to wreck Ty's life, things would *not* be good for Les after this. Not good at all.

"Clark," my dad said, "what are you thinking?"

"I don't know, Dad." I pressed my fingers into my forehead. "I don't want him to get away with anything. But I don't want him...hurt."

I thought of what I had been through—being pushed around by someone I was powerless to stop. How it was the kind of thing that made people say, "I wouldn't wish that on my worst enemy."

I heard Ty whimper a reply to his raging dad, and I thought, It's true. I would not.

"Dad?" I looked at him pleadingly. What I was thinking was not logical. But it felt right.

He looked at me, and then at Blethins. "Counselor, do we have options?"

Her nose twitched, and then she looked over at Denton's office. We could hear him begging with one of his superiors for something. "Well, actually, I wasn't lying when I told Denton I'm in charge of the Disciplinary Tribunal now. Or I will be, as soon as he's gone. So I could, I suppose, approve an in-school suspension. It's kind of like probation. We could attach terms to it—a 'one false move and you're out' type of thing. But that's only if you're willing, Clark."

I looked across the hall. I listened to the shouting. "Could we put his dad on probation too?" Dad looked over at Blethins again.

She thought for a moment, shaking her head. "There's only so much a counselor can do, Clark. Like I said, I'll be contacting some authorities, but I can't force his dad to do much. A judge could, but in my experience, a lot of steps have to happen before we get there." Then her face lit up. "But you know, for starters, we *could* be creative. I *could* offer to let Ty remain here at Festus, and in baseball, *if* they agreed to seek some kind of family counseling. In writing, of course. Yes. I think I could make that work."

I looked at my dad.

"You have a hunch?" he asked.

I nodded.

"Your call," he said. "You've earned it."

I turned to Counselor Blethins. "Tell them I'd be willing to make that deal."

She looked at my dad, who nodded. Then she smiled. "You've got a good heart, Clark. Someone has taught you well." She turned and, with a grimly determined look I had never seen her wear before today, went to confront Mr. Hunter.

I had a feeling I was leaving something out.

"Wait!" I called.

She turned back.

"Can you also make them promise that Les never has to attend another baseball game for as long as he lives?"

She looked over at my dad again. "I can try."

"Clark," he asked, "this is really what you want?"

I thought, Is this something Captain Maxim would do?

And I remembered: In Episode 64, he is captured by a race of beings from a quantum dimension who cage him, torture him and force him to fight a pitched battle with the commander of a Vexon battlecruiser, with the lives of both crews at stake. After nearly a full episode of brutal combat, Maxim gets his enemy by the throat and is ready to snuff the life out of him. You can tell from the look in his eye that he wants to. He doesn't. Why?

"I'm a man!" he yells at the quantum beings. "You can make me fight like an animal, but you will never turn me into one!"

I looked up at Counselor Blethins. "Ty needs help," I told her. "My crew and I will be OK."

"Space is mostly emptiness. Days like today—it feels especially so. But the only way through it, even when we don't know what's waiting at the end, is forward. Forward, guided by that one dim star. Right there. The one called . . . hope."

—Captain Maxim
Star Survivors Episode 69,
"Eulogy"

EXPEDITION LOG

ENTRY 14.01.01

Blethins gave me an excused absence for the rest of the day, and I was happy to accept.

Dad let his friend go write the newspaper story and stayed home with me, Mom and my sister. We had to recap everything for Mom, and at the end of it all she gave me a big hug. Little Gwen sort of applauded, although she might have just been hungry and demanding a cracker or something.

I spent the afternoon catching up on my non-Marine reading and wondering about Les.

That night we drove across town to a hamburger chain that I thought existed only back on the old planet. Sadly, they no longer carried *Star Survivors* commemorative cups, as they had once when I was in first grade. But they *did* have bobbleheads from the new *Star Wars* cartoon. My dad even let me have his. For the first time, this planet was actually starting to feel like home.

But all good times must end. And the next day I had to return to Festus.

I thought I would slip back into my usual anonymity when I entered the building, but I was wrong. It was the first of many surprises.

As I walked the halls to my locker, people stopped and

turned and stared. I felt my face. Had a giant zit formed? I looked behind me. Had someone pinned a *kick me* note to my back?

Then people started coming up to me. "You're Clark, right?" they would ask. And then they would say, "That was awesome!" Or, "I can't believe you stood up to him like that!" Or, "Coolest. Speech. Ever."

One kid whispered, "I wish I'd been that smart when they got on me last year."

And a teacher standing in a doorway smiled and said, "Ding-dong, the witch is dead. Thanks, Dorothy."

I just kept walking.

At my locker, Les was waiting. Beaming. (The smiling kind, not the transporter kind.)

And I was finally able to ask, "How, Les. How did you do it?"

While I loaded books back into my locker, he explained. "It was Ricki. She saw Denton leading you down the hallway, pulled out one of her fake hall passes, then got *me* pulled out of class.

"At first I didn't know what to do. I thought about setting off some kind of diversion, like in your original plan, so you could run for the hills. But Ricki talked me out of it. Then I remembered something that happened when I was building this Heathkit project that I found in my dad's stuff. I read the schematic wrong, and I wired some speakers incorrectly. It turned them into giant microphones—too lo-fi for any serious recording, of course, but they worked. And I realized that the intercom could work the same way.

"I ran down to the basement. It was just a matter of identifying the wires from Denton's office, tracing them to the junction box, then patching them directly into the receiver, reversed. I was trying to figure out how to tell you that you were on the air, but you rendered that step sort of unnecessary."

I shook my head. "You've earned your pay for the week, Les," I said, and started toward class.

He stopped me. "No, you did. You know that we're all going to see a shrink together? Me, my stepdad, my mom, Ty?"

"Yeah," I said, feeling a bit worried. "How's Ty taking that?"

He smiled. "I don't care. I've already emptied the baseball gear out of my closet. I'm done forever, no matter what anyone says. And now, I'll finally have a place to keep my soldering iron and some spare parts I salvaged from the Sanctuary. Maybe in a few months I'll build a real radio station for you."

"No doubt."

I looked for Ricki, but she didn't make an appearance. So I sauntered to the gym. Jerry and Bubba actually cowered when they saw me. Blethins, I later learned, had called their parents in, at which point each boy had stood tough as cotton candy, blamed Ty for everything and pleaded tearfully not to be expelled. The frightened looks on their faces told me all I needed to know, though. They would not bother me again.

When Chambers saw me, he quietly pulled me into his office.

"Uh, look," he said, nervously. "No hard feelings, right?"

I was silent. He fidgeted.

"Look, um, given where we are, I was thinking, you might need, ah, a rest period. So, ah, if you want to spend the day in the bleachers, doing, ah, homework, or with a book or whatever you read, that's fine with me. In fact, ah, you wouldn't even need to suit up. This year. Again. Sound good?"

It did.

I did not find Ricki until lunchtime. She sat with me and Les at our usual table, which had a few extra people at it.

"I guess you're a celebrity now," she said.

"Oh, not really. But I'll bump you right to the front of the autograph line anytime you ask."

She smiled, but weakly, and didn't say much the rest of the meal. Actually, I didn't either; Les was busy retelling some of our new tablemates about how he didn't know *exactly* how the intercom had been hacked, but that it wouldn't be too difficult if you knew what you were doing. Then he proceeded to explain how to do it.

Afterward, Ricki and I walked to the ARC together. "Can you meet me at the rocket ship park today?" she asked. "Alone?"

This was intriguing, but her voice was flat, and even I could tell something was bothering her.

"Ricki, is there—"

"Just—let's talk at the park, OK?" She quickly changed tones and topics. "Did you hear they have almost the whole original crew signed up to do a *Star Survivors* movie? They could start filming in July and have it ready by the time school is out next year."

We walked the halls, talking of stars and survival and summer and the future. Life on Earth, I am telling you, was pretty good.

14.01.02

Ricki and I met at the front doors and walked in the sunshine together.

"Considering how recently we were doomed, this has been a good day," I said.

She nodded but kept her eyes on the trail and said nothing.

After we had gone another half block, she finally asked, "Do you believe in life on other planets?"

It wasn't a question I'd been expecting, but it's one I'd thought a lot about. You ponder such matters when you're alone in a room and think you're the only one of your kind.

"Well, you know, I read that if there's a hundred billion planets out there, and if just one percent of those are capable of supporting life, and if just one percent of those actually had evolved life, that works out to…"

She wasn't listening.

"Why?" I asked. "Do you?"

We were getting close to the park now. I could see the rocket ship.

"I just think the universe can be an awfully lonely place sometimes," she said.

"Yeah, but we've got that taken care of now. I mean, you and me and Les, we've sort of carved out our own space, you know? I mean…" What did I mean? I wanted to say thank you, but I owed her more than that. Which was hard to express.

We were at the base of the rocket now. She stopped walking, turned and looked at me directly. Her eyes were bright and sparkling.

"We're moving," she said.

My first thought was, "No we're not, we're standing still." Then I saw the pained look on her face, the way her lips were thin and tight.

I thought about movies...the wingman getting picked off right as Luke closes in on the Death Star's exhaust port. I thought of films of hydrogen bomb tests, the houses splintered in a rush of nuclear wind. *The Planet of the Apes* guy collapsing before the Statue of Liberty, realizing that everything, everything was forever ruined.

I dropped my backpack and staggered back against the rocket, then slid down, until my tailbone crashed onto the rocky earth.

"No," I coughed.

She nodded.

"Ricki, I..." Two kids whizzed past on their bikes, laughing. If I'd had a blaster, I would have shot them on the spot for daring to be happy in this horrible, rotten world.

Ricki looked up and down the path. "Inside," she said. And she climbed up.

I followed her into the capsule, where we sat shoulder-to-shoulder, staring out at the world through the steel bars.

"When?" I asked.

"I get two weeks," she said.

"Two *weeks?* But what about the end of school?"

"My dad got an offer from some tech company. Bought him out of his school contract. Offered my mom a job too. They need to start right away."

"Where?" I asked.

She shrugged. "California," she said. "Palos Verdes or Palo Alto or Alta Vista something. Doesn't matter. It's all the same."

"Are you…can you…?" I was grasping for a little bit of hope, in something. But there was none, and I knew it.

"We've moved a lot," she said. "I'm used to it." She thought about that for a moment, then added, "No, I'm not."

"We can…we can write each other or something," I said.

"You know we won't."

"Yes, we will!" I said angrily. "Why wouldn't we?"

"Moving ruins everything," she said. "Especially friendships. How many friends did *you* keep when *you* moved?"

But, I wanted to tell her, you're different. I wanted to tell her *we're* different. I wanted to tell her…I can't believe how much this hurts.

So I told her.

"Ricki," I said. "You're different. We're different. You saved my life this year. You made me feel—normal. Which is funny, because you're weird. Really weird. Your defenses are like…like…Iron Man in a Batmobile behind Captain America's shield.

"But you know, you made this planet feel like…home. I won't forget that. Ever."

She looked over at me. Her frown told me she was doubtful. But she didn't tell me to stop. So I didn't.

"I mean, you know, you're my friend. That means…the universe to me."

I didn't know what else to say. So I started to raise two fingers towards the stars. She started to do the same.

"I suppose you're thinking up a Captain Maxim quote that will help us right now," she said, sniffling.

"No," I said. "I'm thinking, I'll bet we figure this out together."

And instead of extending our thumbs in a regulation

salute, we reached out, toward each other, and pressed our fingertips together.

We went from touching fingertips to pressing palm against palm, and then we hugged, tightly. We held on like each of us was about to fall off a cliff, down a chasm, into a rip in the universe.

We held one another as close as we could for as long as we could.

Then we had to let go.

14.01.03

After we parted, I walked off into the sunset. Actually, the sun wouldn't be setting for about three hours. But it felt like it should be.

And then, as I was walking past Festus on the way home, I saw it. In the parking lot. I had to squint to make sure.

The blue Subaru. With the bumper stickers.

She was back!

I then did something I had never, ever expected to do. I ran. *Toward* Festus.

The front doors were locked. But a side door had been propped open. I sprinted down a hall, around a corner, into the ARC. She was behind the circulation desk, wearing a sweatshirt and jeans, carrying a box of books. Unpacking, I assumed.

"Ms. Beacon!" I cried.

She looked up, startled. And then she smiled. It struck me

as a sad smile—clearly another sign that I had not yet mastered the skill of reading emotions. Because what was there to be sad about? Ricki was leaving, yes, but my own triumph over Denton was now complete.

"Hello, Clark," she said.

"I'm so glad to see you," I said. "I was afraid I..."

I took a deep breath. The look on her face said I was speaking much too loudly for the ARC. "Sorry," I said.

She laughed. A little. Which, coming from her, seemed like a lot. "It's OK, Clark. You don't have to whisper."

"Good," I said. "Do you need help with anything? Putting your stuff back? Or are you just unloading now, and we can get it tomorrow?"

She sighed. And now her smile definitely looked sad.

She motioned to a chair. "Have a seat, Clark." Why was she calling me by my first name again?

I sat.

"Clark," she said, "I'm very happy you're here. I heard what you did. You were brave. You did the right thing. I knew you would, and I am proud of you. You made good work of my coded message."

I stared blankly. "Message?"

"The day I was so ignominiously escorted from this building, I had time to scrawl only one note, and nothing that a weaker mind might be able to decipher. Hence, *Colby 359.9*."

My jaw dropped. "*Always Faithful, Always Ready*. That wasn't Denton's idea—it was *yours*?"

She smiled. "Something about his incessant boasting did not match up with the men and women *I* have known who have served in the Marine Corps," she said. "I suspected that you might come to the same conclusion. And thanks to your father's skills and connections, we now know that we were entirely correct."

I was about to laugh out loud. And then I remembered why she had been sent away in the first place. It was because I had been an idiot.

"I screwed things up," I said to the floor. "Massively. With the envelope and all. I'm really sorry." I looked up, saw her smiling and felt a wave of relief. "But I guess it's working out, because you're coming back!"

She kept smiling, but she was shaking her head. "Clark," she said softly, "I'm not coming back."

I leapt out of my chair. "What?" I cried. "That's—that's not fair! Why? Denton is gone! He can't hurt you anymore!"

She nodded. "You're right. He can't hurt me further. Or you.

"Unfortunately," she said, as she turned and started to gather things to put into a packing crate, "he's done some damage that can't be undone. He got me removed on a technicality. It's not the kind of thing that should cost me my job. But I've been smacking heads with some of more calcified members of the administration for many years. About many things. A fair number of those people don't have much use for an old radical like me. And so I am being invited to take early retirement. It's an offer I can't refuse."

I had barely begun to process the loss of Ricki, and now this?

"I hate this place," I croaked, as I unsuccessfully fought back tears once again. "Ricki's leaving. Now you. Next year, at high school, it starts all over again. What's the point in being friends with anybody? They just leave. I should…I should just stay home and watch *Star Survivors*. Or read a book.

They never go away. And they don't hurt. Losing people—*that* hurts."

Ms. Beacon reached into her box and handed me a tissue. Then she said, "Far be it from me to disparage reading books—or even watching *Star Survivors*—but I need to leave you with one more lesson, Mr. Sherman. You are a man of science, correct?"

Just hearing her call me by my formal name settled me down a bit. I wiped my eyes and nodded.

"You understand a bit about atomic physics, then?"

I stared, puzzled.

"Atoms. Nuclei. You understand that they are tightly bound bits of protons and neutrons, yes?"

Oh. That. "Yes," I said.

"If they are left alone, for the most part, what do they do?"

I thought for a moment. "Not much."

"Yes. They sort of drift aimlessly through space. But what happens when you throw them into a mix and make them bounce into one another?"

I tried to imagine what she was asking. "You get...a bunch of atoms bouncing off one another?"

"More than that, Clark. When the right atoms collide, in the proper circumstances, they fuse together. Things fly in all directions. It makes new elements, it creates energy. And when you break atoms apart, and send the pieces flying around, it also releases energy. It's how the universe was made. It's what makes the sun glow. It's what gives us life. Atoms flying around, bouncing into each other, fusing together, splitting apart.

"You and Ricki are splitting apart. You and I are splitting apart. But sparks we created are going to fly around and set things off. You'll take the energy you got from me, and I'll take the energy I got from you, and we'll soar on that until eventually, we'll bounce into something else, and we'll all create something new that will be wonderful, and powerful, and good."

I wasn't sure I understood. But it made me stop thinking about how hollow I felt inside.

She resumed putting things in her box. "What are you going to do, Ms. Beacon? " I asked. "Without a job?"

She held a folder labeled PARENTAL CHALLENGES, briefly examined it, then tossed it in the recycling bin. "Well, it's not as bad as you might think. The district might consider me a bad influence on children, but they have to pay me until my contract is up this summer. In a way, they are paying me to have a nice vacation.

"So my friend Maggie and I—the one who was in the hospital—are going to treat ourselves to a few weeks in Florida. She could use some sunshine, and we've got friends with a spare room. And then—well, something will come up. Maybe I'll finish that novel I started."

"You're going to read a novel?"

"You are good to notice my carelessness with language. I should pay closer attention to the words I use.

"But for now, I need to finish cleaning out this office. I was trying to do so quietly, when nobody was around, so as not to cause a fuss. But it has been very good to see you, Clark. I shall not forget you, or your loyalty. Would you like to help me out, one more time?"

Without speaking, I took one of the boxes she had filled, and she took the other, and we walked to her car.

Once it was loaded, she turned and faced me. She stood

up straight, and for a moment her face was the stern, mighty Beacon of old.

Slowly, she brought up her right hand, extended two fingers and held her thumb out. She touched her heart, and then pointed to the skies.

I watched, in awe, then returned the farewell.

"May you always feel at home, Mr. Sherman. Whichever star you follow."

The growl of her Subaru driving away was not quite as impressive as the *whoosh!* of the *Fortitude* as it flew off into the closing credits. But it was a worthy exit nonetheless.

I held the salute until she had rounded the corner. Then I turned toward home.

14.02.01

The goodbye to Ricki came frighteningly fast. We had a week of school, a few days off for break, and then she had to go.

It was brief. She didn't want anything too complicated. We just stood out in front of the school, me in my best NASA shirt, her in a dress that, for once, did not have any flowers on it. It was all black.

She was holding a small white box with headphones attached.

"New phone?" I asked, hopeful that this might open some line of long-distance communication.

"Old iPod," she explained. "Les rebuilt one for me. Something he salvaged from the Sanctuary. He filled it with music he thought I might be able to use on the drive west."

"What kind of music?"

"I'm not exactly sure," she said, looking down at the box. "It's stuff his mom and dad used to listen to, he said. He assures me it's quite loud. Which is what I wanted. I'm going to enjoy introducing it to my parents. It's about time I broadened their appreciation of the world a bit, don't you think?"

Her voice was spookily bright.

"Ricki," I asked, "are you...are you going to be OK? With them?"

She set her jaw. "Clark, I survived life in a sewer with you, and I took down a wolf pack with my bare hands. I'm ready for anything."

She started to turn away but halted. She looked me right in the eye and said softly, "Thank you for your support."

My throat burned too hotly for me to speak. She touched her fingers to her chest, and as she raised her hand, we touched fingertips one more time.

"I suppose it is ironic that you will go down as the one bright memory I take with me from this place," she said cheerfully. "But you will."

Then she spun away and, with a bouncy stride, was gone.

I wondered whether I would see her again. But I knew she'd know where to find me: I'd written my address inside my copy of *Star Survivors: The Novel*, which I'd slipped inside her backpack earlier.

I like to think that with real friends, hailing frequencies are always open. As Maxim might say—there's always a way.

14.03.01

I still have to report to the gym each morning, and again in the afternoon. But it's not such a bad class when you don't have to suit up. Or run. Or throw anything. Or get punched, kicked or...

It's not so bad having to sit for an hour and read.

In the afternoon sometimes, Les is able to hide in the bleachers with me and talk to me about how things are evolving at his house. How Blethins had gotten them into a counseling center that had a whole shelf of games, funky toys and even free snacks—and how Les's mom had been really interested in this book the counselor had suggested. Also, how Ty had been keeping his distance.

The updates give me hope for Les. But I'm too much of a space veteran to lower my guard. Today, I waited a good long time for the regular PE students to get out of the way before I decided to slip into the locker room to visit the water fountain.

Which is where I ran into him.

We almost collided, there in the doorway. He'd been slow in suiting up because he'd done something to his arm. His right hand and forearm were sheathed in plastic and athletic tape. Maybe he'd sprained it. I didn't know. I didn't care. It still looked as if it could damage me, should he put his mind to it.

Then I remembered he couldn't actually hurt me anymore. In theory.

I dared to look him in the eye.

Ty returned the stare with what I took to be the glow of hatred coming from deep inside his pupils. I balked. I wanted to run.

I stayed.

He spoke.

"I didn't need your help," he said.

"I didn't offer any," I said. "Go ahead, take a drink. I'll watch."

He snorted. "Not the water fountain. With my dad. In the office. I could of handled him."

I spoke to him in a tone that I imagined a mouse would use in conversation with a cobra that was trying to decide whether to strike.

"I'm sure you could have," I said.

"I was in control."

"I know."

"He doesn't own me."

I said nothing.

"When they called me to the office, I thought they were going to kick me off the team. That would have really made him blow his stack." He smiled at this thought. "It would've been great."

"You mean," I said slowly, "you *wanted* to get kicked out?"

"I didn't think so. Until he was there, yelling at me. But after that, yeah. Getting banned from baseball would've been a great way to tell him, 'Screw you,' don't you think?"

I didn't move.

"I mean, even Blethins and the new shrink couldn't get him to talk about much besides baseball at first," he continued. "All he wanted to know was when I could rejoin the team. So to get his attention, I had to do this."

My look must have said, Do what? because he held up his bandaged hand.

"Punched my locker. I'll be out for six weeks."

"Uh, nice?" was all I could manage. My eyes kept darting between his face and his good arm. Which I expected to strike at any second.

Then his shoulders sagged, and he glanced around. "Look," he said in a lower voice, "I, uh, I'm glad you did what you did. With the counselor and all. I'm not sure why you would. I mean, nobody else has given a rat's ass about me. Aside from my arm, I mean. My freaking arm.

"And I—I'm sorry. That I was an ass. It wasn't supposed to be...I mean, we never..."

He huffed. "We were just doing what we did. That's all."

It was not going to win an award for Most Articulate Apology. But I shrugged my acceptance.

"You looked like you needed a break," I said. It was true.

He gave a very slight nod.

"If you're up to visit Les, I'll keep clear," he said. "And I'll tell the others to keep clear too."

"Thanks."

"Just watch out for my dad." And he called him one of those urological nicknames he used to reserve for me.

I cringed reflexively, then remembered I was no longer his target. "I will."

I stepped out of his way. And he stepped out of mine.

"I'll see you around."

"Yeah," I said.

He headed to the field. I headed to the water fountain.

I thought about all he had put me through. I thought about how his wrist would heal a lot sooner than my mental scars. I thought it would be wrong to forgive him for what he'd done. That would be a sign of weakness. And if I had learned one thing on Planet Festus, it was that the universe is far too tough a place to show weakness.

But as I bent down to take my drink, I thought the universe had plenty of meanness in it already, and perhaps it would not be too weak of me to hate him just a little bit less.

14.04.01

Don't get me wrong—even if I hate Ty slightly less, there's still plenty to dislike about Planet Festus.

Classes are still boring. The hallways are still ugly. And when I walk them, sometimes I still feel like a lost spaceman. When I see packs of unfamiliar faces headed my way, I reflexively look for a wormhole.

But there's no denying that life has evolved.

Sometimes somebody will say hi to me. Not often. But more than before. I'm working on how to handle that.

And then there's Les.

When he wired that intercom, I think he electrified himself. Because he has become a magnet. A powerful, human-shaped geek magnet.

They keep coming up to him, showing him tricks on their graphing calculators or printouts from the computer lab and asking his advice.

I found out that I'll have several of these people in my classes next year in high school. Counselor Blethins said she'd put notes in my file to make sure I got the right schedule, even if I would forever be known as an eighth-grade zero.

None of this, of course, prepared me for the greatest cosmic oddity I have ever witnessed.

Les and I had met at my locker after school. We had the remote hallway to ourselves, and he was explaining the bizarre rules of some game that one of his new friends had been describing to him. He kept referring to it as "Dee 'n' Dee." And talking about dragons.

"It's not a video game?" I asked.

"No," he was telling me. "It's all done with dice. And *graph paper*."

"Sooooo...," I said, "it's like gambling?"

He rolled his eyes. "Just come on over to Brad's house on Saturday. It'll all make sense."

"I doubt that," I said. And as I closed my locker door, there was Stephanie Spring.

I doubted that too, so I said nothing.

She was smiling. And wearing a loose-fitting sweatshirt that said Stanford. And not looking lost.

"Hi, Clark," she said.

I tried to say, "Stephanie! What a pleasant surprise!" But what came out was, "Shouldn't you be cheering somewhere?"

She pointed to her right foot, which was in a bulky plastic boot that would have looked right at home on a space station.

"Fractured ankle," she said in response to my obvious confusion.

"How?" I asked.

"I slipped. On a Herkie, of all things."

My face scrunched as I tried to remember whether I had met anyone by that name. Or maybe it was some kind of banana-like fruit? Careless of them to leave the peel on the gym—

"It's a kind of jump," she explained.

"Ah." I nodded.

"It'll heal, but no more cheering for me this year."

"Really?"

"Or next. I missed tryouts for the ninth-grade squad and everything. My mom was pretty upset."

Stephanie did not actually sound all that devastated.

"Sorry," I said. "I guess, well, you know…" It was very, very hard for me to come up with small talk about cheerleading. Maybe I should suggest that she and Ty could compare X rays?

"I'll be OK," she said. "Anyway, Clark, I'm here because I wanted to say…I'm sorry. That I wasn't nicer to you when you got here. That must have been tough."

I shrugged. I realized that her powers over me had diminished. I mean, her type and mine would always be from different planets. And I didn't really need her to help me fit in on mine.

Although…was she reaching out to me? Well, maybe I could find time in my schedule for her to—

"And I was wondering," she continued. "I've been hearing about this guy named Les—do you know him by any chance?"

Les, who had been standing in silent shock at Stephanie's presence all this time, coughed.

"You're Les?" she asked, suddenly lighting up in a way

that made me realize I was about to become the invisible one. "I totally didn't see you there!"

"I get that a lot," he said.

She leaned in and in a hushed voice asked, "Is it true you're the one who hacked the intercom?"

Les drew himself up—he came just barely to her shoulder—put his hand on his chest, and made a slight bow. "I can neither confirm nor deny that. I can merely tell you how it's done."

She was glowing. At Les! "Awesome! Audio—well, it's sort of a hobby of mine. You probably know all about soundboards and amps and speakers, and stuff like that?"

He looked at me out of the corner of his eye. "A little," he said.

She pulled up closer to him. "So I'm in charge of music for the end-of-the-year all-school dance, and I have this idea that would *totally* rock. Do you think you could help me?"

"H-help you?" he said. His voice cracked so harshly that I was afraid he was going to spit shards of glass.

He finally cleared his throat. "Well, what kind of help are we talking about?"

She reached into the gym bag on her shoulder. Several books fell to the floor—I bent to pick them up and saw that they were some of the same electronics books that Les usually liked to check out from the library. Also, a copy of *Starship Troopers*.

She didn't see me gather the books because she had just thrust a wiring schematic at Les. "This is from my attic. It's pretty old," she said. "But maybe you'll understand it?"

I thought Les might fall to pieces under this kind of attention, but as he smoothed out the paper and saw a series of lines that indicated circuits and wattages, he settled down. Briefly. Then his eyes opened wide, and his lips parted in astonishment. He looked so excited I thought he might actually ignite and shoot into orbit.

"This...this is a plan for a tube amp," he spluttered.

"A Dynaco Mark III," she said.

"You're not saying you have one of these, are you?"

"I have two!"

"Two? Two tube amps?" Les's voice was so high this time I think it cracked some nearby windows. "This could be—sonic heaven!"

"*Right?*" Stephanie looked almost as happy. She clapped her hands and started to do a little bounce that reminded me she was still a cheerleader. The boot made that rather awkward, but she quickly regained her composure. "There's a catch," she said, solemnly.

Les looked up.

"They're in pieces. I have all the parts, and I have an old magazine article explaining how to piggy-back them for maximum output. But I don't have time to finish the job myself. Much less find the proper speakers."

"Not a problem," Les said. "Some of my dad's old gear would be perfect with this setup. The sound would be..."

"...awesome?" Stephanie asked, her voice full of hope.

I thought I should say something. "Uh, if you need sound for a dance, couldn't you just do your thing with the intercom again? Wouldn't that be loud enough?"

They both looked up at me with disdain, if not disgust.

"You'll have to forgive Clark," Les said. "He's kind of new."

"Oh, Clark and I go way back." She smiled, the old, polite

smile, and thanked me as I handed her books to her. But then she was back in Les's tube-amped world.

"The dance is in two weeks. Do you have time to work with me?"

"I have time, but, ah..." He looked off in the direction of the park. "My workshop isn't available right now."

"Well," she said, looking up and down the hall, again, as if she were about to do something she wanted to keep private. "If you wanted to, you could, maybe, come over to my house? My dad has a workbench and stuff. He's an audio engineer, and he'd be totally into this."

I got ready to catch Les. I was afraid he would die of bliss on the spot.

"I'll be there," he said faintly.

"Oh cool," Stephanie said, doing her little lopsided bounce again. She looked around, then leaned in. "I never thought I'd find anyone at Festus who was into this stuff. It's like I was the only one of my kind on the whole planet. It gets kind of lonely, you know?"

Les and I looked at each other.

"Yeah," he said. "I know."

14.05.01

My time on Planet Festus is drawing to a close. It would be an understatement to say I am going to be thrilled to fly out of here. Picture Chuck Yeager blasting through Mach 1, with a "Yeeeeee-haaaaaaaaahhhhhhhhhhhhhhh!"

I will not leave with many happy memories, but I did think of Ricki as I walked past the office this morning. Out of habit, I looked in to see whether she was around.

She, of course, was not. But sitting in the waiting area was someone I had never seen before. She had a backpack with a plaid design. She was clearly a newcomer. A pin on her backpack suggested that at her previous school, she had lived in Gryffindor House.

Her hair was mousy, limp and stringy, and her eyes were wide as she glanced around the room. She reminded me of a rabbit in a new cage—twitching, nervous, desperately looking for a place to hide.

I took a breath and walked up to the receptionist.

"Is Counselor Blethins here?" I asked, knowing she would not have time for me.

"Hi, Clark," the receptionist said. "Yes, but she's busy preparing a schedule for our new student. Is it urgent?"

I shook my head. "No, I can come back."

I turned toward the girl in the waiting area. She held my gaze for just a moment, then looked away.

I walked over to her.

"First day?" I asked.

She looked up at me, probably trying to decide whether I was an imminent threat or just a looming danger.

"Yes," she finally said.

"Kind of late in the year to be starting at a new school," I said.

"We just moved. My parents thought I should enroll

for the final weeks, to have a chance to meet people. It's so crazy."

"Everything about this place is crazy," I said. "But you can find ways to cope."

"Really?" she asked, with just a little bit of relief coloring her voice.

"Yeah, although it would probably help to have a guide." I added, "If you need one, I'm Clark."

"That's an interesting name," she said. Then added, "Are you, like, the welcome committee or something?"

I thought for a moment and said, "Nah. I just know a little about this school. And a few things about how to be a survivor."

I didn't tell her what *kind* of survivor.

I could deal with that, and whatever else came up, in the future.

ACKNOWLEDGMENTS

The author would like to thank...more people than will fit here. Because it takes a starship-sized crew to turn a pile of jumbled words into a book. But I will limit myself to thanking:

Daphne Howland, first reader of my first draft, and Maylee Chai, who provided keen insight on a late one. Also, *Dallas Morning News* subscribers and editors, who kept me employed, and the smart, tolerant colleagues I've learned from, particularly Bryan Woolley, whose encouragement and wisdom I miss.

John Freeman; Logan Garrison Savits; and nerd magnet Sarah Burnes, the rock-star avenging angel agent/editor every writer dreams of.

The Richardson Public Library, for quiet spaces, and Carolyn Bess and the Dallas Museum of Art, who brought Norton Juster to town, making a childhood dream come true while also providing me with an epigraph.

Chris Morris, John Hanan, Ken Walters, Scott Dirk Anderson, Mark Bradford and anyone else who answered oddball questions about Marines or electronics or helped me survive junior high. David Innes and Melissa Parsons, for reading my work and providing decades of moral and immoral support.

Kelly Loughman, who edited this book with intelligence, grace and deep concern for characters and readers alike. When

I tell people about her, they say, "Wow, I didn't know editors like that still existed." I am grateful she is not a hologram.

Gene Roddenberry and George Lucas, perhaps obviously. Mom and Dad, also obviously.

When I was Clark's age, I vowed to honor all my *good* teachers—I had many—whenever I wrote a book. The two who shaped me most as a writer were Katherine Starkey, who read hundreds of pages of terrible freewriting journals and listened to my arguments that *Star Trek II* was the greatest movie of all time, and Cheryl Cartin, who pushed me to get real. Also, thank you, Pat Nelson, wherever you are.

Krista, Gabriella and Jacob provided inspiration, put up with Grumpy Dad when the writing was not going well and sometimes watched *Star Trek* with me. Melinda, in general, holds my life together. She does not like *Star Wars* but says she loves me anyway, and my universe is full of wonder and laughter because of them.